THE
TURING
MACHINISTS

M.E. REID

**Canada Council
for the Arts** **Conseil des Arts
du Canada**

 Canadian Patrimoine
Heritage canadien

The publisher gratefully acknowledges the support of the Canada Council for the
Arts and the Ontario Arts Council for its publishing program. We acknowledge
the financial support of the Government of Canada through the Canada Book
Fund (CBF) for our publishing activities, and the Government of Ontario through
the Ontario Media Development Corporation, an agency of the Ontario Ministry
of Culture, and the Ontario Book Publishing Tax Credit Program.

LIBRARY AND ARCHIVES CANADA CATALOGUING IN PUBLICATION

Reid, M. E., author
The Turing Machinists / M.E. Reid.

Issued in print and electronic formats.
ISBN 978-1-77086-466-5 (paperback).— isbn 978-1-77086-467-2 (html)

1. Title.

PS8585.E6018T87 2016   JC813'.54   C2015-907529-7
                                         C2015-907530-0

Cover photo and design: angeljohnguerra.com
Interior text design: Tannice Goddard, Soul Oasis Networking

Printed and bound in Canada.
Manufactured by Friesens in Altona, Manitoba, Canada in June, 2016.

This book is printed on 100% post-consumer waste recycled paper.

DANCING CAT BOOKS
An imprint of Cormorant Books Inc.
10 ST. MARY STREET, SUITE 615, TORONTO, ONTARIO, M4Y 1P9
www.dancingcatbooks.com
www.cormorantbooks.com

To My Beautiful Monsters, Max and Benjamin.

Thanks Mom and Dad for teaching me how to be a good parent.

Thank you Kids Ability for giving Benjamin words.

We were all sitting down for first period Social Education when a woman none of us had seen before walked into our classroom. Mrs. Karroll stood up, and she and the woman exchanged nods. Mrs. Karroll came out from behind her desk and clasped her hands in front of her. She cleared her throat and addressed the class.

"Class, this is Ms. ... Pokolo—" Mrs. Karroll stumbled over the name. A rosy rash started to creep up her neck. "Ms. *Pokolopinison*."

And then she looked out at us and showed us her teeth.

Sometimes when Mrs. Karroll smiles I can't figure out whether she is happy or in pain. I can't find her smiles in the facial recognition charts. I did look in the grimacing section and finally found one that sort of fit Mrs. Karroll's. I discovered that while grimacing is considered a natural response, smiling is not. Smiling is a *learned* behavior. Often what we think is a smile is, in fact, only a reflex, or a reaction to a possible gastrointestinal problem. Does Mrs. Karroll suffer from Irritable Bowel Syndrome?

But I have always been weak on interpretations of smiles. Thankfully, the woman who walked to the center of the room has a recognizable smile. In fact, it is right out of the facial recognition chart book Mr. Valtoody gave us in our Facial Talk/Body Talk Communications class.

"You can call me Ms. Poko," she said. Her voice is a C chord: clear and even and easy to take in. I started to suspect she is one of the trained ASD researchers who have been employed by the government to teach.

"Ms. Pokololo—" Mrs. Karroll cleared her throat. "Ms. Poko is a Social Spectrum Education teacher," Mrs. Karroll told us. "You remember those forms your parents signed last week? Well, Ms. ... Poko will be teaching a Social Spectrum class this year." She was watching us, her face very still and poised. "I believe we went over this last week?"

Social Spectrum classes are mandatory for us; the hope is that they will provide ASD kids with the guidelines needed to act properly in social settings. Only Merryton Public School and a few other schools that teach the entire education curriculum, from Kindergarten to grade 12, have these kinds of classes. In SS classes we learn about what we're supposed to do and not supposed to do in social situations, and courtesy protocols — like how far away to stand when lining up for the bank machine and when to hold the door open for an older person. But also we talk a lot about what is considered illegal behavior in society. Most of what we discuss involves criminal behavior that none of us would even consider thinking about. What we need is a class about how to talk to girls, and dating.

Jeddy's hand shot up. "Ms. Pokolopinison, are you an examiner or a researcher?"

Ms. Pokolopinison's facial expression froze in a smile. "I'm a *teacher*. I will be teaching you, not testing or researching you. Please, it will be easier to just call me Ms. Poko."

"But Social Spectrum classes are sponsored and funded by the government, aren't they?"

Ms. Pokolopinison's brows lowered and came together at the bridge of her nose, which was slightly hooked and pinched. "You're Jeddy Millner, am I right?"

"If we are to be the subjects of your research, we should get paid," said Jeddy, standing up. His hands had balled into fists.

"Jeddy, please sit down," Mrs. Karroll said in her quiet warning voice.

Jeddy was jutting out his jaw, and his voice grew sharper. Wesley Farkle started to rock and make groaning noises. Hannah got up and circled the room clockwise, then sat down. I looked out the window, watching Mr. Yaggi cut the grass. I could hear the muted buzzing of the mower's motor. My ears vibrated with the sound, but for some reason I was not irritated. After a moment, I glanced over at Ms. Pokolopinison, who hadn't moved. Her face was set in the same expression with the corners of her mouth turned up ever so slightly and her heavy-lidded dark brown eyes looking coolly at Jeddy. Her stillness relieved and puzzled me at the same time. I tried to remember if I'd taken my medication at breakfast. I have an unreliable memory for these kinds of things.

"As this is your graduating year," Ms. Pokolopinison announced slowly, loudly, with emphasis on each syllable. "You will all be doing a *thesis* project."

A rumbling started within the classroom. Mrs. Karroll's face started to constrict, losing some of its rosy color. The knuckles on her clasped hands turned white. I wasn't sure how I felt. I was excited about the thesis project. But I was nervous and afraid, too. I wasn't sure why.

And then Ms. Pokolopinison's smile changed ever so slightly. We all saw it. The sudden change in the air was palpable. We didn't know what it all meant, so we were frightened. Wesley Farkle let out a loud fart. Mrs. Karroll rolled her lips between her teeth. She had unclasped her hands.

"Also," Ms. Pokolopinison continued, still smiling, "this thesis project is intended to be a *group* project."

And it was like a nuclear warhead had gone off in the room.

Doctor Bankoy, who has been my doctor since grade five, told me that when I understand the importance of "context" I'll be able to figure out how best to react and act in a particular circumstance. It's usually in the interpretation of the situation where people like me go wrong. I wonder — if I could better understand the context of situations, would that help me talk to girls? Of course, my interpretation of the situation seems to always come out wrong.

Especially when it comes to Petula.

Whenever the Special Education people speak about "contextual sensitivity," we all know what they are really talking about; they are talking about "socially appropriate behavior." Social behavior is what is deemed most important at Merryton Public School. However, the chief subject of almost all of the research done here on autism spectrum disorder has to do with social communication.

ECHOLALIA:
(http://dictionary.reference.com)
(Psychiatry) • the uncontrollable and immediate repetition of words spoken by another person

Everyone in our ASD class knows what echolalia is because we all have it in some form or another. Petula echoes scenes from old black-and-white TV shows like *The Twilight Zone* and *Leave it to Beaver*; Jeddy and Djebar like to quote obscure lines from movies that no one can ever remember; I repeat lines from movies, but I also listen to a lot of books on tape and I sometimes feel the need to echo some passages aloud — especially if they sound interesting in my head. Sogi listens to CBC Radio 1 on his iPod, and once every so often he will repeat a news item, or the weather several times. Wesley Farkle echoes pretty much everyone, even himself. If the teachers and researchers ask him a question, he usually responds by repeating the question. All he is doing, though, is saying out loud what all of us have learned to echo silently in our heads.

"Can't we just have a normal conversation, for once?" my father is always saying to me.

I don't know why "normal" conversation is so hard for us. When Djebar and Sogi and Petula and I talk amongst ourselves, our conversation seems to follow a "normal" route. However, some people have remarked on the "weirdness" of how we talk to one another. I'm not sure if they are commenting on the *way* we speak or the *content* of what we say.

Some research psychologists think that there might be a link between echolalia and memory. Everyone in our ASD class has fantastic memories. When given a listing of items, that list becomes immediately imprinted in our minds, and when asked we can recite all those items in order. Having a good memory is especially good for the math and science courses I'm taking, as memorizing algorithms and formulas definitely gives you an advantage. A lot of high-functioning autistic people speed read because they initially learned to read through memorization.

But not everything we take in sticks. If I am reconstructing a social scene, the memory is almost always fuzzy and off balance, like a hasty snapshot. I have been told this isn't unusual, that childhood memories tend to be unreliable. But this irks me, because when pictures and thoughts are not sharp in my mind, I feel anxious.

And so I have learned to build past events into structured tales with beginnings, middles, and endings so that I can recall them more easily without being suspicious of them. The stories are not permanent, however. I often have to rebuild them in my mind. And there are occasions when I have to shuffle around the truth a little to make everything come out correctly in the end.

Thea, my school ASD counsellor, says she believes my memory is good enough to recall the specifics of my past, but that I am *choosing* to add my own details to make them seem like stories so that I can have more control over them. I'm not sure she is right; but sometimes it does feel like I'm not in charge of where my life is going, and this thought does make me feel anxious.

One of my earliest memories as a child is of a guitar: an electric guitar my father plugged into the wall behind the bookcase where my Thomas the Tank Engine books were later shelved. I remember my father's hands, big and white and blurry. His face is an oval fog in my mind with warbling words circling it. But it is the sound that came from his body that assaults my memory: yowling, baying, groaning, wailing, *tcchhhhhh, reeearrrgh, rutwaaaaang.*

My ears split away from my head and I am trying to hang on to them. But they are hot and buzzing and I am afraid. I scream and scream and scream. Hands pick me up, and I am being pressed against something warm and fuzzy that smells familiar.

The sounds have stopped, but my head hurts, and I bang my face into the fuzzy warmth again and again until the pain stops.

"Geezus H Christ. He hates it. He hates my guitar."

"You were playing too loud."

"Goddammit, there's something wrong with him — and you know it."

"There's nothing wrong with him. And watch your language!"

"Why? Look at him. Geezus, Connie, he doesn't even know we're here."

"He's only three!"

"He'll be four in two months. *Get your head out of the sand!* He's not *normal.*"

GET YOUR HEAD OUT OF THE SAND:
(idiom) • refusing or being unable to confront a problem

IDIOM:
(*New Illustrated Webster's Dictionary,* 1992)
• a group of words whose meaning cannot be understood from the meaning of the individual words; an expression, peculiar to a specific language, that cannot be translated literally

My father told me he *played his music by ear.*

Understanding idioms is not difficult; everything has an algorithm — like the Tower of Hanoi. The problem lies in the persistence of trying to understand the idiom. Literalness has more of a basis in truth for most autistic people, so an idiom, while understood to be an idiom, is still based in the literal for better understanding.

"Real musicians don't need to read music. They should be able to play it by ear, like me," my father told me. The smell of his breath told me he had been to the Busy Pub again after work. "Music is — is, like, *blood* to the real musician. Me? I'm treble clef positive." He cackled loudly, thumped me on the back. But then he looked at me and his mouth drooped and his eyes suddenly turned watery.

"Music stirs your soul, Del. It's like ... falling in love ..."

My mother set down a cup of coffee in front of him and didn't say anything. The lines around her mouth were deeper than usual, and her eyes were red around the rims as if they were sore. When she went to pick up my dessert plate, my father reached out and brushed his fingertips over the top of her hand. My mother didn't look at him or me, but just went to the sink to do the dishes.

I excused myself to do my math homework (which was a lie; as a general rule I never do homework). When I stepped into my bedroom I heard the smash of something breaking in the kitchen. My mother's voice started its inevitable rise until she was yelling so loud the walls seemed to reverberate. I covered my ears, and my sister Bea came into my room and sat on the edge of my bed.

"I wish they'd just get it over with already," she said.

"Get what over with?"

"The divorce, stupid."

"Divorce? Why would they get divorced?"

Bea stared at me, then shook her head and laughed. "You're like this weird genius, and you can't figure out that our parents hate each other?"

"They hate each other?"

"Well, I don't know about hate, but ... hey, you know Dad's moving out, right?"

"Moving out where?"

Bea stood. "He's leaving. You know, Mom and Dad are separating. Getting a divorce."

"I don't understand." My stomach didn't feel good. "Why didn't they tell me?"

"Hey, look. They didn't tell me, either."

"Then how do you know?"

Bea cocked her head, her long brown eyes narrowing slightly. "How could you *not* know?"

I awoke in the middle of the night with this thought: If there is any logical reasoning behind the nature of marriage, then it may be possible that I can do something about my parents' impending divorce. Logic comes about as result of cause and effect, doesn't it? If I can change the cause, I can change the effect. I can stop my parents from leaving each other.

Djebar's parents divorced when he was five. But his father lives ten minutes away, so he's around almost all the time. On Monday nights Djebar and his father go bowling, and every Thursday night Djebar's father takes him to karate class. Every other weekend Djebar sleeps over at his father's house.

"I see my father more than I did when they were together. Hey, divorce is not the worst that can happen. They could stay together and end up like Petula's parents."

I'd only been to Petula's house once, but I could tell her mother and father didn't like each other much. The whole time I was there they shouted at each other. None of them, including her two brothers, who are eleven and thirteen, ever seem to be in the same room at the same time, so they yell at each other too: through the walls or down the banister or up the stairs, from the basement to the top floor, from the upstairs bedrooms down to the cellar. Petula actually wears special earphones at home. They're supposed to tune out the sounds of their voices. But she still walks around the house with her shoulders hunched. It's not just the noise of the shouting or the blow-dryer going, or her older brother's alto saxophone; we can all sense it the moment we walk in — tension. Or as Sogi's mom calls it: "bad vibes."

It has been said that people on the autism spectrum are receptors; they can often sense the "vibes" people put out. That is not to say that we are psychic. It's just that the volume on our senses is turned up a lot higher than what is typical.

We're supposed to use the word *typical* instead of *normal*. Comparing ourselves to *normal* society will give us a complex, my mother says.

"A complex what?" I'd asked.

My mother looked at me and laughed, and then hugged me tight. She's always doing that: hugging me tightly. Not to say I don't like it; the deep pressure eases my tension, in fact. I told her that one night, and her whole face lit up. And then she kissed me. I don't like having my face touched, so I wiped my cheek with the back of my hand, and her face kind of went slack and turned that gray color again.

I don't mean to hurt her feelings, but she is always telling me I'm not hurting her feelings. I know that's a lie. What I don't understand is while she doesn't want me to lie to her, she lies to me all the time. For one thing, she told me that she and my father were "fine," and that it was very sweet of me to ask.

Maybe I didn't ask the right question? Or maybe I didn't ask the question the right way?

"If they've decided to break up, you can't do anything about it," said Djebar. "When my parents decided to separate, I went through a million scenarios, calculated risks and probabilities. None of them panned. I realized that what it comes down to is that you have no say in what they do. Besides," he grimaced, "they were really stressing me out. That year before they divorced I got a B+ in chemistry. And I spent all my time going to the therapist and sitting in the Plum Room. Remember? But it's way better now," he said. "I'm left alone more, I get to watch more TV, my computer's been upgraded again thanks to Dad, and Mom lets me eat sugar cereals." The bell rang and he started down the hall, heading towards our fourth period. As I followed him to class, I thought maybe Djebar hadn't succeeded in keeping his parents together because he hadn't tried hard enough. I knew then that all I needed to do was to come up with a perfect plan and try as hard as I could to see it through.

One day, while I was organizing the garage for my mother this past summer, I came across a notebook. On the front cover it had a picture of a banana riding a bicycle. The banana wore a red bandana and dark sunglasses. When I opened it an earwig and a flat-bodied centipede fell out. I watched them scurry away. I'm not afraid of bugs. But I don't like cats, and birds make me nervous. Dogs are all right, so long as they don't bark.

Anyway, some of the pages of the notebook were stuck together, and I was going to throw it out — until I came across a doodle of a man in a porkpie hat smoking a cigarette. Underneath, someone had written: "There are no normal dreams. Only dreams."

I looked at the other scribbling. Not everything was legible, so it took me a while to decipher. But I was halfway through the notebook when it occurred to me I was reading something written by my father. I put it down right away. Then, not knowing why, I picked it up again, went inside the house, and hurried up to my room. I slid the notebook under my mattress where I had hidden some of my Thomas the Tank Engine books.

Later that night, when everyone had gone to bed, I read the rest of the notebook (at least all the words that I could decipher). Did it make me understand my father more? I'm not sure. He had written these things before I was born. I only knew him as my father. I only knew him in relation to me.

But one thing I did get from reading the notebook was that at one time my father had had a dream: he'd dreamed of becoming a rock star.

Usually, I only surf Internet sites that have already been cleared by a closed security system. But what I was looking for I knew I wasn't going to find on any of my regular sites. So the following night I forced myself to ignore the warning signs and ventured past my safety perimeter. It took me almost two hours to find it. But I knew it was the one I was looking for because my heart was pounding so hard my ribcage hurt: *DON'T DREAM IT; BE IT! A CHANCE TO WIN ROCK STARDOM!*

I carefully read through the advertisement to make sure it wasn't a hoax. I read it three more times, memorizing the details of the contest requirements. After I bookmarked the site and printed out the information, I paced around my bedroom for a while because my whole body was humming with too much excitement. When I finally calmed down I folded the printout and tucked it into the side pocket of my knapsack.

I now had an actual plan of action: I was going to live out my father's dream by forming my own rock band.

Alan Mathison Turing died in 1954. He was forty-two years old, the same age as my father. He often told people that his dream was to see his Universal Turing Machine used in every household in the world.

I tried to explain to my parents how a Turing Machine works, but when I started in about how Turing had developed this device to read symbols on a paper strip of tape, my father said it sounded more like something from Doctor Seuss. I didn't get the reference, or why they both started laughing when I pointed out that the strip of tape had to be of infinite length. But when I explained about the device reading individual cells carrying specific symbols from a table of rules, my mother said something about how maybe Turing was trying to design a human brain. I thought that was pretty insightful of her, and told her that if this was true the *Universal* Turing Machine would be a brain reading another brain, a Turing Machine that can simulate another Turing Machine by reading another machine and then input data from its tape strip.

After our discussion my parents didn't ask anything more about Alan Turing or the Turing Machine. I guess they got it, finally.

Even though Alan Turing thought of himself primarily as a mathematician, we don't study him in any of my math classes at Merryton High. And even though he cracked the Nazi Enigma code in World War II, he's not mentioned in history class, either. Come to think of it, he's absent from our computer science studies, as well.

I wonder what he would think of some of the mathematicians living today? I am betting he would have liked to sit down and discuss Fermat's Last Theorem with mathematicians like Andrew Wiles. He and Yuri Matiyasevish could have chatted about the Entscheidungsproblem and argue about his negative solution to Hilbert's tenth solution.

But, of course, if Alan Turing were alive today he would be exactly one hundred years old. He would probably be sitting in a nursing home and not thinking at all.

I was eating my Corn Flakes and milk when my father strode in. His hair was sticking up, and there were crease lines on the left side of his face. When I had come down to have breakfast I had noticed my father sleeping on the green couch on the living room.

"Why were you sleeping on the couch?" I asked.

"Huh?" He scratched his belly. The odor he was exuding had a faintly familiar smell. It wasn't the couch smell.

Bea glared at me, but said nothing. I looked back at her, puzzled.

"Oh." My father suddenly uttered a groan, then arched. He pressed his palms into his lower back so that his rounded belly stuck out further. "Bad back."

Later, as I was heading out the door to school, I wondered if my father still dreamed of becoming a rock star. Thea, my counsellor, once asked me if I had any dreams for the future. I wasn't sure if I did or didn't. It just wasn't something I thought about. I don't know anything about dreams, but one thing I do know is that if my father still wants to be a rock star he will have to take better care of himself.

My father now sleeps every night on the couch in the living room. He says it's more comfortable and better for his back. Our couch is pretty old, and it's a sectional. How can the couch be more comfortable than the bed? I considered this for a while, calculating the slope of the springs of the bed and the contoured shape of the couch using polygonal equations. Bea told me I was wasting my time. Didn't I understand that Dad was sleeping on the couch because he and Mom didn't want to sleep together anymore?

"This is what adults do when they are getting ready to divorce each other," she told me.

Her words lingered in my room and stayed there. I didn't want to think about my parents, so I pulled out my geometry book and spent the next couple hours working and forgetting, until my eyes got heavy and I felt tired enough to go to bed. I turned off the light and almost immediately went to sleep.

But when I awoke a few hours later, I had a terrible stomach ache. I sat in front of the window with my binoculars. The man who lives on the fifth floor in the building at 88 Margaret Street was up. He was playing his guitar again. My anxiety lessened and I began to relax. As I spied, my mind began to spin; I began to put ideas together. By the time I was ready to go back to sleep I knew the man living at 88 Margaret Street was the person who was going to help me keep my parents together.

I have never hacked into a database, but I know how to do it, and I needed to find out the guitar-playing man's name. It didn't take me long; Cloudburst Housing hadn't updated their security protocols, so accessing its database was easy. I wasn't interested in anything but the man's name, so I didn't access any other data on the site. I thought about updating their security protocols, but thought this might cause the company some problems. After I exited the database I wondered if Mrs. Karroll would consider computer hacking an illegal act or a social wrong?

So I learned the man who lives at 88 Margaret Street is named James Comfort. He is an American musician. The information I got from the Internet told me he was once the lead singer and guitar player in a band called the Magic Horse Marines. I downloaded some of their music and listened to it. It made the skin of my scalp hurt and my ears ring. But my heart was also pumping with excitement.

Now all I needed was to meet James Comfort.

And come up with a plan.

HORSE MARINE:
(New Illustrated Webster's Dictionary, 1992)
* a member of an imaginary corps of mounted marines;
  one who is as awkward and out of place as a mounted

marine would be aboard ship; a mounted marine or sailor on duty ashore.

At lunch, Jeddy told us his parents had been invited to attend a lecture at the Perimeter Institute (of which they are honorary members, he reminded us). The lecture was about evolution and genetic mutation, but its main theme centered around autism. The key lecturer, a professor from Princeton University, stated that "autistic people are the wave of the future." He believes that our highly attuned sensory capabilities are, in fact, valuable early warning detectors that classify people with autism ahead in the evolutionary chain. Jeddy's father is a prosecution lawyer, and he and Jeddy's stepmother are lobbying to get this professor to speak to the Merryton School Board. But Jeddy told Mrs. Karroll that the members of the school board have all got "their pointy little heads stuck up their lubed assholes." Mrs. Karroll was unfazed. This is the way Jeddy's dad speaks, and Jeddy, with his echolalia, repeats it word for word.

Sogi's mom had him on another one of her sugar-glucose-wheat-gluten-dairy-casein-peanut–tree nut–soya-free diets, so Sogi begged me for my Lindt chocolate bar. He was in a bad mood, but this was the opportunity I was looking for. It takes me eleven bites to finish my Lindt chocolate bar. He ate it in five. When he was finished I unzipped the front pocket of my knapsack and pulled out the folded piece of paper with the website and contest information. I'd been meaning to show it to him for weeks now, and I was nervous as I unfolded the printout and thrust it into his hands.

CUBGROUND PUB ANNUAL BATTLE OF THE BANDS
Rock your way into fame and fortune!!
$10,000 in cash prizes
April 24–26, 2012
Register by December 15, 2011
See eligibility rules @ www.cubpubbattleband.ca

Sogi glanced at the paper, then handed it back to me. "So?"

"It's a competition."

"So?"

"I want to enter it," I said.

Sogi's expression didn't change. "Why?"

"You play the bass guitar, don't you?"

"And the cello."

"I want to put a band together."

"Why?"

"I want to win this competition. You play the bass guitar. I need you."

"I didn't mean why're you asking *me*. I meant why do *you* want to be in a band?" Sogi's eyes narrowed and they moved back and forth for a second, which bothered me. "I thought you didn't like music?"

"I like music," I said truthfully. "It's just … the instruments scare me."

Sogi's long, straight brows lifted a little, and he stared down the hall for a long moment. His hands started to twitch and flap at his sides, and he made a couple squeaky sighs. Doctor Bankoy calls this "self-stimulatory behavior." Everybody else just calls it "stimming." Most of us in the ASD class stim; it happens whenever we're having sensory processing issues or our brains are craving some form of stimulation. I tend to pace and rock. I also flap my hands a little. A few people, like Hannah, spin. She can spin for ten minutes and not get dizzy. I used to do a lot of spinning when I was little. But I actually do get a little dizzy now. Thea says that some typical people also stim, but not to the same degree as autistic people. Stimming for us is a way to help sort out the sensory chaos that builds up in our brains. It helps us think better, and for a while it keeps the world from crashing in on us. But because stimming makes us feel so good, it can be addictive, too — and sometimes it's hard to remember to stop. Sometimes, you don't *want* to stop. I guess that's when it can become a problem. Doctor Bankoy thinks my running might be a form of stimming. I'm not so sure.

Sogi started down the hall towards his locker. He was still flapping his hands a little, but he wasn't making the squeaky noises anymore.

I didn't call after him, and he didn't turn around. I did wonder, though, if he understood what I had just asked him. I got out my "Dream Sweeter" assembly instruction booklet for the R29863 king-size bed and sat with my back to the wall reading it. After a while, the noise in my head settled, and I went to the math room to wait for fifth period to start.

I hoped Sogi would get back to me, because I knew I wouldn't ask him again.

There are only two students who play violin for the Merryton Public Symphony: Martha Yin and Darrin Relowski. Both Martha and Darrin are in the twelfth grade, like me, but Darrin is in my ASD graduating class. The problem is he's only sixteen, a year younger than me and the rest of the class. But Martha doesn't play the electric guitar; Darrin does.

We were in line for the cafeteria when I asked him if he had ever played the electric guitar in a band. He told me he'd never been in a band other than the school band and that they didn't allow him to play the electric guitar.

"Would you like to?" I said, stuttering and looking down at my feet.

"I don't know what you mean," he said.

"I'm putting together a … rock band."

He looked worried and started tugging on his ears. We're class-mates, but in the four years we've been together we've never socialized, not inside nor outside of school. I was sure he was going to say no, and I was about to take back the invitation when he took out his iPhone and asked me for my address and phone number. I started to get a bit anxious; I don't socialize much, and I don't know Darrin all that well.

"Darrin's okay. But his parents are weird," said Sogi.

"My father says Darrin's parents are 'hippies,'" said Djebar. "They don't eat meat."

"That means they're vegetarians, idiot," said Petula.

"They tried to get the school to sponsor a rodent sanctuary or something," said Djebar.

"It was a *dog* sanctuary," said Sogi. "Darrin's okay. He had an autistic dog, but it died. It got cancer or something."

"What?" Djebar blinked. "You mean there are such things as autistic *dogs*?"

"No, idiot. It wasn't autistic. It was one of those dogs trained for people with autism."

"You mean, people like us," said Sogi.

Petula rolled her eyes. "Anyway, Darrin's okay. He's really changed, don't you think? Remember how he used to stim all the time? He barely does it anymore — just plays with his ears."

I'd noticed this about his ears; but I don't ever remember seeing Darrin stimming. And I didn't know about the dog. I guess I hadn't really taken that much notice of Darrin before now. Like I said, I didn't know him that well.

I hoped he would join the band. But at the same time, I was nervous about having to get to know someone new.

Of all the people in my ASD class, I knew Djebar the best. He doesn't take as many math courses as me, and he is nowhere near the same level. But we're both in the top levels in physics and chemistry and computer. Djebar's good at art, and does okay in the mandatory English/history/geography courses. I'm okay in the mandatory classes, but I only get the minimum grade in art. Neither of us likes biology or gym. Djebar and I have known each other since the third grade.

Djebar's mother is East Indian; his father is from Nairobi. They both speak very fast, and I find it difficult to understand them, so I just stop listening to them. But while Djebar's father has blurry features to me, I find his mother very easy to look at. When Djebar's mother smiles, you can see her front top and bottom teeth, and the laugh lines that bracket her mouth are about an inch long on either side. It is, in fact, rare to have such a symmetrical face, let alone a symmetrical smile. I don't smile very much. That is not to say that I don't smile. But sometimes by the time I think I might smile I have already thought of something else that makes me forget to do it. I smile as a reflex when my mother tickles me or when my father wrestles with me pretending to be the Incredible Hulk. My father doesn't do that anymore. I don't know why he stopped. But he doesn't smile as much as he used to, either.

Our Social Spectrum group was waffling about our group project. We'd told Ms. Pokolopinison we were doing a board game that would accommodate at least six people. This was Djebar's idea. His folks were currently marketing a new board game in Canada called *Milk and Cookies*. It had something to do with pairing up objects with people and places. Djebar was vague on the details, but neither he nor I are very interested in board games.

Petula and Sogi, on the other hand, are hobby gamers. They play tournaments of cards called *Magic* every Sunday afternoon at the Grog. Petula has won almost every tournament the Grog has ever put on. Sogi also paints these plastic miniatures of skull people and warriors with swords and armor for a game called *Warhammer 2000*. He doesn't play the game, though. He tried once, but he told me he just couldn't reconcile toppling an entire army with a throw of the dice. But then, *Warhammer 2000* is about role-playing; autistic people are not supposed to be adept at taking on roles or pretending. I'm not so sure this is true; from what I've heard, a lot of movie and theater actors have Asperger syndrome, like me and the majority of the students in my class. Being an Aspie, I'm supposed to be able to function better in social situations and have more neurotypical speech pattern skills than those people diagnosed with other kinds of autism. I think I'm okay with language, but socially — I'm not so sure. I do have an anxiety problem, and I tend to be clumsy and awkward, so it's little wonder I have trouble socializing. Anyway, Doctor Bankoy says Asperger syndrome is being absorbed into autism spectrum disorder because it turns out none of us are fitting into just one syndrome type.

Anyway, since Petula was crowned Merryton *Magic* Champion everyone's been pushing her to go to Toronto to play the Dragon Lord's Grand National Tournament, which brings in people from all over Canada. But Petula says she's not interested. Jeddy accused her of being afraid. She punched him and gave him a black eye.

Petula might've been afraid, but she was also procrastinating — just like we were all procrastinating on the Social Spectrum project. I was also procrastinating about asking Djebar and Wesley if they wanted to join the band. I told myself I was waiting for Sogi and Darrin to get back to me about joining, but I was now beginning to think it was a stupid idea. Unfortunately, it was a stupid idea I couldn't get out of my head.

"I don't want to do a board game," said Djebar.

"I don't want to do a board game," echoed Wesley.

"But it was your idea, Djebar!" Petula protested.

"I don't want to do a board game, either," said Sogi.

"Well, I do!" Petula said, her face getting red and puffy. "Del, what do you want to do?"

This was it. This was my moment! "I — I —"

"Okay. See? He doesn't want to do it. No board game," said Sogi. "And because Del is our leader he has the final word."

Leader?

Petula threw her pencil case at him. "Eat shit!"

Ms. Pokolopinison was suddenly standing in front of her. "Petula, dear, why don't you take a walk over to the Plum Room and calm down?"

Petula muttered some obscenities under her breath and stalked off.

"How is everything going in the group?" Ms. Pokolopinison asked in her cool, C-chord voice.

The others shrugged, returned to their school com-pads. I gritted my teeth and looked down at my feet.

When Ms. Pokolopinison was out of earshot I said, "I want to put together a rock band."

After a moment when no one said anything, I got up and walked out of the classroom. My eyes felt like they were being pricked by needles, and my heart was pounding so hard I didn't hear Djebar running up behind me in the hall.

"Hey! Hey, Del! I play keyboard, you know."

"It's a music competition," I said.

"Yeah, Sogi said. Hey, you know Wesley plays the drums, right?"

I nodded.

"Ms. Pokolopinison said you need to come back." Djebar grinned and gave me that loose wave he does that makes his hand look like it's going to fall off at the joint. "She said you have to ask permission to leave from now on." He turned and started back towards the classroom. "You gotta have faith, Del!" he shouted, and went back inside the classroom.

I leaned against the wall, waiting for the rims of my eyes to cool down and my heart to return to its regular beat before I went back to class. It took a while.

During Emotional Recognition Training class, Sogi suddenly turned around in his seat and yelled, "Okay Del. I'll do it!"

Jeddy perked up, narrowed his eyes at Sogi then at me. "Do what?"

"None of your goddamn business," said Sogi. He had eaten half of Djebar's cherry Jell-o package during math class and now he and Djebar were both on sugar highs and acting giggly and stupid.

"Sogi! Language, please," said Mrs. Karroll.

And then Petula tapped me on the shoulder. "I'm in, too, Del."

My heart jumped at her touch, and I got that weird frustrated feeling in my gut when I turned around and looked into her face. "What?"

"I can play the xylophone, you know. You'd be lucky to have me."

I could feel my face heating up as I stared at her.

"Well?" she said, her brows lowering over her dark eyes.

"How does *she* know about this?" said Sogi.

"Know about what?" Jeddy frowned at me.

I turned around and fixed my gaze down at the photographs lined up on my desk.

"See, Del? You did it!" Djebar leaped up. "I told you. You gotta have faith!"

"Faith in what?" Jeddy demanded. "What are you idiots talking about?"

"We're going to rock the fucking world!" Sogi cried.

"Sogi!" Mrs. Karroll exclaimed. "Language, *please*!"

Ms. Sabine, the Computer Studies 3 teacher, explained to us that when Alan Turing wrote about a "computer," he was in fact describing the person doing computing, not the machine. Essentially, when he came up with the idea of the Universal Turing Machine, he was creating a model of a human mind at work.

But his colleagues wondered at the amount of time he was investing in this machine of his. "After all this time and effort, what if it doesn't work?" they asked.

"It will work," he insisted.

"But how do you know it will?"

"Because I have faith that it will."

"Faith? And what if your faith lets you down? What if it doesn't work? What then?"

Turing gave a laugh. "Then I will start again."

My plan to put together a band and win the Cubground Pub Battle of the Bands competition was underway. I don't know what frightened me more: my plan failing — or *succeeding*.

THE ENTSCHEIDUNGSPROBLEM:
(Wiktionary)
(mathematics, logic) • A decision problem of finding a way to decide whether a formula is true or provable within a given system.

When Alan Turing conceived of his Universal Turing Machine, did he really intend to build it? Or was he just interested in challenging himself to find solutions to what seemed to be unsolvable problems like the Entscheidungsproblem?

When we sat down for lunch, Jeddy looked at me and declared, "There is no valid algorithm for the Entscheidungsproblem, so why bother looking for it? It's a waste of time."

"*Entscheidungsproblem* means 'decision problem' in German," said Sogi. "My mother says there is no problem in this world that can't be solved."

"Your mother's a kook," said Jeddy.

Sogi surged to his feet, his eyes narrowing. "What did you say? Did you just call my mother a *gook*?"

"*Kook*. I said *kook*. Are you deaf or something?"

Darrin suddenly appeared at our table. He stared at me for a few seconds, then looked down at his feet. "All right. I'll join." And then he hurried away.

Jeddy looked at me. "Join? Join what? What's he talking about?"

"Darrin can't join the band," said Djebar.

"Band?" echoed Jeddy.

"If Jeddy joins us, I'm quitting," said Petula.

"Well, Jeddy can't join anyway; he's not in our Social Spectrum thesis group," said Sogi.

"Neither is Darrin."

Jeddy frowned. "Join what?"

Petula was twisting and twining a lock of her long, dark hair around and around her fingers. "Wait. I didn't know this was our thesis project."

Djebar frowned at me. "How come you asked Darrin, anyway? You're going to have to talk to Ms. Pokolopinison, you know. There's no way she's going to let Darrin come into our group. There're ten people in our class. It should be five and five. But with Darrin that puts the class at six and four." He was rubbing the tips of his fingers with his thumb, blinking. "It's not balanced. It won't work."

"We can give them Wesley Farkle," Sogi suggested.

"Do you hear me? It's not even," Djebar repeated. "It's unbalanced. It won't work."

"Hey, Wesley's better than *Jeddy*," said Petula. She had begun to twist the hair on the other side of her head. Petula is part Assiniboine; her hair is shiny and dark brown. Her eyes are brown with gold and green flecks in them, and sometimes when she looks at me I get a feeling like I'm hanging from a high place.

Jeddy stood up. "You guys are dicks. I'm going to repeat this word for word to Ms. Pokolopinison and then we'll see what happens. And no way are we trading Darrin for Wesley Farkle."

"Go ahead and repeat it," said Djebar. "You don't even know what we're talking about."

Jeddy smiled. "No, but Darrin does."

A year after the Canadian Research Association for Autism Spectrum Disorder moved into Merryton Public School, an anti-bullying/zero-tolerance program was implemented. Monitors were posted in washrooms and on playgrounds, in the gym and in the cafeteria. Anyone caught bullying another student received an immediate suspension and a personal reprimand that went on their permanent school record.

This new program came about largely because of Sogi's mother, who complained to the principal that Sogi was being targeted by bullies. These bullies were supposedly extorting money from Sogi and stealing his lunch. If the principal knew what Sogi actually brought for lunch she might have investigated the complaint a little more thoroughly.

However, that is not to say that bullying didn't happen at the school. It's always there. When you think of it, the pattern of bullying is algorithmic: the big guys go after the small guys and then the small guys go after the smaller guys, and so on and so on. A student who stands out, who decides to walk a different path outside of the groups's protection, is often targeted. Our class didn't seem to have those protective instincts. We did not group together; we did not protect one another. And we did stand out. So we were seen as prime bully meat.

There was a boy named Raymond Arbuckler who used to delight in tickling my neck because the sensation would make me whoop out loud. This was extremely annoying to me, but it didn't seem a big enough deal to report to the principal.

Raymond Arbuckler did eventually get bored of the tickling. However, that didn't mean he was through with me. One day he decided to shove my head into a urinal before tickling my neck, just to see what would happen. What happened was that I vomited. As I jerked back, I head-butted Raymond Arbuckler so that he fell back through one of the stalls and banged his chin on the flusher. I remember looking around the washroom and seeing everyone just standing there, watching me. No one thought to look for the bully monitor; they were never around when anything actually happened. But someone must have reported the incident because a few days later I heard Raymond Arbuckler had been transferred to another school.

Everyone in our ASD class has been the victim of bullying in one way or another. Some of us have also been the bully. Jeddy, being taller and bigger than all of us, likes to push his weight around sometimes. When he used to pick on Wesley, we all kind of stood around watching. It wasn't that we didn't feel badly for Wesley, it was just that we had no context for the situation and didn't know how to react. And I suppose a part of us, too, was afraid. If we helped Wesley, would Jeddy then come after *us*?

Thea says bullies have low self-esteem and are insecure — "they're just reaching out for friends." I'm not sure she is correct; I don't think Jeddy is looking to be friends with anyone.

My theory is that it runs in families: if you look at kids who bully, most often you will see that their parents are bullies in one form or another. But Mr. Valtoody points out that bullies are usually people who have been bullied themselves. Mr. Valtoody doesn't strike me as a person who would ever be bullied, just because of his size. But he told us physical size doesn't necessarily determine whether you become a bully or are the victim of one.

My father is five foot, eleven inches tall. I am now a half-inch taller than my father, and taller than most of my teachers except Mr. Valtoody, my fifth period teacher. Mr. Valtoody stands six foot, eight and a half inches tall. I know this because his height was a detail Mr. Valtoody shared with us at the beginning of the Facial Talk/Body Talk Communications class. He predicted correctly that we would be asking the question, and that we would be preoccupied for the rest of the class estimating and trying to measure his height in our minds. But what he didn't understand is that once he'd given us his height, he became an algebraic equation. Now we had to figure out his weight and the proportionate angles of his body. That his nose was as long as my baby finger intrigued me, as I know that the nose continues to grow throughout a person's lifetime. But Mr. Valtoody couldn't have been more than thirty. In my mind, I began to formulate quadratic equations to measure the features of his body, all of which were untypically large.

"Mr. Valtoody, if you were thinking categorically, would you consider yourself to be a giant?" Petula once asked him.

He laughed then, and we all sat silently in our seats, gripped by the marvelous sound that bellowed from his mouth. He grinned at us as the school bell buzzed. "Ho! Ho! Ho! Happy Holidays, everyone!"

Santa Claus! I thought.

But then Djebar leaned towards me and whispered loudly. "He's the *Jolly Green Giant*!"

"Were you a bully, Mr. Valtoody?" Petula asked one day.

Mr. Valtoody's Jolly Green Giant face went slightly pink. "We all do things we regret in life."

In Jeddy's case, I don't think he ever regrets his bullying. I think he enjoys it. He's also the only one in our class who is physically coordinated and strong enough to bully (except for maybe Hannah, whom Jeddy leaves alone).

But it's not just us Aspies who are targeted for bullying.

Once when I had stayed late to log in an algorithm program for Computer Studies 3, I cut across the small campus houses on my way home and came across two boys beating up another one. I wasn't sure what I was seeing or what I was supposed to do, so I just stood there and watched.

"Get the hell out of here, geek!" one of the boys snarled.

"Help me!" cried the boy on the ground. He was smaller and skinnier than me. In the grass, less than a meter away from where I stood, I spotted a pair of eyeglasses. The lenses had been smashed.

I didn't know the boy, and I wasn't sure what I was feeling because the wind in the surrounding trees was rustling the leaves and the evening shadows were beginning to stretch across the field like a hand closing over the world. I glanced at my watch. If I didn't go now I would be late for dinner.

The boy screamed as he was kicked in the ribs by the bigger

youth wearing the green army jacket.

"You better stop. Mr. Pilking is coming," I said.

The boys glanced up at me. I immediately looked down at my runners, hoping they didn't see my lie. I think I was more shocked by my interference than they were.

"Hey! It's an *Ass Burger*," one of them said, laughing.

"Come on, let's go before Pilking gets here," said the boy wearing the army jacket.

"Aw, he's lying. Pilking's not coming —"

"What's going on here?"

I think I jumped about a foot in the air when I heard the voice. It was Mr. Bowden. Upon seeing the shop teacher, the two bullies scrambled away into the shadows. Mr. Bowden pushed me aside and went to the boy lying on the grass. The boy got up, said he was all right. But when he picked up his eyeglasses his voice made a crackling noise. Mr. Bowden patted his shoulder and told him to be brave. Was he okay to go home? the shop teacher wanted to know.

The boy looked past Mr. Bowden to me. I didn't know what to do, so I stayed where I was.

Mr. Bowden followed the boy's gaze, and looked at me. "You there. Did you see what happened here?"

For a second I froze. And in the next second I ran. I don't know why, but I kept running even when Mr. Bowden called out to me to stop. I ran all the way home. When I arrived, I went straight up to my room. My mother called to tell me that dinner was in five minutes. I told her I wasn't hungry. The truth was I thought I was going to be sick.

When I didn't come down, my father came up to see what the problem was. I told him I had done something wrong.

"What did you do?"

"Nothing."

My father looked at me sternly. "I don't have time for your games, Del."

"I wasn't sure what to do. So I did nothing," I said. I was searching for a way to describe this strange feeling inside me. But words just got in the way. "I feel … bad."

"Bad? You mean sick?" He felt my forehead. "Well, I don't think you have a fever. Do you feel like you have to throw up?"

"I don't think it's so much my stomach," I said quietly. I was reliving the scene with the bullies and the skinny boy and his smashed eyeglasses over and over in my mind. It was almost like I was a character in a video game trying to make my way through a maze. But I kept getting lost and having to start all over again. There was something I was missing. Only I had no clue what it was …

Jeddy ambushed me on the way home. "Wait a second, will ya, Del?" I turned around, and his hazel-green eyes stared at me. "Tell me what you're doing."

"What do you mean?"

"This thing you're doing with Djebar and Sogi and the others. What's it all about?"

"Why do you want to know?" I asked.

"Because I want to know."

There was something in his eyes that made the hairs near my ears bristle. A funny feeling was starting in my stomach.

"I'm not telling you."

"Tell me."

"No."

"Yes! Tell me!"

A sudden dizziness overtook me. I felt a throbbing pain start up from my occipital bone and move across my skull. I wanted to sit down, but there was nowhere to sit.

"If you don't tell me you'll be sorry," Jeddy said, advancing towards me.

My arms flung out, and I hit him with both palms in the chest. Jeddy stumbled back, and his face got red and tight. My heart was pumping, so fast I couldn't catch my own thoughts and figure out what to do next. But in my mind something flashed, a pattern that rearranged itself into an algorithm, a polynomial equation. My heart slowed, and the pain in my head ebbed. I closed my eyes to catch my breath.

The next thing I knew, I was on the ground and Jeddy was standing over me, his face all red and sweaty. "Darrin said you and your group are putting together a board game. But I know he's lying. I know it." He put his knee into my chest and blocked out the sun. I tried to push him off, but Jeddy is at least thirty pounds heavier than me. His pupils were big and dilated. "What do you think Ms. Pokolopinison will do when she finds out you lied to her? That you *all* lied to her?"

When I get excited or when I'm cross or afraid, I blink a lot and my stutter gets worse to the point where spittle comes out of my mouth. "Jeddy, g-g-get off ... m-me!"

Jeddy started to laugh. I shut my eyes tight, waited for whatever was coming. But almost instantly I felt the weight lift from my chest. To my left I heard Jeddy cry out. I shielded my eyes with my forearm and rolled over. My eyes stung as if they'd been pricked by a hundred wasps. A wave of sensation swept through me; my throat was so tight I could barely draw a breath.

"Hey, kid. You okay?"

I squinted up at the figure standing over me and recognized him immediately. It was James Comfort.

James was looking through my polynomial workbook. It gave me an anxious feeling watching him, and I thought about snatching my workbook away from him, but I resisted the urge.

James set down the book. I wanted to put it back where it was supposed to be, but he was blocking my way. "You know, Einstein believed imagination was more important than intelligence," he said.

"He said imagination was more important than *knowledge*," I corrected him.

James looked at me. One of his eyebrows lifted with the corner of his mouth. It was an odd expression. "Right."

"But don't you have to have to be intelligent to be imaginative?" I asked.

James looked off to the left for a few seconds. He was looking at my poster map of the Island of Sodor. He blinked, cast a glance around my room, and suddenly looked uneasy. "You sure it's okay for me to be up here? Where are your parents?"

"My father works at Balm Life, and my mother is the assistant manager at the Merryton Community Arts and Book Center."

Bea passed by my door. James caught sight of her and got a funny look on his face. Bea came back, stared at James.

"Hey, aren't you —?" Bea's hand went to her mouth. "You live on the other side of the block. You're ... James Comfort." She grinned. "Hey, I really like your music — even if it is a bit retro. But I like the late nineties stuff. You're American, right? I've seen you play the guitar —" She suddenly stopped, looked at me, then shot a glance towards my window where the curtains were drawn back. James followed her gaze. The funny look on his face got funnier. I was frustrated; I couldn't read him at all.

He approached the window, hunched, and looked through. "Oh. Fuck."

I was startled by his response, and looked to my sister. Bea had turned bright red and pressed her fingers to her mouth. "Excuse me," she muttered, and fled the room.

James turned to look at me, but his attention was suddenly diverted by something on my desk. He paused, then turned his washed-out blue eyes on me. His expression puzzled me. I still couldn't read him properly. But I did sense that he might be cross, which confused me all the more since we didn't even know each other and there wasn't really anything to be cross about.

"Tell me you haven't been spying on me, kid."

"You're the only one on the fifth floor who doesn't have curtains," I said. "Why do you play your music while everyone is asleep? Do you have sleep problems, like me?"

"Oh, shit." James rubbed his chin a few times. "What is this? Some kind of set-up? Did you set me up?" He was looking around the room now with a kind of fearful look. "Where are the cameras?"

"I don't know what you mean."

"That fight out there. It was all a set-up, wasn't it?" He ran his fingers through his long sandy blond hair. "You're filming this, aren't you?"

"I don't know what you mean."

"Listen, I don't do the fan-groupie thing anymore, okay? I'm through with all that. Finito. I just want to be left alone, you capisce, kid?"

I shook my head. "I don't know what you mean."

"Okay, I'm just going to skedaddle out of here. Okay? Nothing to talk about here, right? Everything's cool. Okay? We're all cool here. Nothing happened." He walked around me towards my bedroom door.

"I don't know what you mean." The words came out strangely. My throat felt tight. My eyes were stinging.

James Comfort paused in his step. His forehead creased as he squinted at me. His eyes were like bits of blue noon sky, and they made me stare back at him. After a moment he said, "What's wrong with you, kid?"

"I have Asperger syndrome."

"What's that?" And then he immediately waved his hand at me. "No, no. Never mind. I don't want to get involved. I'm out of here." He slipped out my bedroom door, and I could hear him clomping down the stairs. He was taking them two at a time, which, in descent, is quite difficult.

Bea came racing out of her room. "Del! What was *James Comfort* doing in your bedroom?" She shook her head in disbelief. "Wow! They say he's a washout because of the drugs and stuff. But he looked even better in person! And he's *old*. I mean, he's got to be about … thirty-five?"

"He's thirty-seven," I said.

"Whatever. But, you know, if I were famous like him, I would be out having as much fun as possible. Not hiding out here, in *Merryton*. He's got to have loads of money; he could go anywhere. But he comes *here*? Why?"

"Do you think he'll come back?"

Bea frowned. "What do you mean? Come back here? To the house, you mean?"

I started to cry. It just happens sometimes. It's like a big wave of sensation washes through me and I start to cry.

"Hey. What are you crying about? What's wrong?" Bea took my hand. "Del, did — did James Comfort hurt you?"

I snatched my hand away and shook my head. "It's nothing. I — I just wanted to ask him something."

"Yeah, well … I think you kind of freaked him out. He knows you've been watching him."

"You watch him too, Bea."

My sister's face turned red again, and her mouth scrunched up at the corners. "I only did it that once, when I couldn't sleep and I caught you looking through your stupid binoculars." She went over and picked them up. "I'm going to tell Mom and Dad. This is … *perverted*."

I got a scared feeling in my chest and I lunged at her, grabbed the binoculars from her hand. She fell down, bumped her head on the bed. She had on her really cross face when she stood up. I backed away.

"That's it. I'm telling on you for sure now." She started to walk out of the room, then suddenly stopped at the doorway. She whirled around. The look on her face frightened me. "Why are you like this? Why do you have to be such a *retard*! It's *you* they fight about all the time. It's because of *you* they're getting a divorce!"

The following day I took a different route to school. This may not sound like a big thing, but in my world it is a big thing. I am, as my mother says, a creature of habit. I like routines, schedules, instructions, rules. These are things I can count on. These are the things by which I can feel safe. When I am following my routines, it is as if I am connecting the dots through that day of my life. I told Doctor Bankoy this, and he told me I needed to change my routines so that I can enjoy the variety of life and gain more confidence in the way I conduct myself. Doctor Bankoy will be pleased that I took a different route to school.

There was another reason I did this, however. I had planned it two nights before, in fact. I was taking a different route to school so I would have a greater chance of running into James Comfort.

The houses on this street were smaller, squat, with straggly shrubs and mugo pines whose long finger-cones hadn't been snipped. I was sweating, that fluttery feeling in my stomach beginning to intensify and the scalp of my head prickling with alarm. Sometimes I get this sensation. Doctor Bankoy says it has something to do with my sympathetic hormonal system. But I like to think of it as my Spidey-sense. The colors around me were wrong; the smells were wrong; the sidewalks were wrong. I looked at the cars that were parked in the driveways, but it was difficult to focus. Was I going the right way? There was a compass on the right-hand side of the middle drawer of my desk. I hadn't thought to bring it. I tried to visualize a compass in my head, but everything had taken on a reddish-orange hue, and I was frightened.

I was lost. I was sure of it.

Ask someone for directions.

But when I passed a man getting into his car, I just kept going. Wait. Up ahead. A girl. Someone from Merryton Public, maybe. Yes, I think I recognized her. *Follow her.*

I hurried along behind the girl, but all of a sudden she turned and started up a driveway and knocked at the front door of a white house with dark brown shutters. Someone opened the door and the girl slipped inside.

What should I do? I thought. *I'll wait. I'll wait until she comes out.*

I remembered then why I had opted to take this route. James Comfort. Where did he live? I closed my eyes, visualized him in the sitting room playing his guitar. Oddly, the image calmed me. *Margaret Street.* That's where he lived. What street am I on now? In my mind's eye I pictured the street sign as the yellow van with the painted dragon had passed me: *Carbunkle.*

I know Merryton because I've studied and memorized the "Tried n' True Handy Map of Merryton." Carbunkle Street intersects with

Margaret, nearest to Flora Drive. The map in my head told me it was further ahead. I was sure of it.

I waited another three minutes, but when the girl didn't emerge from the white house with the dark brown shutters, I went on. When I saw the intersection ahead, I ran to it. I looked at the sign: Flora Drive. A wind rushed through me, and I felt suddenly lighter, cooler. I started to run. I only had thirty-eight minutes before the bell would ring.

I ran until I was running down Margaret Street and I saw the building where I knew James Comfort lived. I ran towards it, looked at the panel of buttons. *I will ring his doorbell,* I thought. *I'll ask him to help me with the band and he will say —*

Out of the corner of my eye, I saw the beast coming. A dog. A big one. It sprinted across the grass, flying towards me as if it had been shot from a canon. Its big white head hurled towards me, its eyes tiny and black and sunk deep into flapping folds of skin. It loosed a snarl that sounded like wood splintering, and suddenly all I could see was its bared teeth. I heard myself shriek as I slammed into the panel of buttons.

A woman's voice sputtered through the speaker. But she spoke in code. "He-e-elp me!" I screamed. And then I think I heard James Comfort's voice, but I couldn't be sure because the dog sank its teeth into my calf and everything shut down.

It is not uncommon for autistic people, while in the throes of extreme stress, to suddenly zone out or suffer fainting spells. Most of the students in the ASD class suffer from syncope, which is sudden faintness. I rarely faint, but Wesley used to faint all the time just from swallowing. When I go to places like malls, I have moments when I think I will faint. But I just stop and sit down and put my head between my legs and I'm okay.

I was staring into James Comfort's face, watching his mouth move. My thoughts were jumbled, spinning in the wrong direction, and I was trying to clear the gray in my brain.

"Kid? Hey, kid." He snapped his fingers in front of my face. "Can you hear me? Did you hit your head? Because I can't find anything wrong with you." He patted my cheek. "Hey, kid. Snap out of it, will you?"

His touch jolted me. "My name's not 'kid.' It's Del. Delmore William Capp."

James looked at me. I couldn't read his expression. "Right … Del." He glanced up, his gaze arrowing past me.

"We should call an ambulance," said a voice behind me.

I jumped, startled. I twisted my body so that I could see two fat stockinged legs standing at my back. "Go away! I don't want to talk to you!" I said loudly.

"Hey, no need to be rude, Del. Mrs. Agee's only trying to help. She's the one who found you lying on the front stoop."

I looked around me. I was on a navy rug that smelled like Alphaghetti and cigarette smoke. My perimeter consisted of greenish-blue walls with an encased fire alarm on the wall to my right. I saw the stairs then, and realized I was inside the building on the main floor landing. "How did I get here?"

"I carried you."

"I weigh one hundred thirty-seven pounds," I said.

"That much? I would have put you at a hundred — one-ten at the most," said James.

"I'm five foot, eleven and a half inches. If I weighed one hundred pounds, I would be considered seriously underweight," I said.

James cocked his head. Again, I couldn't read his expression. "Yeah, okay." He clasped my hand. "Can you sit up?"

"Do you think that's a good idea? He might have a concussion," said Ms. Agee.

"I don't want to talk to you!" I said. "Leave me alone!"

"Rude bugger, isn't he?" Mrs. Agee said. "Kids these days. No manners."

I could hear her moving her feet behind me, and it made me anxious. "Get away from me!" I warned.

"Thank you, Mrs. Agee." James smiled up at her. "I'll take it from here."

When she was gone, I felt the tension dribble out of my shoulders. But I felt suddenly frightened because it was at that moment that I remembered the dog. "It bit me. I got bit."

James clasped my hand. "Can you sit up?"

"Yes." I sat up, and immediately checked my right calf for dog bites. "Where is it?"

"Where is what?"

"It was a bull terrier mix — part mastiff, I think. It came at me and bit my leg. But I don't see the bite." I frowned. "I am certain he bit me."

James laughed. "Well, you're partly right."

"I don't understand."

"The dog did bite you — only it didn't have any teeth."

"The dog did bite you — only it didn't have any teeth," I echoed. I felt a throbbing sensation in my right leg. I looked down. Near the bottom of my brown cargo pants a dark stain had pooled around the calf. I made a sound deep in my throat. My stomach didn't feel well. James squeezed my hand.

"I already checked. The bite didn't break the skin or anything," James reassured me. "But it might've bruised you. Do you want me to look at it?"

I let go of his hand, pushed him with my other hand. "No!"

James nodded, scratched his chin, and didn't say anything for a long moment.

"Can you get up?" he asked finally.

"Yes." And then, as an afterthought, I muttered, "Thank you."

He showed his teeth in his smile. They were yellowish, but even on the top. "Hey, no problem. Uh, listen, if you need a drive somewhere —"

"I need to talk to you," I said. My words surprised me, and when I looked down the inside of my head swirled a bit and my face suddenly got very hot.

"Oh? Uh, what about?"

I had memorized this bit of dialogue, written it like a script the two of us were supposed to follow. But he wasn't following it, so I got frustrated.

"You're supposed to ask me: *Why do you want to start a band?* And then I say: *Because my mother and father are divor—*"

"Whoa! Slow down a second, kid," he stopped me. "I have no idea what you're talking about."

I started again, repeating what I'd said, but he stopped me in mid-dialogue.

"All right. Let me get this straight." James scratched his head. "You want to start a rock band, am I right?"

"Yes. And I'm —"

"— looking for a band manager?"

I hadn't said as much, but he had guessed right. "Yes. You see, we need a Neural Typical who knows about music. And you were in a rock band —"

"Past history, kid. I'm ... well, I'm on vacation from that life."

"But you have experience. We need you."

"Look, Del, I don't do that kind of thing." His brow crinkled. "Wait a second. What's a *Nerval Typical*?"

"Neural Typical," I corrected. "A Neural Typical is someone who's not on the autism spectrum."

"You lost me."

"I'm an Aspie. I'm a person with Asperger syndrome, so I'm on the autism spectrum. You're a Neural Typical. Or a neurotypical person. You're ... *not* on the autism spectrum."

James looked at his watch. He was biting his lower lip. "Shouldn't you be in school?"

"Yes." I had already looked at my watch. If I didn't leave now I was definitely going to be late. "I should go."

"Are you sure you're okay?"

"Yes." My head was groggy and my heart was beating a bit faster than normal, but I didn't think I was going to faint again.

James shook his head. "You sure seem to get into a lot of trouble, kid."

"My name isn't 'kid.' It's Del."

"Right. Well, you'd better skedaddle, Del." He scratched his head. "Listen, I'm sorry, but I don't think I can help you."

I looked down at my shoes. Tightness sneaked through my chest, and I could feel a panic attack coming. I kept my gaze on my running shoes, willing the tightness in my chest to go away. "You have to help me." I tried to blink away the sting in my eyes.

"I *have* to help you? Look, Del, you don't even know me —"

"I don't ... do well with people," I said. A part of me just wanted to run away, but I took a deep breath and thought about Hero Boy from *The Polar Express*. "I believe," I said loudly.

"Huh?"

I suddenly remembered my knapsack. I jerked around, looking for it in sudden panic. But it was right there, sitting by the door. I walked over to it, took out the notebook, and extracted the papers I had stuffed in it last night. I thrust them at him. "Here."

"What's this?"

"My email address is on the top. I have to go. I'm going to be late for school." I shrugged on my knapsack and sprinted out the door. My right leg felt a bit numb, but my heart was pounding so hard I couldn't hear the street sounds. When I crossed the street, I very nearly ran into the side of a gray minivan backing out of a driveway. I looked at my watch. I was going to be late. I would have to go to the main office and get a late slip. My thoughts crowded inside my head, and I could feel the anxiety rising inside me. I started to cry. I hate being late.

"Del, honey, would you like to try some mustard?" My mother was feeding Bea pureed peas, and she was systematically spitting them out. My gaze fastened on Bea's mouth, watching the peas spew from the cavernous hole between her lips.

"Del? Did you hear me, sweetie? Del? Would you like —?"

"'Suddenly, an idea flew into his funnel!'"

"You might like it. Here." My mother placed a dollop of yellow mustard. My reaction was to push the plate away.

"I don't like it!"

"You didn't even try it," said my father.

"Would you like to dip your hot dog into it?" My mother forked her own hot dog, dipped it into the mustard on her plate, and took a bite.

"'Li-ily white and cle-ean, oh!'"

My father growled under his breath. "Talk properly! When we ask you a question, just answer it."

I stared at the mustard. It was too yellow, and I didn't like the smell. "'Talk properly! ... just answer it.'" I echoed. But the words shot out of my mouth like bangs from a cap gun, and it startled me.

"Geezus." My father leaned towards me with a strange expression on his face. "Now he's *stuttering*."

Alan Turing was a stutterer like me. But while many believed back then that the cause of stuttering was primarily psychological, Turing came to understand that his speech impediment was caused by malfunctioning signals between the brain, speech nerves, and interacting muscles. To him, it seemed only logical that if one could mend these faulty signals, one might be cured of one's stammering. However, when World War II broke out and Turing decided to take up the challenge of cracking the German code Enigma, his stutter improved so much that it disappeared altogether.

In trying to understand his proposed connection between his stuttering and the brain's speech nerve signals, Turing asked of himself the one question he knew he would never be able to answer with full certainty: "Do I stutter when I think?"

I thought about this. Do I stutter when I think? I don't know. Doctor Bankoy says I don't have a real stutter, that I stumble over my words because I have so much anxiety.

I guess I'm not too anxious when I sing or laugh or write because I don't stutter.

And then it occurred to me that I also didn't stutter when I talked to James Comfort.

The logic of mathematics is something I can count on. It provides solutions to problems. Just *knowing* that a problem has a solution helps organize some of the chaos in my mind and alleviates the anxiety in my belly. When I am stressed I calculate basic quadratic and polynomial equations. After a while the fruit flies buzzing inside me start to settle and I stop feeling so afraid.

Turing argued that mathematics should be seen as one of the natural sciences, which focus on experimentation and quantifiable information and value objectivity and accuracy. Turing said he did not believe there was anything abstract about mathematics. I'm inclined to agree, as abstractions often muddle my thinking, but mathematics does not.

But Picasso is considered, by some, to be an abstract artist. And yet everyone in our ASD class seems to be able to identify with him. But maybe it's not so much that we understand Picasso's paintings as that we see what he is trying to do. He is trying to show us all sides, all perspectives of things in a two-dimensional medium. I had the thought that maybe this is how an autistic person experiences the world; the difference is the perspectives are coming at you *all at once*.

I told Doctor Bankoy about my theory, and he told me he was impressed, if not quite a bit surprised that I had thought up such a theory. Autistic people normally don't do well with abstract concepts, he told me. I wasn't sure Picasso's art was an abstract concept, but I didn't say that as he admitted to me that he himself had never been able to understand Picasso's art. I wondered if that might be because he wasn't autistic. But I didn't mention that, either.

Doctor Bankoy asked me how I felt about my parents divorcing. I said I didn't know. I didn't tell him that I had planned to keep them together by winning the Cubground Pub Battle of the Bands competition and living out my father's dream to become a rock star. I don't think he's the kind of person who would have understood.

"So, you want to put a band together," said James.

We were sitting on the stone bench in the park just outside his apartment building. He didn't invite me into his apartment, he said, because he didn't think it would be appropriate. I didn't know what he meant. But in any case, I was already familiar with his apartment.

When I didn't say anything, he asked, "Are you thinking about studying music?"

"No."

"Oh. So what are you thinking of studying?"

"Mathematics."

"Huh." James made a face. "I wasn't too good at math."

A beat of silence stretched between us so that I could hear the pulse in my own neck. Then suddenly he started scratching his arms and wriggling on the bench, crossing then uncrossing his legs. I wanted to ask him if he was okay, but sometimes when I ask people that they get angry for some reason.

Finally, he spoke. "Your email said you want to put a band together to, uh, enter this battle of the bands competition in Toronto, right?"

"Yes."

James rubbed the blond stubble on his chin. "Help me out, here, Del. I still don't know what you want from me."

"I told you yesterday — in the email I sent." The day was overcast, and my skin felt dry and itchy. But the bugs weren't crawling up and down my arms and legs, so it wasn't an Orange Day. Most of us give our moods and sensory issues colors or animal names; it's something mental health therapists encourage. Orange is a color I don't like: it's a color that hurts me, and it's the color I see when I'm not feeling good. So bad sensory days for me are Orange Days.

But even though it wasn't an Orange Day, my scalp was tingling, and I could feel the beginnings of a strip headache. A strip headache is one that runs from the occipital bone to the frontal, and involves cervical nerves and the sternocleidomastoid muscle at the back of the neck. I get them a lot, usually when I'm stressed or anxious.

"To tell you the truth, I'm not really sure I understood your email," said James.

"You didn't email me back."

"I'm not a computer kind of guy," said James. "I don't email or text a lot."

I looked at him. I knew he had a computer. And a smart phone. I'm not good at reading faces, and James's face was especially difficult to read. I didn't know why.

"Okay," he said. "Why don't you start by telling me how I can help you?"

"There's six of us, that includes me," I said. "We're all in the same class."

"Who? Your friends?"

Friends? Were Djebar, Sogi, Petula, Wesley, and Darrin *my friends*?

"You're talking about your band, right?" he asked when I didn't answer.

My band? "We're all in an ASD class together," I replied.

"ASD? What's that?"

I suppose I had taken for granted that everyone knew about ASD. "Autism spectrum disorder. The people in my class, we're all autistic."

"Oh. Right. Right. You said something about that before, I think …" His expression changed. But I still couldn't read it. "And *you* think — you think you won't be able to enter this competition because you have a, uh, mental illness?"

"Autism is a neurobiological disorder," I said.

"Oh." James scratched his head. "Right." He looked directly into my eyes, and for a moment I experienced a jolt of anxiety. It took everything in me to not look away.

"So, can you help us?"

"Help you do what, exactly?"

"Manage our band." I glanced at my watch and sprang to my feet. "I have to go. So will you do it?"

James shook his head, laughing. "You've got me totally confused, Del."

"I do that to people, I know."

"Look, if you need some help — sure. I guess I can give you some advice about a few things —"

"I have to go." I tugged on my knapsack and sprinted down the street. My heart was pumping a little too hard in my chest, and I was getting that pins and needles feeling in my fingers and toes, which meant I was hyperventilating. I began to recite the "Dream Sweeter" assembly instruction booklet, and in my head I pictured myself putting together the R29863 king-size bed.

By the time I arrived at Merryton Public, I was calm again.

The first time I heard about the Canadian Research Association for Autism Spectrum Disorder was when I was twelve, and it was four days before Valentine's Day (a day of anxiety for me). As I wedged myself into the cupboard under the stairs, I heard my mother telling my father about the specialized research departments that were being set up in Merryton Public School.

"Del will be going into grade eight, so he's eligible to apply to their ASD program."

"I'm not so sure I want him enrolled in this research program thing," my father said. "Why can't he just keep going to normal classes like Bea?"

"Do you know how many applicants this research program gets?" said my mother. "This is a wonderful opportunity for Del. It could change his life!"

"I'd like to know a bit more about it before I commit him to something like this," said my father.

"If he's accepted, he will have access to all the behavioral therapies he needs."

"I'm not so sure he needs all that stuff, Connie. He's doing fine as he is."

"No, he's not, Tom." My mother's voice had changed, growing more abrupt and impatient. "Let's face it, we're tapped out. We will never be able to afford all these expensive behavioral therapies. And he's not our only child, remember. Bea is going to want to go to university, as well."

"You think Del is going to go to *university*?"

"He's smart enough, Tom. All the teachers say that. He's already doing advanced math and computer programming. But he needs help. And with this program, Del will not only be helped, he'll get a free ticket to a university education! And let's not forget that the government will be paying *us*, as well."

"I don't know. It seems like so much trouble. And what about all these computer gizmos they want us to buy for him? Geezus, Connie, have you seen this list?"

"It's government-funded. They'll reimburse us," my mother said. "I think this is what he *needs*, Tom. Academically, he can hold his own. But socially ... maybe — maybe this program will help him make some *friends*."

"Friends? Look, the kid doesn't *want* any friends. And if the other students are like him, they're not going to want to make friends, either."

"That's not true. Children like Del want friends. They just can't ... make friends very easily. And that's what breaks my heart."

My father made a sound at the back of his throat. After a moment he said, "I just don't like him being an *experiment*, that's all."

"That's not what this is —"

"Bea told me what the other children in school are calling kids like Del. *Ass Burgers*." I heard my father make a groaning sound. "*Ass Burgers*. Geezus."

"Tom —"

"It's meant to be some kind of joke, I guess. Something they picked up from some television show or something."

"Kids can be cruel —"

"*Ass Burgers*: now there's a name for a band." My father suddenly laughed. But it wasn't his regular laugh, and I was suddenly frightened by its cold sound.

The microwave buzzer interrupted him. My mother got up, and I could smell spaghetti sauce. I don't like pasta or any kind of noodle. But I do like spaghetti sauce.

"Connie, I just want him to be *normal*."

"Normal? Tom, be realistic."

"Well, he won't have a chance to be normal if we put him in this program, will he?"

"Tom, this research they're doing is *important*," my mother protested. "By being a part of this, Del will get the help he needs — and at the same time he'll be helping others like him. And … he'll be helping people like *us*, too. Maybe — maybe this will help *you* get to know Del better. Maybe this will help you finally accept him for who he is."

"Geezus, Connie. You want me to *accept* this? He's my *son*. I'm not going to let this thing take over our lives."

"Tom, you need to know more about this disorder —"

"I know enough to know I want to beat this thing! I want Del to be a regular kid. I want *us* to get back to normal so we can get on with our lives."

"This is about Del, not you or me. We need to do what's best for Del," my mother said in her "dark" voice. "I already put in his application. If they accept him, he's going into the program."

There was a sudden sound of chair legs scraping against linoleum. "Why do you even bother to involve me in these discussions? It really doesn't matter what I think, anyway, does it?"

"Where're you going?"

"You know what? I'm tired of talking about it. I'm tired of fighting about it, goddammit! From now on don't even bother asking my opinion. From now on you make the decisions. I don't want any part of it!"

A moment later the kitchen side door slammed shut.

"So, where is everybody?" James asked, sitting opposite me at the picnic table.

"They went home," I said.

"They left?"

"Yes. You were late."

James looked at his watch. "I'm … I'm *ten* minutes late." He glanced around the park. "They couldn't wait — just for ten minutes?"

"You're *fourteen* minutes late," I corrected him.

"Okay. So my watch is a bit slow." He rubbed his eyes, sat back on the bench. "You want to get a coffee?"

"I don't drink coffee."

"A ... hot chocolate, then." James yawned.

"No."

James looked at me out of the corner of his eye. "Hey, I was just a little late."

"Yes."

"Look, I'm doing this as a favor, okay?"

I didn't say anything. After a while, I glanced at my watch and stood.

"All right, listen," said James. "If you still want my help, why don't we meet *after* school?"

"Okay."

James yawned, then yawned again. He blinked up at me. "I'm sorry, kid. It was a rough night."

I nodded. "I'll see you tomorrow morning."

"What? Uh, I thought we said we'd meet *after* school."

"Yes, we can do that. But I thought you and I had agreed to meet in the mornings at 8:15."

"We did?" James gave a short laugh. "Well, I didn't actually —"

"I'll be here at 8:15." I looked down and began to trace circles in the leaves with the toe of my running shoe. "But it'll just be me. The others won't be able to come to meet you in the mornings."

"Oh. Okay." He frowned. "Uh, why not?"

I didn't answer, because what I had just told him was a lie. Djebar and the others would probably come if I told them to. I just didn't *want* them to.

"You'll be here?" I said. "At 8:15?"

"Sure."

"At 8:15."

James's brows lowered slightly. "I said I'd be here, didn't I?"

"I have to go." I started across the grass, my gaze fixed to the ground.

The pulse in my neck was throbbing. Why was my heart pounding so hard? As soon as I reached the sidewalk I broke into a run. I was going to be late again.

It is said that autistic people love rules because rules can regulate time limits, organize routines, and manage what happens around them. Following the rules can also be seen as a method of controlling the content and context of our everyday lives.

In all the special ASD classes, we use "curriculum menus" that tell us exactly what we are going to do in the class that day. People often see this as being too dependent on rules and routines. And while it is true that autistic people rely on regular routines, one might say that Aspies aren't any different from Neural Typicals in that respect. We're *all* dependent on schedules of one sort or another.

But the difference between Neural Typicals and autistic people is that when the routine is suddenly disrupted, or the rules are abruptly changed, we can sometimes freak out. Autistic people typically have problems adapting to transitions, and some of us get very emotional and suffer degrees of anxiety that can be disturbing to Neural Typicals.

I don't think it's the rules and routines per se that autistic people are attracted to, but the clear logic and predictability that run behind them. Logic and predictability, after all, are tools that can help us cut through all that disorder and confusion that surrounds us.

My Aunt Shirlee, who comes to visit once a year from Berne, Switzerland, once asked my parents what it was about trains, specifically Thomas the Tank Engine, that fascinated autistic children so much. Neither my mother nor father could come up with a satisfying answer as they, too, were puzzled by my obsessive interest.

When I was younger, I don't think I knew why Thomas the Tank Engine or trains meant so much to me. Even now, I find myself wondering what that magic was that held my attention so rapt. However, when I think about Thomas and trains in general, I feel an instant defogging in my brain. It is as if the train tracks are able to cut right through all that chaos that is continually bombarding me from the outside world.

There is something about the routines of the trains of Sodor that simultaneously excites and calms me. I feel a sense of reassurance when I see the trains all lined up symmetrically in their sleeping sheds, or when I watch them being arranged one by one on the tracks waiting to be coupled with trucks of cargo. I often made my mother be the signalman waving his green flag. I made elaborate train schedules so that all the engines would arrive at the station, unload their cargo, and depart on time. I think it worried my parents the way I controlled every aspect of my play with the engines. But it was when something went wrong with my train schedule that they became truly concerned. My emotional outbursts were sudden and explosive, and no matter what my parents did to try to stop or deter them, it never helped. Back then I was like Gordon smashing my way through the station wall in search of a new panoramic view.

However, for autistic people, I think the biggest attraction to the Thomas the Tank Engine trains is that all the engine models are equipped with faces whose expressions are actually readable. I've always preferred the live action models, with their eyes rolling, their expressions changing with every story plot. I always knew when Thomas was happy or when Percy was surprised or when James and Gordon were cross. I knew how they were *feeling*. Consequently, I was able to understand the world they lived in and the rules by which they lived. The truth was I couldn't help but be a little bit envious; these engines already knew their place and function in society. They knew what they were supposed to do, and they knew what their roles were in the world of trains.

But isn't that what we are all ultimately striving for? To figure out *who* we are?

Who are we? What are we supposed to be doing? Where are we supposed to be going?

The other day my mother asked me if I was interested in any of the girls in my class. My face became very hot, and I looked away from her, scared she might read what I was thinking.

I told her there were only two girls in the ASD class: Hannah and Petula.

My mother grinned at me. "So which one do you like?"

I looked down at my keyboard and didn't say anything. After a couple of minutes my mother got up from the edge of the bed and patted my shoulder. "That's all right. I respect your privacy, Del. But if you ever want to talk, you know where to find me, okay?"

"Talk?" I felt a jolt of panic. "What do you mean? Talk about what?"

My mother shrugged. "Anything. We can talk about anything you want."

"I don't understand."

My mother sighed. "Yes. I know." She smiled and blew me a kiss before shutting my bedroom door behind her.

My mother often seems to know things about me even before I tell her. I wondered if she knew how I felt about Petula.

But then, even *I* didn't understand how I felt about Petula.

Petula is a NDC, a Non-Denominational Christian.

"But that doesn't make sense," said Sogi. "Saying you're a Non-Denominational Christian means that you actually *do* have a denomination."

"We're about living the *idea* of Geezus Christ, not worshipping him," said Petula.

Sogi laughed. "You think living the idea of Christ is *not* worshipping him?"

"What do *you* know? You're an atheist." She snorted, tittered as if to herself. "An autistic atheist."

Sogi's narrow eyes shifted back and forth. "My mother says your mother thinks autism is a sign from Geezus."

Petula's mother is the manager of the Monastic Experience Therapy Center in Mississauga, and she says things like, "Faith in love creates harmony in life" and "Lift your eyes to see your purpose in the world." Whenever Petula's mother sees me she embraces me and says, "Joy of spirit is there if you believe and reach for it, Del." Petula's mother is part Assiniboine. Her eyes are a deep dark brown, and I have to look down at the ground to not feel so overwhelmed by them. I know she can't read my mind, but I can't help feeling that sometimes she is trying to.

Petula has two younger neurotypical brothers who are smart, good-looking, athletic, and popular. Although they don't pick on Petula, they — like both her mother and father — tend to forget she's there. I'm not sure they neglect or abuse her, but I do know they don't take much notice of her. Sometimes I wish my parents would ignore me more, but I don't think I would ever wish for parents like Petula's.

My parents do not practice any religion. This doesn't bother me. I have no interest in religion. Perhaps this is because the entire concept of religion continues to confuse me. I'm not sure if that's how everyone else in the ASD class feels. Wesley Farkle is Jewish, and he celebrates all the Jewish holidays and performs the rituals. If you ask him about the Jewish faith, however, he won't answer you. I'm not sure if it's because he doesn't understand Jewish faith or because he just doesn't like to talk about it.

The problem with religion, at least for people like me, is that it does not feel safe. I mean that it is not grounded on anything dependable or consistent or *certain*.

But is there anything in life that is certain? I don't know. Mathematics, maybe.

But even mathematics has its inconsistent moments. The difference is that these inconsistencies are not impossible to discern. Girls, on the other hand, are a bit more difficult to figure out.

Ol' Ben, my windup clock on the bedside table, told me it was fourteen minutes after three. I had promised James I wouldn't watch him anymore, so I had stuck my binoculars in the closet. I didn't feel like going online or doing my math, so I lifted the mattress and pulled out the notebook with the banana wearing the bandana and sunglasses. As I flipped through the notebook, I wondered if my father had written his journal in the early hours of the morning, because after a few pages I began to feel annoyed. My father hadn't been very organized. There were no dates, and the writing wasn't structured or styled in a regular prose fashion. He'd written in the margins, on the tops and bottoms of pages; there were doodles and little notes and quotes and poems jotted everywhere.

I realized my father had jotted down whatever had come into his head. Like notes to himself, I thought. Like *dreams*. My father's dreams before I was born.

But he had thrown them away. Forgotten them.

I turned on my computer and decided I would use the notes and make my father remember.

One morning I found my father in the kitchen wearing my mother's apron and frying eggs. Bea was sitting in her chair at the breakfast nook cutting up her eggs. She looked over at me, bit her lip, and didn't say anything.

"Good morning!" my father greeted me. "What's your 'up-over,' eh?"

"What do you mean?"

"How would you like your eggs? Sunny side up? Over easy? Over medium? Over hard? Boiled? Scrambled? I do it all!"

"I don't like eggs for breakfast."

"Sure you do!"

"I want Corn Flakes and milk."

"What the hell? Corn Flakes and milk?" My father's face scrunched up, the color of his skin darkening a little. His eyes were veined, and there were dark blue semicircles under them. My father's face is not symmetrical. I correct it every time I look at him. He once grew a moustache when I was four, and I struck out at him whenever he came near me. He tried it again when I was seven. It gave me anxiety. I tried to get used to it, but the sight of his uneven moustache agitated me. My father finally shaved it off. He has never since tried to grow facial hair.

"Tell you what," he said. "I'll make you an egg, and if you decide not to eat it, then you don't have to eat it. Okay?"

"I'll just have Corn Flakes and milk, if that's okay."

"It's not okay. I am making you an egg for breakfast."

"I don't want an egg. I don't eat eggs."

"Since when?"

"I don't like eggs."

"Really?" My father put down the spatula, looked at me. "Where the hell have I been?"

"I don't know, Dad."

My father sighed, came over and put his hand on my head, and rubbed it hard. It felt good. I remembered when we used to wrestle together. He called it "strong-arming." My father has very strong arms and he used to lift me like one of his barbells then pretend to squish me against his chest. My mother would tell him to be careful, but she would laugh with us. Bea was a baby in her arms then, and she would make strange noises that made me clench my teeth together sometimes. But when my father was strong-arming me she laughed too, and it was okay.

"Okay. So this time *you* are late," said James as I approached the bench.

I looked at my watch. It was 8:19. "I am. I apologize."

James laughed. "That was just a joke. I was teasing you."

"But I am actually four minutes late."

James shook his head, gazed at me with an expression that might have been curiosity. But his face is unsymmetrical with odd angles and planes, and his expressions confuse me. I looked away and said, "It'll be five of us: Darrin on lead guitar, Sogi on bass guitar, Djebar on keyboard, Petula and Wesley on percussion."

"You've got two on percussion?"

"Petula plays the xylophone and the triangle."

"Huh. Okay. So, you need ... a sound man, is that it?"

"And a place to rehearse."

James stroked his chin. "I know of a couple of studios in Toronto who might help you out. I can make some calls —"

"We can't go to Toronto.

"Why not? It's, like, a half-hour's drive away."

"We're not going to Toronto."

James frowned. "But you're going to have to go to Toronto if you want to enter this competition. The Cubground Pub is in Toronto."

"None of us drive. And we don't travel well."

"You don't travel well? What's that supposed to mean?"

I was quiet for a moment. "We need a place to rehearse the band here. And we also need to send in a video recording for entry into the competition by December 15th."

"December? That doesn't give you much time."

"We need someone who can ..." My words faltered. "*Organize* us."

"You mean a manager," said James. He shook his head. "I hate to disappoint you, but I'm not the most organized person in the world —"

"It's not about organization. It's about dealing with ... other people."

I couldn't read James's expression. But for a flash of a moment I thought maybe he was going to tell me he couldn't help me. When he didn't say anything, I said, "Djebar's mother travels to Toronto sometimes, so Djebar says we can use his garage to rehearse on the Saturdays when she's away. But she won't be away every weekend, so we're going to need somewhere more ... reliable."

"Okay," said James. "Let me work on it."

"So ... you'll help us, then?"

James made a sound in his throat, then gave an abrupt laugh. But it wasn't a happy laugh. "Well, it's not like I have a career pursuing me." He looked at me, and his cheeks pinked a little. "I'll let you know tomorrow. How's that?"

"Let me know what?"

"I have a place in mind where you might be able to rehearse your band."

It was already twenty minutes to nine. I shouldered my knapsack. "I'll see you here tomorrow?"

"Sure. Just don't be late, okay?" James gave a light laugh.

I started off, and then stopped when he suddenly called out to me: "Wait a minute, Del!"

I turned around.

"You told me about the others, but what will *you* be doing in the band?" he asked.

I froze, turned the question over and over in my head. In fact, I had no idea what I was going to do in the band.

I turned and ran.

Can a machine, Turing wondered, be capable of original thought and independent action like a human brain?

Some people believe that human brains are just organic computers. I'm not so sure this is true. And I don't think Alan Turing believed it, either. For one thing, when a machine makes a mistake, it is more often than not caused by the human inputting information. Human brains are not infallible, to be sure; they make mistakes. But this is how they learn. Can a computer learn from its errors? Can it alter and improve itself without a human *inputting* the correction?

I wonder what Turing would make of the Internet? If he were alive today, would he agree with Jeddy's father, who calls the Internet the Human Brain Network?

I think Jeddy's father is wrong; human brains may be very similar to computers, but computers are not, and will never be, human brains.

In the summer of 1987 my father formed a rock band. There's a photograph of them in my parents' bedroom. My father's hair is down to his shoulders and he is wearing a black-and-white tie and a black jacket with rounded shoulder pads, with the sleeves pulled up to his elbows. If you squint really hard you can see a bit of a tattoo on the inside of his left forearm. He doesn't have a tattoo now, so my guess is it wasn't permanent. In the photograph it looks like a bird with its wings spread, but I can't be sure.

They called themselves Dynamoelectric. This surprised me a little; my father is not at all scientific-minded. He did very poorly in school and very nearly didn't graduate. Not because he didn't have the smarts, my mother explained, but because "your father was lazy."

Dynamoelectric is an adjective used to describe the relationship between electricity and mechanical force. I thought it was a great name for a band. In fact, it was even better than the Turing Machinists.

"The Turing Machines?" James scratched his head. "*That's* what you want to call yourselves?"

"Machinists," I corrected. "Meaning that we are *designers* of the Turing Machine."

"Oh. Uh, does this name have any significance? Is this Turing Machine a real machine of some kind?"

We all stared at him.

"It's the Turing Machine," said Djebar. "You know… Alan Turing?"

James shook his head. "Sorry, I don't know who that is."

Wesley made a sound like he was going to throw up. None of us spoke for a few minutes.

James cleared his throat. "Wait a second. Does this guy, Alan Turing, have this Asperger disease as well?"

Was Alan Turing a Neural Typical or an Aspie? He was known to be socially awkward, he didn't have very many close friends, and people considered him an eccentric. Djebar says this was because he was a homosexual. In those times, being homosexual was seen as being caused by mental disease. But what does his being homosexual have to do with his being eccentric? Did Turing believe his homosexuality caused him to be different from other people? Did he, like all those experts of his time, believe he possessed faulty brain circuitry?

I spoke my first word when I was nine months. At ten and a half months I was speaking short sentences. My mother jokes that I came out of the womb flapping and kicking, and reciting Shakespeare. At eleven months I skipped the crawling stage and went directly to walking. By the thirteenth month I was running.

However, I wasn't able to climb stairs until I was two and a half. I didn't learn to jump until I was three, or ride a bicycle until I was ten, and to this day I still have trouble balancing on one foot.

My mother and father were reassured that all children develop at different times, and that one day all my developments would even out and I would be just like all the other typical children. They waited for this to happen. The day after I started junior kindergarten my mother stopped waiting.

I think my father, however, is still waiting.

I was four and a half years old, and that year I had started spinning. When the woman with the white steel wool hair tried to stop me spinning I struck out at her. At the time I was also spitting at people. This latter behavior seemed an effective way to get people to leave me alone.

"Oh! How rude!"

My mother rushed onto the scene, apologizing as she always did.

"You should teach your little boy some manners! That is not the way we behave in public."

"He knows that, but I think you startled him."

"I did no such thing! He hit me, then *spit* at me."

"I'm really sorry. He —"

"That boy will grow into a real bully if you don't put a stop to that behavior!"

"For your information, my son has autism. He's *autistic*," my mother said, putting her arm around my shoulders.

"Oh. Well …" The woman looked at me like she'd just smelled something rotten. "I thought autistic children didn't speak." Now her eyes were narrowing as if she didn't believe my mother. "Are you sure? He *seems* normal enough."

"Well, it's difficult to confirm —"

"He seemed to understand me fine," said the woman, gazing sternly at me. I remember feeling an urge to strike out at her, to make her stop looking at me.

"It's not … an intelligence thing," my mother explained. "I mean, he's not mentally challenged or anything. It's more *developmental*. It's his emotions, you see. He gets upset easily. And the autism makes him really sensitive to everything like sounds and flashes of light. And right now, he doesn't seem to be doing so well with people …"

How does a doctor test for autism? He can't. Not really. Yes, there are the observations, the questionnaires, the behavior analyses. But there is no simple test that will come back positive or negative and confirm a diagnosis of autism. Even with the genetic testing for autism, such as the newer chromosomal microarray genetic test, verifying a diagnosis of autism is not possible, as it is only effective in detecting less than 10 percent of known genetic disorders. And what if you don't believe that autism is genetic?

Alan Turing was purported to state that his sexual preference was a "dart thrown in the dark." It had nothing to do with the world and the people in it. I think, maybe, I believe the same thing about autism. Genetics does make the most logical sense in the puzzle. But if autism is a dart thrown in the dark, it can hit anywhere and anyone.

Social etiquette is part of every ASD academic class. It comprises 5 percent of our overall marks, so it is deemed important. At one time social etiquette was an official class in itself, but Jeddy's father argued that it was unfair to include it in the academic curriculum as most of us do not achieve very good marks and it would bring down our overall average. (Jeddy was doing poorly on account of his X-rated language and refusal to say "please.") Wesley and Darrin always get the best marks in social etiquette; Djebar, Sogi, and I do average; Petula and Hannah are usually tied for the worst. One time Djebar tried to pull out Hannah's chair for her, and she kicked him in the stomach. Djebar told me later that he was more in love with Hannah than ever.

"She's in love with me," he said. "I can tell about these things."

I wish I had Djebar's confidence; I can't tell whether Petula even notices me.

"Have you ever been to the Minotaur before?" Petula asked me.

I shook my head.

"I have," said Sogi.

"I wasn't asking you," Petula snapped.

James knew the owner of the Minotaur, and he told us he could arrange it so we could come in on Sundays when it closed after the dinner crowd.

"I don't think my parents will like me going there," said Darrin.

"Mine either," said Petula. "It's a *bar*."

I was thinking about the Busy Pub where my dad hung out. I'd always wondered what it'd be like inside. But from what my mother has said about the pub, I hoped the Minotaur was a little more sanitary.

"It's the perfect place." James glanced around the park. "We're eventually going to need somewhere to rehearse, right? Other than Djebar's garage, that is. And the Minotaur has a stage and a sound station."

"Why do we have to meet at all?" said Sogi. "We can always video conference using an MCU, or even Skype each other."

"You want to rehearse ... over the computer?" James wrinkled his nose so that we could see his front teeth. It was an odd expression, and it made Wesley laugh.

James shook his head. "This is *music* we're talking about. If you're going to be a band, you need to learn to all be in the same room for more than —" he glanced at his watch "—twenty minutes."

"Speaking of time, I have to leave," said Sogi. "I have spiritual yoga in half an hour."

"Okay. Uh, Del? You said something about rehearsing in Djebar's parents' garage?" James looked at me, then at the others. "I'm thinking once a week at The Minotaur isn't going to cut it. So if we could get in more rehearsal time —"

"Djebar's parents are divorced," Petula informed James. "He lives with his mom."

"Oh. Well, I guess rehearsing at The Minotaur will have to do —"

"We can rehearse in my parents' garage," Djebar spoke up.

"Great!" said James. He suddenly frowned. "Wait. You talked to your folks about this, right?"

We all looked at Djebar. As far as I knew, none of us had told our parents about what we were doing. Forming a music band was all well and good, but if we told our parents, they would take over and make us do it their way — just as they do with everything we do. The other, much more important thing was that not in a million years would they ever let us go to Toronto alone to compete in the Cubground Pub Battle of the Bands.

"Yeah, of course." Djebar bobbed his head, twisted his fingers together. None of us are good liars. But of all of us, Djebar is the best.

"Okay, then. We have a place to rehearse the Turing Machinists." James rubbed his hands together. "Now we just have to agree on *when* to rehearse."

"We can rehearse at my house this Saturday," said Djebar. "My mom's gone for a whole week."

"I don't understand poetry."

Mr. Levinson adjusted his wire-rimmed spectacles. "I think you might surprise yourself, Del."

"I don't like surprises."

"What about the sonnet?" Mr. Levinson asked. "Or perhaps haiku poetry would interest you?"

"Haiku?" I echoed. Issa. Japanese. *It followed a formula.* "Yes, haiku." I nodded earnestly.

Djebar's chosen topic was the stage play. His favorite playwright, Neil Simon, wasn't on the list, but Mr. Levinson approved it. Djebar loved anything to do with Neil Simon. Djebar and I are both into movies, although we differ in what we like. He likes action/blow 'em up films; I mostly like science fiction. We do both like Charlie

Kaufman a lot. Maybe because we don't quite understand his movies.

Djebar watches *Being John Malkovich* every Tuesday night, and he says he still doesn't totally get it. But it is less a routine than a compulsion for him to watch the movie. It's just something he has to do. And I totally understand it. A lot of my classmates have their obsessions and compulsions — like Jeddy, who has to line up his pencil grips in the groove on his desk every morning before the bell rings; and Hannah, who walks around the room, first clockwise, then counterclockwise, then clockwise again. She used to do this three times each way, but Mrs. Karroll asked her to keep it to only once in both directions as her pacing was taking up a lot of class time.

Although I am a big fan of *Being John Malkovich*, I would have to say my favorite film of all time is *Zero Effect*. It's about this private investigator named Daryl Zero who investigates this mystery involving blackmail and missing keys. Jeddy thinks *Zero Effect* is a loser movie because it never actually addresses the zero effect. (Any number added or subtracted by zero always remains the same; if it is multiplied by zero it will become zero.) I'm not sure the title is about the actual number zero, but in any case, I think Jeddy is wrong because, on principle, I very rarely agree with Jeddy.

The main character in the movie is played by Bill Pullman, and he kind of reminds me of me. Maybe. I don't think the character Daryl Zero is autistic, though. He had a pretty traumatic childhood, and I think he's also just naturally eccentric. Sometimes I like to think of myself like that: just a bit weird and different. Not autistic.

The other thing I like about Daryl Zero is that he's awkward around people — especially girls. I've been wanting to ask Petula out for three years now, but I just can't seem to get around to it. It doesn't help that every time I try to talk to her, I stutter so bad I sound like an electric typewriter.

"Life can be confusing, Del." Perched on my bed in the dark, my mother took on the shape of a grand harp, but with all the angles softened, and the light that shone through the window formed a kind of halo around her. "It's not always as simple as we'd like it to be, is it? I mean, everything can just go … wrong, you know? You make plans and — well, they don't always turn out like you want them to, do they?"

I wasn't sure if she was asking me a question, so I didn't say anything.

After a moment, when I did not respond, she said in a low, quiet voice, "I think you know what I'm talking about, Del."

My heart suddenly lurched and began to thump hard. Two minutes ago I had been feeling sleepy because I had taken two melatonins after brushing my teeth. But now I was wide awake. How had my mother figured out my plan? How had I given myself away? I immediately braced myself for her reprisal and began formulating a Plan B.

"Well," my mother sighed. "I just want you to know that whatever happens, none of this is your fault. Do you understand? All you need to know is that we — your dad and I — we love you very much. Okay, Del? Do you understand?"

I didn't understand. Now I was confused. But I nodded and smiled reassuringly when she stroked my cheek and bent down to hug me. Smelling her smell calmed me a little.

"You're not cross with me, then?" I asked.

My mother stared at me for a moment. "Why would I be *cross* with you? Del, I'm *proud* of you. I want you to know that."

"So, you're okay with all of it, then?"

My mother sighed wearily. "Well, Del, I wouldn't say I'm *okay* with it. But it's just the way it has to be, right? Life is like that. You just have to accept it, like I accepted —" She reached out and squeezed my hand. Her palm was hot and damp. I pulled my hand away from hers.

"We will all get through this, Del. But it will take time. This is harder on your father, I think. So, be nice to him, okay? But …" Her words trailed off. After a long moment she reached over and smoothed the hair back from my forehead. I experienced a prickling sensation and flinched. "Listen, Del, if you have any questions about this, you ask us, all right? The one thing that won't ever change is that we are still both your parents and we love you and Bea very, very much."

I was really confused now, and suddenly my stomach wasn't feeling right.

My mother pulled up the quilt the way I like it — with the silk ribbon nestled just under my chin. She looked back at me and smiled just before she closed the door behind her.

I lay in the dark, going over and summarizing my mom's words, mimicking her gestures, her intonation. But my bedside lamp had been turned off, and so her gestures and facial expressions had melded together with the shadows in the darkness, the moonlight, and the light from the hall. I have never been good at voice detection or recognition.

However, I did arrive at two hypotheses: 1) neither my mother nor my father knew about my registering for the Cubground Pub Battle of the Bands contest in Toronto, and 2) while insight #1 relieved my anxiety somewhat, I realized that in order to complete my plan to keep my parents together, the Turing Machinists' recording submission would definitely have to be accepted into the finals.

The other side of Djebar's double garage was stacked with boxes of dolls. But some of them were out of the boxes, with most of them wrapped in protective plastic. Djebar had told me he used to have nightmares about them.

"I can't play with all of them staring at me," said Petula, gesturing.

James followed her gaze to the other side of the garage. "Huh? They're only *dolls*."

"Make them stop looking at me!" Wesley was cringing behind the snare drum. Sogi put his bass guitar in front of his face. Djebar stared down at his feet with an anxious look on his face, and I was standing by the garage entrance preparing to bolt. Darrin was already halfway out of the garage.

"Ah, hell," James muttered as he spotted me. "Come on, Del. They're *dolls*. They're not real."

"We all know they're not real, James," said Djebar. "But they're ..."

"They're *distracting* us," said Sogi.

"Just turn them around so they can't see us," I said to James.

"They can't see you," said James. "They're not real people. They —"

"Just do it, okay?

"It's like being in a *Twilight Zone* episode," James muttered.

"Hah! Which one?" Sogi asked.

"'Mirror Image,'" Petula said, casting a glance at the dolls. She shuddered. "Doppelgangers."

"Doppelgangers?" James scratched his head.

Djebar snorted. "Why are you so stuck on 'Mirror Image' all the time? There are a lot better episodes, you know."

"It's probably the only episode she's watched," said Sogi.

Petula ignored them, lowered her gaze, and made her face go slack. "*Like most young career women she has a generic classification as a, quote, 'girl with a head on her shoulders,' end of quote.*"

"What does that mean, anyway: 'girl with a head on her shoulders'?" Sogi shook his head. "She wouldn't be a girl if she didn't have a head."

"She wouldn't be alive," said Djebar.

"Not necessarily," said Darrin. "Being brain dead doesn't necessarily kill you. The rest of the body can live."

"But we're not talking about brain dead, we're talking about not having a *head*," said Sogi.

"It's just a saying," said James. "You don't take it *literally*."

"Stop looking at me!" Wesley suddenly shouted at the dolls. He was circling the drums.

"James, will you please —"

James threw up his hands. "Okay, okay! Keep your pants on!" He whirled around. "Right! I know you have your pants on. Just ... give me a minute, all right?"

"I'm not wearing pants," said Petula. "I'm wearing a *skirt*."

Djebar tittered. A few seconds later all of us, except James, were laughing. Even Wesley, who hardly ever laughs, giggled.

Djebar's parents are both entrepreneurs. They sell stuff. Almost anything you can think of, they have sold it. They are divorced now, but they are still business partners. This means when there is a business convention in Toronto, they both go. So Djebar is home alone quite a lot. We all envy him his situation, but we don't expect him to invite us over. We don't do that kind of thing. None of us. Sometimes Djebar comes to our house because my mother feels bad about him being alone. He won't sleep over, though. Which is better for me, actually, because I don't sleep well as it is. And I can't sleep with someone else in the room. I don't mind Djebar coming over, but I don't think I could handle inviting any of the others in our class to visit. And really, I don't think they'd *want* to come over. My parents don't get this. I'm just more comfortable being by myself than they are, I guess.

James helped us set everything up. I had emailed him saying Wesley needed drums. I don't know where he got them, but they were in better shape than the ones at school.

"I know you're probably used to your own set, Wesley. But these are in pretty good shape," said James. "But please don't beat them up too badly; they're on loan."

Wesley just stared at him, his long caterpillar brows practically hooding his eyes.

"I have to call my mother in half an hour," said Sogi.

"Me too," said Petula.

"Me too," said Wesley.

"Me too," said Darrin. "I have to be home by nine-thirty at the latest."

James frowned. "Your parents have a pretty tight grip on all of you, don't they? Hey, you guys are *nineteen*. You're adults, right?"

I cast a quick look at the others, cringing, praying they wouldn't say anything about their real ages.

"Nineteen isn't an adult," said Petula.

"It is legally," said Djebar.

"The point is, you can make up your own minds, right?" said James. "So maybe you can make your own curfews, huh?"

Everyone had on puzzled looks — although with Sogi it was harder to read his expressions. I looked down at my shoes, my face feeling like it was going to burn off.

There was a long stretch of silence, as none of us seemed to know what to say.

"Well," Sogi suddenly blurted, "at least I don't spend forty-two minutes in the ladies washroom every lunch break, say like *Petula*."

James's brows drew together. "Huh?"

"I do not!" shouted Petula.

"You do. I timed it."

"You're a shit *bastard*!"

James jumped in. "Whoa! Okay, okay! We only have a couple of hours —"

"Two hours and twelve minutes," said Sogi.

"Yeah, whatever." James let out a long breath. "Look, I turned all the dolls around so they're not watching. Time's a-wasting, guys. Can we start rehearsing already?"

As I got older I stopped getting invitations to birthday parties. "Del doesn't know how to play" was what children said to their parents.

The last birthday party that I remembered attending was for a Karen Updike who was turning seven. I don't remember Karen, really, just her name. But I do remember what happened when Karen's mother insisted I participate in a game of *Snakes and Ladders*.

"Del, you have to wait your turn, dear."

I was confused and grabbed the die from the boy's hand.

"Del, it's not your turn … Remember, I explained the rules to you? … Yes, it is your turn now. Roll the die … Oh no, you landed on a snake, you have to slide down … Yes, those are the rules — Oh!"

In a fit of frustration I had upended the game and had struck out at a little girl who was trying to calm me down. I cried and cried — until my mother came and took me home.

"He needs to spend more time with kids his own age," Karen's mother was saying to mine.

"I'm sorry he upset Karen. I know he didn't mean it," said my mother.

"Connie, why don't you enroll Del in the Wilderness Pack? He's not in soccer, is he? You should put him in as many group activities as possible so he can learn how to act."

My mother said nothing. The reality was she had tried putting me in swimming and soccer and tee-ball and bowling and skating and hockey and gymnastics. I did poorly in all of the activities, and my social skills, in fact, seemed to worsen.

Finally, my mother took me to Doctor Campella (still my current occupational therapist). She took one look at me and said, "Your son is under extreme stress. He cannot learn under such anxiety. My advice is to take him out of all those group activities until he has learned a social skill set. But I am going to be truthful with you, Mrs. Capp, even when Del does learn more social skills, I cannot guarantee he will be able to engage in or enjoy group activities."

A lot of experts are saying now that it is not a matter of autistic people not being interested in socializing and friendship, it is a matter of autistic people not having the skills to engage socially or make friends. Since socializing causes extreme anxiety in most autistic people, it only stands to reason that they should avoid social situations altogether.

The truth is, I am interested in friendship. I've always wanted a best friend. I only wish I didn't have to actively socialize to make friends. Entering into my adolescence, I began thinking more and more about Petula. I began to think that having a girlfriend might be a good idea, as well.

On the other hand, most times I just want to be alone. In fact, I *prefer* to do things on my own. Everyone in our ASD class is more comfortable doing their own thing. The problem is that neurotypical people don't think we're telling the truth.

What Djebar, Sogi, Petula, Darrin, Wesley, and I didn't take into account was that despite our individual talents, despite all our individual music practice and memorization of the composition, in the end the Turing Machinists had to play together *as a group.*

Individually, they were very skilled: Darrin on the lead electric guitar, Sogi on the bass guitar, Djebar on the keyboard, Petula on xylophone and tambourine, and Wesley on drums. I was the only one not playing an instrument. But a minute into the song, James waved his hands in a frantic motion. "Stop! Stop!"

It took another minute for them to stop.

"It's not working," said James.

It's not working. My music isn't working.

"What do you mean?" said Petula. "We're playing it as it's written."

"That's not the problem," said James.

Something in my chest constricted. My head reeled a little, and I felt that familiar sting starting to rise up in my eyes. *My music isn't working.*

James was looking at my music sheets. He shook his head. "Okay. This is not going to work."

I turned and started to leave the garage.

"Del?" James called after me. "Hey, Del! Where are you going?"

"Let him go," I heard Djebar say. "He'll be back."

I just kept walking. I didn't want to cry in front of everyone, but most especially I didn't want to cry in front of James.

When I came back I didn't look over at anyone, but just sat in the far corner of the garage, my head between my knees.

James looked over at me, sighed, then said, "We need a lead singer. How about it, Del?"

I stared at him, stunned.

"Del can't sing," Sogi said. "He stutters."

"He does?" James sounded surprised. But his expression was unreadable to me.

"He only stutters when he's nervous," said Petula.

"People don't stutter when they sing, do they?" Djebar asked.

"He also cries when he's nervous," said Petula.

"Oh, yeah. He does," said Djebar.

"He doesn't cry that much," said Darrin.

"Well, he can't cry and sing at the same time," said Sogi. "Or can he?" James looked at me. "Hey, come on. Let's give Del a chance. How about it, Del? You want to try singing for the band?"

"I can't," I said.

"Sure you can," James said encouragingly. But there was a tweak in his voice now that reminded me of my father whenever he was losing patience.

"No, I can't." I shook my head. "I haven't written the lyrics yet."

"Or finished the music," Sogi pointed out.

"Bloody hell! How are we going to rehearse with you guys arguing about every little fucking thing?" James rubbed his face, closed his eyes for a couple of seconds.

"But how can we rehearse without music and lyrics?" said Petula.

"Or without anyone to *sing* the lyrics," James muttered. "Look, we have most of the music, right?" He looked at me. "What we need now is a lead singer ... a front man for the band."

"Front man?" I echoed.

"Look, you're the one who got everybody together. You're going to lead this band," he said.

Lead? "I don't want to do that," I said.

"Plus, you're the only one who's not playing an instrument."

When I didn't answer, he drew in a breath, rubbed his palms together. "Okay, I'll tell you the truth: this may sound corny, but I have this gut feeling you can sing, Del. I really do." .

"Really?" said Sogi. "You can really feel that in your *gut?*"

"Yeah." James nodded. "Really."

Everybody turned to look at me. I turned my gaze downward, stared at my white Nikes with the black stripes that didn't intersect. For a second I thought I was going to throw up. But when the feeling passed, I glanced over at Petula, who was watching me with that funny smile I like so much, and I heard myself say, "Okay. I'll do it. I'll be the band's front man."

"What does a 'front man' actually do, again?" Djebar asked.

"Never mind." James gestured to the microphone. "Okay, Del, give me a sound check."

I stared at the microphone uncertainly.

"Just say something into it. I want to check the sound."

"What should I say?"

"Anything."

"I'm not sure —"

"Bloody hell! Just count to three!"

"From zero? Or one?"

"What?" James glared at me for a moment, drew in a breath. "Just say: 'Testing 1-2-3.'"

I leaned in and started to speak, and a piercing shriek bellowed back at me. We all cowered in startlement and covered our ears until the noise went away. Wesley was shaking his head from side to side, moaning, "No, no, no ..."

"See? I was right," said Petula. "He can't sing."

"I think there might be something wrong with your gut, James," said Sogi.

James lifted his hands and shrugged. "That was feedback, that's all. If you guys keep freaking at the smallest thing, we're not going to get anywhere. Okay, Del. Let's try it again."

I hesitated. "Maybe I'd better not. I don't want to harm your equipment."

"Bloody hell! Get a set of balls, will you?" James looked at me, then sighed. "You can't run away from everything, Del. Look, this was your idea, right? This is your *dream*."

My throat felt tight, and my eyes began to sting. "This isn't *my* dream."

"Then whose dream is it?" James glared at me. "Why the fuck are we *doing* this, huh?"

Djebar and Darrin and Wesley were huddled in the far corner, looking wary. Petula and Sogi still had their hands covering their ears. "Why are you getting cross with *Del*?" said Djebar.

"I'm not. I just —" James threw up his hands. "Bloody hell! I'm your manager, right?"

We all nodded.

"Right! Well, as this band's manager, I say Del sings. And that's the end of it."

My lips were trembling, and I was gulping for air. *Don't cry. Don't cry.* "But … but what if I'm terrible?"

"Then you get better. Bloody helllll!" He pointed to the microphone. "Let's get this party started. Del, give me a fucking sound check."

We all cowered and pressed our palms to our ears.

During a survey communications lab test, one of the education research assistants was trying to calm Hannah. The assistants and their assistants were asking us each a bunch of questions that involved different inflections in the voice. But Hannah was getting irritated by the process, as sometimes they would repeat the question and place emphasis on a different word or part of the question.

"You already asked me that!" Hannah protested.

"But sometimes words can have multiple meanings," the assistant said. "What I said means something *different*."

Hannah looked at him, her nose wrinkled, her upper lip puckered like she'd just eaten something sour. "Well, why don't you say what you *mean*, then?"

Social Spectrum classes were a puzzle to all of us. The ill-defined curriculum caused us some consternation and anxiety, and we could not help but suspect that Jeddy might've been right about us being used as guinea pigs. However, when we addressed our concerns to Ms. Pokolopinison, she replied, "What do you think this class is about? Anyone?"

After a moment Petula spoke out. "We're asking *you*, Ms. Pokolopinison."

"What do *you* think, Petula?"

Jeddy surged to his feet. "You're the one getting paid! If I want to hear what Petula thinks I'd pay *her*!"

"Okay." Petula stuck out her hand, palm up. "Pay me and I'll tell you what I think."

"Screw you."

"Jeddy, language, please." Ms. Pokolopinison got up and started to move along the side of the class.

"Ms. Pokolopinison?" said Petula.

"Yes, Petula?"

"*Screw you* is an idiom, isn't it?"

Ms. Pokolopinison stopped in front of my desk, smiled her calm, composed smile. "Del? You're always so chatty during this class. Why don't you tell us what you think this class is about?"

"I don't know what you mean."

"Come on, Del. This is a social communications class, isn't it? What does that mean to you?"

I was confused. Why did she say I was chatty during class? I barely spoke a word.

"I'm not chatty, Ms. Pokolopinison," I said.

Her smile got a little stiff and that look came into her eyes that made them glaze over and wander. Then suddenly her eyes brightened and her smile broadened. "Ah! *Sarcasm*. Do you know what sarcasm is, Del?"

"Yes."

"Then you know when someone is being sarcastic?"

I didn't say anything.

Ms. Pokolopinison suddenly snapped her fingers. "Aha! Therein lies the problem! How to recognize when someone is being sarcastic." She strode to the front of the class. "Yes! Let's go with this! Let's talk about *sarcasm*, shall we?"

We all listened to her, growing more and more perplexed while she became more and more animated as she lectured us about the uses of sarcasm and humor and irony in conversation.

Finally, Djebar threw up his hand. "Ms. Pokolopinison?"

"Yes, Djebar?"

"Is it okay if I go to the washroom now?"

"Of course, Djebar. You don't have to ask. Just go."

"Okay, thank you." He didn't get up.

Ms. Pokolopinison gestured to him. "You may go now, Djebar."

"Yes, I just went, thank you, Ms. Pokolopinison."

Ms. Pokolopinison's smile wavered slightly. "Excuse me?"

"I just went."

Ms. Pokolopinison's face became very still, paling as she stared at Djebar. "You *went*? Am I to understand that you just went —" She looked at the rest of us, touched her face. Normally it was a very symmetrical face; now it was lopsided and disturbing to look at. "Oh. I see ... Djebar, why don't you go to the washroom to ... clean up. I'll, uh, call Mr. Hawkins ..."

We all tittered. Ms. Pokolopinison's brows drew together as she tried to understand our reaction. This tickled us all the more, and our giggles turned into laughter.

"Ms. Pokolopinison," said Petula in her loud, flat voice, "Djebar was being *sarcastic*."

Ms. Pokolopinison blinked. A strange color of pink was seeping into her face. "That is *not* sarcasm!" Her C-chord voice took on a different kind of lilt, like she was running out of breath. "If you want to be sarcastic, you don't say something that you necessarily *mean*."

We didn't understand. Why wouldn't people want to say what they mean? Or, for that matter, mean what they say?

SARCASM:

(New Illustrated Webster's Dictionary, 1992)

- a keenly ironical or scornful utterance; contemptuous and taunting language;
- the use of biting gibes or cutting rebukes.

IRONY:

(New Illustrated Webster's Dictionary, 1992)

- covert sarcasm or satire, the use of words to signify the

opposite of what they usually express;

- an outcome of events contrary to what was, or might have been, expected.

I have always had trouble sleeping. It has something to do with my internal clock, my circadian rhythms being counter to other people's. Most of us in the ASD class have sleep problems. "It just comes with the autistic territory," Doctor Bankoy assures my mother.

At three o'clock in the morning there is a dead stillness to everything. It is easier at this time of night for me to order my thoughts and make them spin in the right direction. I said this to Thea, and she wanted me to explain the spinning part. But I can't explain it. The closest I've come to describing it is in the image of a bunch of gears and wheels, like the inside of a clock. But that's only an image. It doesn't say or signify what I mean.

At night I can better hear my compositions in my head. So composing is much easier at night. I have yet to attempt to write the lyrics, though. For some reason even thinking about writing the lyrics gives me a fluttering of anxiety. I am befuddled. Why should the simple writing of lyrics be so difficult and complex?

Yesterday, at 2:46 a.m., I attempted Mr. Levinson's haiku assignment. But I got so flustered and anxious I started pacing the room. My head was booming, and words were getting all jammed up in my mind. Where to begin? I was utterly lost.

And then, suddenly, I heard a noise downstairs.

I listened, straining to hear familiar sounds: the sound of footsteps, clunky, a scraping of a chair leg against the linoleum in the kitchen, a blurting of curses. I thought the voice might belong to my father. But I couldn't be sure.

It was a question I shouldn't have asked myself, because all at once I became frightened. I had read somewhere that most house break-ins occur between two o'clock and six o'clock in the morning. I had already worked myself into such a state that all rational thought was burning with anxiety.

I snapped off my desk light and quickly folded myself into the lower part of my closet. I could feel my heart pushing against my ribs and hear my breath inhaling and exhaling like the carbonation in root beer. My eyes were staring wide into the darkness, waiting. They started to itch and sting, but I dared not rub them. When I blinked, swirls and splashes of orange and purple pulsed in front of me.

I could hear my bedroom doorknob turning. I gasped. A wave of nausea swept over me, and I suddenly became dizzy. I wanted to cry, but I was too frightened.

The door slowly creaked open, and a tall figure tiptoed inside.

The room started to thump and thud around me like a headache.

The figure leaned over my bed. "Del? Del?" A beat passed. There was a rustling sound, and I heard cursing. "Del! Shit! Where are you?"

I recognized my father's voice, but I didn't answer.

"Del! Answer me!"

"Here I am," I said from inside the closet.

"What the —?" My father went to the closet. The moon was waxing, and the light that came in from the window was bluish, but bright. It illuminated the spot where I was hiding. My father's face was shadowed, so I could not see his expression.

"Del! Geezus! Do you know what time it is?"

"Yes. It's three o'clock in the morning."

"Get into bed!"

I could smell the Busy Pub on his breath as he tucked me in. I thought he was going to leave, but he sat down next to my bed. I waited. After about five minutes he finally said, "Del, there's some things we need to discuss."

I stared down into his moon-streaked face, which became very still all of a sudden. The bluishness had turned to gray, and for a moment my father had turned to stone. My mother is always saying how much I look like my father. I traced his profile. I tried to find myself in this man sitting next to my bed. The idea confused me. Was that me?

My father started to get up. "Listen, I —" His elbow brushed something from my bedside table. The tinkling sound that reverberated up from the hardwood floor startled me. I bolted up. My father cursed. "Shit! Where's the light —?"

I reached up and turned on the bedside light. We both blinked. On the floor beside my bed was Ol' Ben, my windup alarm clock. I had selected it because of the spiral etching in the metal exterior of the face and the adjustable ring of the alarm. I touched the winding mechanism in the back. It didn't turn. A sudden surge of panic gripped my chest.

"It's broken." My voice had gone up an octave. My stutter made my tongue loll back in my mouth.

"Here, give it to me." My father held it up to the light. "Looks like the lever in the back got pushed up a little. I'll fix it for you in the morning."

"I need it. I need it fixed *now*." I could hear that whine of fear coating my voice, and I cringed inwardly.

"It's late, Del. And I …" He sighed. "Look, I'll buy you a new one, okay? An even nicer one than this."

"I don't want a new one!"

"Keep your voice down," he hissed.

"I want my alarm clock! I need it!" I snatched it from my father's hands. "I'll fix it!"

"Okay, *okay*! Just stop shouting. You're going to wake up the whole friggin' neighborhood!"

I tried to turn the windup lever. It was stuck tight. "It's broken!"

"Del, calm down, will you? It's only a clock."

"I need it!"

"Look, how about I wake you up in the morning? What time —?"

"No! I need to fix this clock!"

My father stood up abruptly. "All right. You fix it." His fingers twirled at his sides, then clenched and unclenched into fists. "I'm going to bed."

After he left I got up and turned on my desk lamp. A whirlwind was whipping about inside me. I closed my eyes, did the breathing exercises we practiced at school in the Plum Room.

"Del?"

I jumped and gave a yelp of surprise.

My father put his hands on my shoulders. "I'm sorry, Del. I'm sorry for yelling at you … sorry for everything."

I stared ahead at the clock, waiting for his hands to lift from my shoulders.

"What is that? Is that —" He reached out and picked up the sheet of music I'd been working on. "Is this yours? Are you writing music?"

"Yes."

He squinted at it. "Hey, this is something!"

"I thought you couldn't read music."

"I can't — but, Del, I didn't know you could actually *compose* music?"

I didn't say anything.

"Is this for school?"

I hesitated. "No."

"What kind of music is it? Classical?"

"No."

When I didn't say anything more, he stood and grinned at me. "Well, this is really cool, Del. Maybe I did pass on a bit of the music gene to you after all, eh? Don't laugh, but there was a time when I thought I was going to rock the world. I even formed a band —" He stopped himself, shrugged. "Well, that time has gone and passed. No sense talking about it now, eh?" He rubbed my head. "I just wanted to say I'm sorry for breaking your clock and yelling at you. Are we okay?"

"Yes." I nodded.

When he left I debated whether I should fix the clock or work on the composition. I decided in the end to go to bed.

What do autistic people dream about?

In one of his papers, Turing points out that philosophers and mathematicians make the mistake of assuming that when we are presented with a fact or problem, all consequences and solutions will immediately spring to mind. The reality is, sometimes the answers never come.

"You're all very good musicians," said James, "but together you make one *lousy* band."

It had never occurred to us that we would have problems playing *together*.

"And what's with those earmuffs?" James shook his head. "How the hell can you play in a band when you can't hear the others play? I thought you all played in the school band or something."

"We do. Well, all of us except for Del," said Petula.

"I play timpani in the Merryton Public Symphony," said Wesley.

"I play first violin," said Darrin, playing with his ears. "They won't let me play the electric guitar. And the dogs don't like the sound at home, so I can't practice there."

"So where do you practice?" James asked.

Darrin tugged on his ears, lowered his gaze, and stared at something on the carpet.

"I play the piano," said Djebar. "But nobody actually *pays attention* to Mrs. Biegler when she's conducting." He shrugged. "We just ... play."

"Well, if you want to be a rock band, you have to pay attention to your fellow band members," said James. "A music band is like a ... like a *family*, you know? You have to work together, take cues from one another. *Listen* to one another."

We all looked at one another. I think we understood what James was telling us, but that didn't mean we knew how to go about implementing what James was directing us to do. One thing was evident, however: James didn't understand us. Not yet, anyway.

We tried explaining again.

"Stop! I can't hear you if you're all talking at me at once." James growled, waited for us to quiet down. "Look, all I know is that if you want to be a rock band, you have to play *together*. And in order to do this, you have to be playing at the same time, on the same page, and you have to *listen* to each other. Which means you can't be talking. Understand?"

We stopped talking and looked at him. Several minutes passed.

Finally, James sighed. "Great. That's great. You guys are good at the long silences. But —"

Then Sogi suddenly blurted, "When Del finishes the song he can give us copies of the entire composition. Then we could memorize *everyone's* part."

"Well, you don't have to go so far as to memorize *everyone's* part —"

"Will I need to learn how to play the guitar, then?" said Wesley. "I can't play guitar. My finger joints are too stiff. Keyboards are difficult for me, as well."

James laughed. "That's funny, Wesley."

Wesley blinked at him. "What do you mean?"

"I've always wanted to learn to play electric guitar," Petula said. "But do we have time?"

James laughed. "That's a good one."

"When's the deadline for the recording submission?" Darrin asked.

"Five weeks," said James.

"Thirty-eight days," I corrected.

"I learned to play the acoustic guitar last year. It took me sixteen days," said Sogi.

"Really?" Petula frowned, looked deeply puzzled. "But I've heard you play. You're actually *good*."

"Okay, let's focus on this rehearsal, all right?" James vented a long breath.

"Well, we can't really do anything until Del finishes the song," said Djebar.

"It's not finished, yet," I said.

Sogi slipped off his bass guitar. "I guess we'll call it a night, then."

Wesley got up. "I guess we'll call it a night, then," he echoed.

"What?" James frowned. "It's only a quarter after eight!"

"It's only a quarter after eight," Wesley repeated.

James gazed at Wesley, sighed. "How about we rehearse what we have so far? Look, you guys need practice."

"If Del can get the rest of the song done by tomorrow I can have it all memorized by Sunday," said Sogi.

"I don't have to campaign for AR this weekend so I can take time to memorize everyone's parts," said Darrin.

"You're kidding me, right?" James shook his head. "What's AR?"

"Animal rights," said Darrin. When he said this, a sudden fierceness came into his face. He fixed his gray-green eyes on James. Darrin has a really good stare. Better, even, than Petula's. I'd noticed, though, he only uses his stare when he's talking about animal rights. I'm not sure who would win in a staring contest between Darrin and Petula, but James and other Neural Typicals always have to look away. I'm not able to do the stare. I'm always the one who looks away first.

James shot me a glance. "Well, it's up to Del. He may need a bit more time ..." He made a gesture towards me and lifted his brows in what I took to be a signal of prompting. But what was he prompting me to do? I cocked my head, puzzled.

"So, Del is definitely singing?" asked Petula.

"I thought we already established this," said James.

"Well, *Petula* is definitely not singing," said Sogi.

Petula sneered. "Shut up! I'll have you know I have a fabulous voice."

"I have a fabulous voice," Wesley echoed in Petula's voice.

"Well, I do," said Petula angrily.

"Well, I do," echoed Wesley.

Petula bunched her fists against her hips. "Stop repeating what I'm saying!"

Wesley mimicked her movements. "Stop repeating what I'm saying!"

There was a whirling going on in my head and I was feeling a bit nauseous, and before I could stop myself I snapped at Wesley, "Oh, Wesley! Just shut up!"

Wesley flinched, wrapped his arms around his chest, and started to rock back and forth on his heels.

Djebar glared at me. "Don't be a shit, Del."

"Sorry," I mumbled, looking down at my feet.

James cleared his throat. "Yeah, okay. Let's calm down, huh? We're all a little excited and on edge here —"

"I don't w-want to s-sing," I cut in. My eyes were starting to sting, and my voice was breaking into a stutter.

"Hey, now, Del. It's only a rehearsal —"

"I'm not singing."

"Del, you said you wanted to sing —"

"I changed my mind. I don't want to sing."

"I'll sing!" Petula piped in.

James scratched his head. I couldn't tell what he was thinking. His expressions are just too difficult for me to read. Finally, he said, "Okay. Why don't we cut this rehearsal short and get back together when Del has finished the music? Del? When do you think you'll have your song done?"

"I don't know."

"Can you have it done by next Saturday? No, wait, that doesn't give you much time —"

"Next Saturday?," I said. "Yes, I can do that."

"Really?" James frowned, shook his head. "No. That's not enough time —"

"Yes, it is," I said quickly. The truth is, a deadline challenge is the best way to get me to finish anything. Of course, I have to *want* to finish it.

"Okay ... Then we'll reconvene here next Saturday?"

Djebar nods. "Mom won't be here."

James' brow wrinkled, and he scratched his chin. "But your mom knows we're using the garage for —"

"So, will we be rehearsing at The Minotaur next Sunday?" Petula interjects.

"Uh, yeah. I guess. Eight o'clock okay?"

"I have to leave by ten to feed the dogs," said Darrin.

At this second mention of dogs Djebar suddenly looked at Darrin with more interest. "I didn't know you had dogs."

"We have fourteen of them in the house right now. It's just temporary until they can make room at the rescue unit in Nestling," Darrin told us.

"Dogs are dirty," said Petula.

"No, they're not," said Sogi.

"No, your mom just likes to eat them."

"Shut up!"

"Okay, let's settle down —"

"Can we meet at the Minotaur at seven instead of eight?" said Petula. "I have to *be home* by ten, so I'll have to leave by 9:45 p.m. at the latest."

"I can stay *until* ten," said Sogi.

"I can stay until ten, too," said Wesley.

"Ten to what?" asked Petula.

"What do you mean?" asked Wesley.

"Well, you said ten *to*. Ten to what? You didn't finish your sentence."

Wesley looked confused. "Ten. I have to go home at ten."

Petula twirled her dark hair around her fingers. "Then why did you say ten to —?"

"I don't know what you —"

"For Chrissake! He said ten, *too*. T-o-o! Bloody hell!" James threw up his hands. "Never mind. I'll see you all here next week, okay? Let's just ... call it a night."

"So, are we still meeting at the Minotaur at eight on Sunday?" Djebar called after him. James exited through the side door of the garage. We heard his Hudson Italia start up. It was tan with shiny chrome. James told me he'd won it in a bet. He never told me what that bet was, and I didn't ask. I don't like cars in general, but I do like James's Hudson Italia.

"He didn't confirm we were meeting at The Minotaur on Sunday," said Djebar. We all looked at each other, suddenly filled with uncertainty.

After being arrested for practicing homosexuality, Alan Turing wrote this haiku:

> *Turing believes machines think*
> *Turing lies with men*
> *Therefore machines do not think.*

Mr. Levinson wasn't sure Alan Turing was writing a haiku. But he could not dispute my analysis, which pointed out the nineteen sound units divided into a 7-5-7 syllabic rhythm, which were typical of an English haiku. But he asked me if maybe I thought the poem might have been intended to be *ironic*. I told him I had highlighted its faulty logic and sophist philosophy, but I had not seen any irony.

Mr. Levinson left it at that.

The second part of my assignment is now to write an original haiku poem. I understand the haiku's syllabic rhythm requirements. But I'm not sure what words to select or what sentiment Mr. Levinson wants. What if the words I choose don't go together? What if they don't sound right? Don't make sense? "Compassion, silence, and a sense of temporality"; I'm not sure I actually understand these ideas, so how can I write them? He gave me a poem to study by Issa:

> *The distant mountains*
> *are reflected in the eye*
> *of the dragonfly*
> — Issa (1762–1826)

But how would a person go about seeing reflections in a dragonfly's eye? We might actually have the technology to peer into a dragonfly's eye. But how would you make the dragonfly cooperate?

The Japanese haiku has a 5-7-5 syllabic rhythm. I wonder if my father wasn't influenced by some Japanese poets like Issa, because a lot of his song lyrics have the same haiku rhythm. Maybe my father could help me with my haiku.

But when I asked him how he felt about poetry, he said it wasn't his thing. So I decided against asking him.

James was stretched out on the bench sunning himself in the fall sun. He asked me how my song was coming. I told him that I had finished the music, but that I was having trouble writing the lyrics. I had already decided I would write using a haiku rhythm. But *what* would I write?

"Write about what you know — wait, scratch that." He sat up, rubbed his neck. "You know a bit too much for your own good. Write … write about you. About how you *feel*."

"About how I feel," I repeated. After a moment I said, "Feel about what?"

"I don't know. How you feel about … life. About your disease —"

"Autism is not a disease. It is a neurobiological *disorder*."

"Disease, disorder, syndrome — whatever." James gave his head one of those little shakes that made me think he might be becoming annoyed with me. I wanted to talk more about the differences between disease and disorder, but I forced myself to get up off the bench and head for school.

DISEASE:
(New Illustrated Webster's Dictionary, 1992)
• Disturbed or abnormal structure or physiological action in the living organism as a whole, or in any of its parts. Disease is the general term for deviation from health; in a more limited sense it denotes some definite morbid condition.

DISORDER:
• Derangement of the bodily or mental functions
Verb: to throw out of order; disarrange; to disturb the natural functions of, as body or mind.
(Synonyms): anarchy, clutter, confusion, disturbance, irregularity

When Turing accepted an academic posting at the University of Manchester he rode a bicycle to work every day. En route, the chain would always come off. Recognizing this pattern, Turing began counting the number of times the pedals went round and instead of getting the bicycle fixed, he would jump off and adjust the chain by hand before it fell off.

His colleagues asked him why he didn't just get the bicycle fixed. Turing replied that as far as he was concerned his method of repair was more reliable and cheaper, and therefore more practical. It also forced him to clear away the clutter and clean off the mud that collected in his chain.

Wesley Farkle laid down his drumsticks, took off his earmuffs, and looked up at us. His pimples seemed to have disappeared, and his face seemed to light up from the inside. "How was that?"

We were all impressed. I looked at James. He wore one of his unreadable expressions, but for an instant I thought I saw tears well up in his eyes. But I'm certain I was mistaken; sadness would be an inappropriate reaction to Wesley's awesome drumming.

"Where did you learn to drum like that, Wesley?" James asked.

"It's just a three-rhythm drum time," he said, wrinkling his nose. "My dad won't let me have real drums at home, so I practice on the basement couch and dining table."

"Real drums, huh?" James was running his palm across his chin. Back and forth. Back and forth. "But you took some lessons, right?"

"I learned to play at school."

"I showed him Neil Peart," said Sogi. "The Thirtieth Anniversary and the Buddy Rich concert."

"Oh." James scratched his head, suddenly laughed. "So that's what you were playing?"

Wesley frowned, leaned back suddenly. "No."

James waited, looked at me. "Well, the thing is, Wesley," he said finally, "you didn't exactly play what Del wrote, did you?"

"Yes, I did."

James frowned, reached for the drum score. "You did?"

"Yes."

James shook his head. "No, you didn't, Wesley. You see here?" He got up to show Wesley, but Wesley suddenly lurched out of his seat and retreated to the wall. "Hey, it's okay. I just wanted to show you —"

"Get away from me."

"Wesley, I —"

Wesley's face was darkening, and he was making gurgling noises in his throat.

"Leave him alone," said Djebar. "My mom will kill me if she smells puke in here."

James hesitated, his eyes shifting to me. I gazed back at him, puzzled. Why was he looking at *me*? He seemed about to say something, but stopped himself, shut his eyes for a few seconds, and returned to his chair. "Okay, okay. We'll deal with it later. Petula? You want to go next?"

"I can't play D or E today," she said.

"Huh? Why not?"

"The bars have to be fixed."

"Your xylophone is broken?"

"No, not yet."

James shook his head. "I'm sorry. Why can't you play?"

"The D and E bars come loose after 157 strikes," Petula explained. "I'm already up to 138 on D and 142 on E. I won't make it through this song."

"Well, why don't you fix the bars *now*?"

"Well, I only have eighteen strikes to go. And it takes me approximately forty-two minutes to fix."

"Approximately, huh?" That look on James's face I'd seen before, and I recognized it as disbelief. I suppose I would have been feeling the same had I not understood Petula's pattern fixation.

"It's a pattern," she told him. "On the one hundred fifty-seventh strike the D and E bars come loose, and it jars the back plate and I have to realign the C and F bars."

James stared at her. After a moment he said, "Why don't you just get the xylophone fixed? Look, there's a good music shop in Toronto that does instrument repairs. I know the owner, and I'm pretty sure he'd fix your xylophone for cheap —"

"I can fix it myself," said Petula.

"But you said yourself the bars keep coming loose," James pointed out. "If you get a professional to look at it —"

"But I know *when* to repair it!" said Petula. Her voice had risen an octave.

James backed away, ran his hands through his hair. "Okay, okay. Djebar, how's your keyboard?"

"The D and E keys are loose."

"You're kidding me!"

Djebar laughed. "Of course I am. I was being *sarcastic*." We all tittered quietly.

James glared at all of us. "That is not fucking sarcasm!" He shook his head. "Bloody hell! What is it with you guys? Are you being idiots on purpose?"

I looked down at my Nikes, traced the non-intersecting black lines. When people yell I get anxious, and I have this sudden need to run. I also cry when people get mad at me. I didn't want to cry or run. But I was feeling bad because I still hadn't finished the lyrics of the song, and my head was vibrating with too many thoughts. I needed some air to think and pull myself together. Darrin must have had the same idea because he started towards the garage exit a few seconds before I did. His hands were clamped over his ears.

"Hey, where are you two going?" James called. "We're just starting rehearsal!"

"I'd like to spend some time with you, Del," my father said. "How about we go to a movie, eh?"

"No, thank you."

"Aw, come on. Movies are fun. Let's see what's playing ... *Spider-Man*! Well, that should be fun."

"I don't like Spider-Man."

"You don't like Spider-Man? But that's ... insane. Every seven-year-old boy loves Spider-Man. He's a superhero!"

"Will he take off his mask?"

"What do you mean?" My father watched me with that look that warned me he was going to raise his voice. "Look, I'll buy you some popcorn."

"I'm going to go out and run," I said. As I stepped through the patio doors I heard my father tell my mother that he was going out. A strange feeling filled my belly, but when I started running it went away and all I felt was relieved.

None of us go to theaters because we talk before, during, and after movies. It's a kind of compulsion that hits us when actors are talking in the movies to start talking ourselves. That is not to say we don't talk during small-dialogue action movies. We just don't talk *as much*. Many people think it's an attention deficit issue — that we can't sit still — but for me it's a combination of being nervous around people and feeling a compulsion to communicate back to the actors and the action on the screen. Do I talk when I am watching a movie alone? I'm not sure. Not as much, certainly. That could be the reason most of us like to watch movies by ourselves.

To not talk while someone else is talking is difficult. Waiting your turn to talk is something we have to continually work on and practice. But behavior therapy can only stretch so far.

Darrin sat out on the front step of Djebar's house while I ran around the front lawn for a bit. After we calmed down we returned to the garage, and James sat us all down so he could talk to us about rehearsals at The Minotaur. But then, Sogi started talking about this new website he'd found about Alan Turing and Artificial Intelligence, and suddenly we were all talking about that.

"Stop!" James surged to his feet, his hands in the air. "You're all talking at once. And my head is full to the brim with this Turing guy."

Djebar cleared his throat. "But I'd like to point out that the actual Turing Machine which Alan Turing conceived of in 1936 was merely a way for him to make a point about the Entscheidungsproblem —"

"But ultimately it became the blueprint for a general-use computer —"

"— which makes him the founder of modern computer science."

"But let's not forget that he was a *mathematician* first —"

"Enough!" James interrupted. "That's all this Neural Typical wants to know about this Turing guy and his stupid machine."

"The Turing Machine is hardly stupid," said Petula. "It manipulates these symbols on a strip of tape in accordance with a set of rules —"

"*Table* of rules," Sogi corrected Petula.

James growled. "Well, you know what? I don't give two shits about Turing or his stupid machine."

"It's not stu—"

"Can we not have a *normal* conversation for once? We're here to discuss the *band*. Notice I didn't mention the *name*. Because if you don't mind I would like us to discuss *music* at these meetings."

We all looked at him, waited silently for him to go on.

"That's better. Now, I spoke to Archie, the owner of the Minotaur, and, as I explained to you the other day, he's going to —"

"Speaking of names, I motion that we change the name of our band to Turing's *Universal* Machinists," said Djebar.

"— allow us to practice at the Minotaur on Sunday nights after seven o'clock, which is —"

"I like the name we have now. I think I'll stick with the Turing Machinists," said Sogi.

"Me, too," Darrin and I said.

"Me, too," said Wesley.

"— when The Minotaur closes. He's also agreed to let you store your instruments in the back room. But the best part is that The Minotaur has —"

"I can't be here any earlier than eight," said Darrin.

"I can be here by seven-thirty," said Sogi.

"— sound equipment that we can use. Also, the acoustics are great in there, so it will be the perfect place to record your submission for the contest"

"I'll have to leave by ten, the latest," said Darrin.

"Me too," said Petula.

"Petula? What do you think about changing the name to Turing's Universal Machinists?" Djebar asked her.

"Do you mind?" Petula snarled. "I'm still thinking."

There was a long beat of silence.

Finally, James got up. His face was flushed and he was making little circles with his fingers around his temples. "Great. I'll see you all tomorrow at The Minotaur at, uh … seven-thirty?" And then he sort of sprinted for the garage exit. "I can't be there until eight. I have an AR meeting with my parents," Darrin called after him.

"I can be there at seven-thirty," said Sogi.

"I'll have to leave by ten," called Darrin.

"Me too!" Petula shouted after him.

But James was already gone.

Our first rehearsal at the Minotaur was, as James called it, a "bust."

Djebar was starting what he calls a Green Dog Day, which means you can expect him to argue about everything. Wesley threw up in the bathroom because his home care worker had given him a hotdog for dinner. Djebar argued that the nitrates in hot dogs have no affect on the digestive system. Darrin complained about the smells in the Minotaur, but we couldn't open a window because the heating was on, so he went to sit outside on the doorstep. Djebar argued that odours could not induce nausea. Sogi wanted me to change the bass guitar parts so that the song had a more "jazzy" feel. Djebar argued that there was a difference between pop music and rock music and jazz music. Then Sogi and Petula and Djebar argued about whether we were a pop band or a rock band.

After a while, Darrin came in and said he had to leave. Petula and Sogi and Djebar were still arguing. James got up and went into the kitchen to talk to Archie.

Archie is short and pear-shaped, and has one of those droopy handlebar moustaches. He doesn't smile a lot, but there's something in his eyes that makes me think that he is not an unhappy man. But I'm not sure I'm reading him right; I'm just no good at that sort of thing.

After about a half hour, Archie came in to tell us James had left. He told us we could stay until ten if we wanted.

Sogi and I looked down at the floor, unable to meet Archie's gaze. Djebar argued that there was no point in staying. Petula got mad and stomped out. Sogi and I and Djebar followed her. Much to my surprise Wesley decided to stay behind with Archie.

Of all of us, Wesley is the most people-wary. But you never know when a person's going to rub you the right way.

The following Sunday, everyone was in a better mood. I still hadn't written the lyrics, but everyone had memorized the music and we were ready to play.

James smiled at us. "Archie's going to sit in on this rehearsal, okay?"

Petula threw down her xylophone sticks. Darrin looked down at his feet, his face turning red.

"We're not ready, James," I said.

"If you want to enter this competition you're going to have to play in front of an audience, guys." James smiled. "Hey, stage fright is *normal*."

It's funny how one word — the *right* word — can change everything.

We were all still really nervous. I was feeling so anxious I was nauseous. And yet, at the same time, there had been a shift somewhere. It was like one of those cool breezes that comes out of nowhere on a hot day. A *normal* cool breeze.

In Djebar's garage we were okay. We felt safe and comfortable, and there was no pressure, nothing at stake. Consequently we played with a sense of abandon and ease.

But now we had the completed composition in front of us, and tonight we were going to play my song in its entirety *for the first time*. We were going to play here, in the Minotaur, in front of an audience of one. This tiny audience might sound insignificant, but in truth it was a momentous occasion for us. The reality of what we were doing and its consequences were just dawning on us; and yes, it made us terribly anxious.

But at the same time, we were, in fact, really, really excited.

When Alan Turing was asked to consider the question "Do machines think?" he replied by replacing the question with the analogy of what he called his "imitation game." The point of the game is to establish whether the machine should be credited with intelligence if in playing the game it cannot be distinguished from a human while it is imitating the intelligence of a human.

The criticisms of the imitation game held that Turing himself was too socially awkward and too much of an eccentric to understand the rules of multi-player games, and that even if people's actions were predetermined, as Turing believed, their actions are still much too complex to solve or predict with a mere algorithm.

"Life is like a game, Del. You understand? A *game*? Like ... hide and seek, or *Monopoly*, or, uh, *Sorry*." My father was sitting across from me at the kitchen table. His face had a saggy look. His eyes were bloodshot, and I noticed some silvery-gray strands of hair on the left side of his head. He had his hands palms down flat on the table. There was a sound in his voice that made me uneasy.

I didn't know how to respond, so I didn't.

"And you know a game has rules, right? So if you are going to play the game, you have to play by the rules. You understand? Do you understand me, Del?"

I was silent.

"You're almost seven years old, now. All the other kids your age are learning to swim. You want to learn how to swim, too, don't you?"

I shook my head.

"Sure you do! You can do it, Del. You can play the game. Trust me. The sooner you start playing this game, the easier your life will be. Come on. Be brave for Daddy."

I stared at him, then after a moment I said what he wanted me to say. My father smiled.

"Great! So let's go. Your swimming lessons start in half an hour."

"I don't want to go," I said.

"Hey, life is a game, remember? We play by the rules?"

"I don't want to go."

"Let's go, Del."

"No."

"I said let's go!"

"No!"

"I paid for these lessons and you're going!"

"NO! I DON'T WANT TO GO!"

"Stop crying!"

I could hear myself screaming. The air around me had taken on a reddish-orange color. My skin felt prickly. The top of my head hurt, and my eyes stung. Through the haze of tears my father's face changed shape, and I felt afraid. The room swirled around me.

"Look, you can't always get what you want!"

I felt myself being picked up. I bit down hard on the arm that grabbed me across the chest. A metallic taste filled my mouth. I wanted to run. Run. Run. Run.

"I'm sorry, Del … for what happened this morning."

"It's okay."

"You bit me. Look."

I looked. It was an oblong bruise, dark purple and gray with bits of yellow. My teeth had pierced the skin, but it had already scabbed over.

"Are you sorry you bit me?"

My mother was hovering in the doorway. "Yes," I said. The hall light illumined my mother's face. She had a dishtowel in her hand and she was wringing it gently back and forth. I felt calm and sleepy. I leaned over and gave my father a hug. He hugged me back tightly, ruffled my hair and grinned.

"Maybe we can try going to the pool next week, eh?"

I tensed. My mother stopped wringing the dishtowel, standing very straight and still. My father grinned encouragingly down at me. Something nudged at my thoughts, beckoning to me, drawing me towards it. *Fear.* My scalp felt as though it were lifting from my skull.

"I don't like the water," I said.

Bea came bouncing towards me. "Dellll!!"

I got up and ran away. Behind me I heard my mother hiss, "Leave him alone!"

I sat on the stone bench and cast my eyes about the park. I was on time. James was not. I sat back, fixed my eyes towards his apartment building, and waited.

After fifteen minutes, a girl came up to me.

"Hi, Del."

I looked at her. She looked vaguely familiar, but I couldn't place her face.

"What are you doing here?" she asked.

"None of your business." As soon as I said the words, I knew they were the wrong ones because of the way her face expression changed.

"Wow, I was just *asking*."

Before I could say anything else, I blurted loudly, "Leave me alone."

The girl's face got pink and her eyes got small. "Your sister's right; you are an idiot." And she stalked off.

I stared down at my shoes. Why did she have to come talk to me *now*? I looked down towards the road to see the girl bobbing up and down the sidewalk. She carried a navy knapsack with pink flowers all over it. She was younger than me, I think. I couldn't figure out who she was or how she knew me.

My watch vibrated at 8:39. I waited another minute, then gathered up my knapsack. Where was James? I cast a last glance in the direction of his building, but he wasn't there. As I turned to head to school, it was like a blanket was suddenly thrown over me. The world got dark and I stopped in my tracks. I closed my eyes. When I opened them again everything was tinged in orange. I walked with my arms tucked into my sides. I didn't care if I was late today.

Wesley has what he calls Red Hot Days where he is afraid to touch anything with his bare skin. On those days he wears mittens or gloves and hats and scarves — no matter the temperature. He throws up a little more than usual, as well — as if he's trying to get rid of everything he has touched.

Djebar's moods are less about fear and more about anger. He's not as explosive or volatile as Hannah, but he does lose his temper a lot. When he's having a Green Dog Day he spends a lot of time away from school or in the sensory room. When these days are on him, we all stay clear of him — even Hannah. Hannah's moods are explosive, but they can be more easily contained. And her moods are pretty much ever-present; I've never heard them referred to as anything.

During my Orange Days everything is shaded and edged with an orange glow. Sometimes there are barbed wire fences around everything and everybody, and I'm afraid to touch anything. Sometimes Orange Days turn into Foggy White Days and I experience a sensation as if I am lost. Doctor Bankoy says I'm disassociating myself because of a chemical imbalance in my brain, likely a depletion of serotonin. I asked him about the recent studies about neurogenesis, the growth of neurons in the use of antidepressants, and he said not to worry about it, that it was just some left-wing theory without any scientific merit. I like Doctor Bankoy, but sometimes I have to wonder if he's keeping current with medical science.

James waved at me from the bench. I approached, but I didn't sit down.

"Hey, Del. Sit."

"You weren't here yesterday."

"No. I had an appointment."

"You should have told me."

"I told you, I don't do the texting thing."

"You could've emailed me."

"Yeah. But I just didn't have time. Sorry."

"You were supposed to meet me here at 8:15."

"Yeah, yeah, I know. But I do have a life, you know. Things do come up," he said. "Hey, I'm here now, so sit, will ya?"

"But will you be here tomorrow?"

James eyed me. "I don't know, Del. I could get hit by a bus for all I know. Things happen that you can't always control."

I stared down at my feet. I was beginning to feel anxious. My face felt hot. I closed my eyes. *Things happen that you can't always control.*

"Del? You okay?"

I sat down. I'm not good at putting on faces, and so I didn't even try to pretend to look okay. "I can get ... attached to a routine, that's all."

"So I'm a *routine*, am I?" James grinned. "I'm not sure that's a compliment." He leaned forward, put his hands on his knees, and gazed at me so that I had to look away. "Del, is something on your mind? You know you can talk to me."

"I can't sing."

"Neither can I."

"But you were the lead singer in the Magic Horse Marines."

"Only because everyone else's voice was worse than mine." He tilted his head, squinted at me. "Is that why you're having so much trouble writing the lyrics?"

I shrugged. "Maybe Petula should sing."

"I've heard Petula sing. She's not a lead singer."

"But you haven't heard me sing."

"With a unique voice like yours, it's got to be good," said James.

"In a rock band, interesting and *unique* are what counts."

After a long moment I looked at him. "I'm afraid, James."

James laced his fingers together and squeezed so that the fingers turned white. "Aren't we all?"

"Hey, look! It's an *Ass Burger*!"

I looked down the street and watched as two guys and a girl with long reddish-blond hair approached. I had a vague recollection of seeing them before, most likely in the high school. The girl I knew by her reddish-blond hair. But as they neared none of their faces registered; I had no idea what their names were or what grades they were in.

"Hey, *Ass Burger*!" The one with longish dirty blond hair made a gesture I didn't understand. They were just a couple feet away now. "Need some ketchup and mustard with that ass?"

The girl and the other guy laughed. I suddenly didn't feel good. I was beginning to wobble like I was a spinning top running out of spin. My stomach hurt and I felt afraid. My eyes began to sting. I wanted to run, but I cringed instead, hiding my head.

I was smart to cover my head. The first blow came to my middle back. A thrown object. A stick, maybe. Then one of them kicked me in the rear and I stumbled forward onto my knees. They laughed. I began to cry.

"Oh, come on. Now that just isn't cool," said a voice behind me.

"Get the fuck away from us, creep," said one of the boys. I think it was the one with longish dirty blond hair.

The person behind me laughed. It was a different kind of laugh, and it made me stop and think.

"I'll give you fifteen seconds to beat it out of here."

"Hah! Or what?"

"Hey, wait! I know who you are! You're that American musician from that band ... the one with the horses ..." The girl was quiet for a beat. "Hey, can we score from you?"

"You've got ten seconds."

"You're kidding, right?"

"Five seconds."

"Whaddya gonna do? Cough on us, old man?"

"Nope. This old man is going to kick your ass so hard you're going to have to wear an inner tube in your pants."

"Go fuck yours—"

I heard a scuffle, a cry, and then the sound of footfalls heading to my right.

"Okay, Del. You can get up now."

I got up, looked at James, then down at the side of my hand, which had scraped against the pavement when I fell. I started down the street to Djebar's house.

"Whoa! Wait a second, will ya?" James caught up to me. "Are you all right?"

I nodded.

"Did you know those idiots?"

"No."

"Have they harassed you before?"

I didn't say anything.

"You get this a lot?"

I shrugged. The faces of the two guys and the girl were already fading from my brain.

James swore. When he gets mad he clenches his fists like my dad. "Don't be cross," I said.

"I just hate bullies. They … piss me off." He went on muttering about what he would do to these "shit-heels" if he ever ran into any of them again.

I have pretty good recall. Better than the others in my class. But the thing is, as hard as I tried I still couldn't remember what any of those bullies looked like.

Mr. Ephron and Mr. Levinson both talk a lot about inspiration. But most of us are puzzled by the concept. How does it work? How do we know when we are being inspired? They both tried to explain it to us, but we didn't get it.

And then one day I felt this kind of shiver zip up my back and fly around my head. I thought maybe it was just an electrical impulse or a reaction to my standing up suddenly. But then I began thinking about how ideas would suddenly fly into Thomas the Tank Engine's funnel, because all at once I had words bouncing around in my head, and they were dancing to the finished melody of the Turing Machinists' first song.

Was this inspiration?

I went to my computer and opened my music document program. But as I drew my fingers over the keyboard, the words suddenly shot away from me and narrowed into vanishing dots — just like when you switch off the old television set in the den where my father sleeps. I don't typically swear, but I heard myself say a couple words I don't usually say.

I don't know how long my father was standing in my bedroom doorway, but he didn't say anything about my swearing, even after I let out a startled cry and knocked over the pen organizer on my desk.

"What are you doing?" my father said in that voice that told me he was trying hard not to be annoyed. "Your mother's been calling you for dinner."

"I don't want dinner."

"Don't be stupid. Come down to dinner."

"I'm not hungry."

"I'm not giving you an option, Del. Come down to dinner, or else."

"Or else what?"

"Don't be snide."

"What do you mean?"

"Just stop —" My father drew in a deep breath, rubbed his palms through his hair. He was doing that a lot lately. "Forget it." He smiled, crossed his arms across his chest. "So, what are you doing?"

I could feel my face getting hot. "Nothing."

My father's eyes narrowed. "You're not on the adult net, are you? We put that parental guidance thingy in, I thought." He crossed the room to my desk in three strides and peered at the screen. I'd minimized it, but on my desktop I'd pasted the photograph James had taken of the Turing Machinists at our first real rehearsal at the Minotaur. Only Wesley was actually looking at the camera, but we were all in it.

"Hey, is that your class?"

"Some of them." I was nervous that he might notice the Minotaur's giant mural of the Labyrinth in the background of the photograph.

"It's a good picture of you." My father grinned. "Ah! I see that boy — Djebar, isn't that his name?"

I nodded.

"So you're friends with these people, huh?"

For one brief moment I considered telling him about the Turing Machinists and the band competition in Toronto.

"It's good to have friends." My father suddenly had that strange expression on his face where his eyes kind of gleamed. "You know, those years when I was in a rock band — they were the best years of my life." My father's sudden laugh startled me. I instinctively flinched and bent away from him. "Believe it or not, we were actually pretty good. We played a few gigs, you know. Nothing big or anything. Maybe if we had chosen a different name ..."

"I like the name Dynamoelectric," I said.

My father looked at me. I couldn't tell if he was cross or surprised. "How did you —?" He gave his head a shake. "Never mind. I'm probably just repeating myself, aren't I? I've told you all this before, right?"

I wanted to tell him I didn't mind, that I wanted to hear more about his band, his life before me. But I wasn't sure it was the right thing to say.

"Listen, Del, we're going to have to talk about what you're going to do after you ... graduate. The school called today. They're setting up meetings with all the parents for after Christmas." His face took on an expression that made me think he might have an upset stomach. "Look, I won't be disappointed if you don't get into college or university. When I was your age I didn't know what I wanted to do —"

"I know what I want to do."

My father looked at me tiredly. "Yes. Of course you do."

Sometimes a person can get lost in the maze of his own thoughts. Most people, when they realize this, immediately try to backtrack to return to their original thought. What Alan Turing advocated was to remain lost in thought until the path eventually circles back to the problem you began with. In taking this journey of thought, what most often happens is that the person gains a new way to think about the problem he originally started with. Turing pointed out that it is not the journey itself, but *surviving* the journey that gives a person the inspiration and innovation to solve the problem.

"So, Del, you want to tell me why you're doing this?"

"Doing what?"

James laughed as he studied my face. "No, don't tell me. Hey, I remember what it was like when I first started. You think being a rock star is going to get you laid, right?"

"Uh, I don't —"

"Yeah, okay. It is true, actually. Being in a band is a bit of a chick magnet. But if that's the only reason you want to do this, forget it. Women are trouble."

"It's not the reason I'm doing this," I said, looking down.

"No?" I thought I detected skepticism in his tone. "Then why are you doing this?" he asked.

"Because I don't want my parents to divorce."

By nine-thirty only James and I and Archie (who was in the back office) remained at the Minotaur. I had drunk two coffees, but I didn't feel as excited and nervous as I thought I would. I wasn't allowed to have caffeine. Still I couldn't seem to stop talking. Finally, James looked at me and said, "Okay, enough already. Change the subject. I've had my fill of Turing and his infernal Machine."

"*Universal* Machine," I corrected. "Did you know that when he was working —"

"When you say 'he' you mean, *Alan Turing*, right?"

"Yes. When Alan Turing was working on the Enigma Code in World War II —"

"Enough, Del! I don't want to talk about Alan Turing anymore, okay?"

I stared down at the floor. It had a diamond pattern that distracted me momentarily. I started to speak, but James intervened: "If this is about that Turing guy and his machine I don't want to hear it."

"Okay."

James sighed. "Why don't we just have a *normal* conversation for once?"

"I ..."

"You look like you have something on your mind."

"I ... do."

"Okay then. Spit it out."

"I'm not supposed to have caffeine."

"Hey, I'm not your father."

I turned my head, gazed at him out of the corner of my eye. I never knew when he was joking or not. And how was it that he was able to read me so well? "My father's leaving at the end of this school year," I blurted.

James scratched the back of his head and looked over at the clock behind the counter. "Hey, I'm sorry to hear that."

"Well, it might not happen," I said.

"Look, I've been there. Divorce is tough on everybody. I come from a broken home myself."

"Yes, I know. I read about it on the MusicCan website."

"Oh, yeah?" His facial expression got really tight all of a sudden.

"Yes. It has everything about you. About your girlfriends and your ex-wife —"

"Don't go there."

"Go where?" I waited a beat. "You know, Alan Turing was a homosexual, so I don't have anything against your ex-wife being a lesbian —"

"Will you just shut up for a moment? Goddammit!"

"I'm sorry." I was puzzled by his reaction.

James shook his head. "No, no. I'm sorry. It's just … I hate the way my personal life is torn open for everyone to see, you know?"

I waited a couple beats, then asked him, "What did you do to try and stop your parents from divorcing?"

James blinked. His brow wrinkled, and then his whole face crinkled up for a few seconds. "Hey, there's nothing you *can* do about this, Del. This is between your mom and dad. They'll figure it out."

"Will they?"

"You shouldn't beat yourself up about it. You're just … a kid."

"I'm not a kid. I'm seventeen years old."

"You're seventeen?"

"Yes."

James stared at me for a long moment until one of his strange expressions seeped into his face. "You're kidding me, right?"

"No. I don't kid very much."

"I thought you were graduating high school this year."

"I am."

"But shouldn't you be *nineteen*?"

"I'm seventeen."

"Are you telling me you … *lied* to me?"

"Technically, yes."

"*Technically*," he echoed. He ran his fingers through his hair. "Shit."

"I had to lie to you. Otherwise you wouldn't have helped us."

"You're damned straight I wouldn't have!"

"Don't be cross with me."

"*Cross* with you? You *fucking* lied to me!"

I didn't say anything, just looked at my feet. I really didn't know what to say. The fact is, all I could think about now was that if James decided not to drive us to Toronto, we would have to make our own way there.

"You're going to have to withdraw from the contest, you know."

"Why?"

James stared at me. "Are you kidding me? You're breaking the rules."

"But we've already been accepted to perform."

"They're going to have to disqualify you, Del. The rules state that each member of the band must be nineteen years of age or older. Bloody hell. I thought you were a stickler for the rules." He frowned. "Wait a second. If you're only seventeen — What about the others? How old are they?"

"Petula turns eighteen years old in February; Djebar turned eighteen years old on September 14; Sogi is seventeen years old; Darrin is sixteen years old; Wesley Farkle is twenty-one years old."

"Wesley's *twenty-one*?" James gave his head a hard shake, made a face I'd never seen before. I thought, just for a second, he was going to laugh. But he didn't.

"Actually, James, you're wrong about the competition rules," I said. "The rules don't state that *each member* has to be nineteen years old. Just at least *one* member of the band."

James folded his arms across his chest and fixed me with a hard blue stare. I forced myself to look into his eyes.

"Contestant Rule number 2b," I quoted from memory. "'At least one inclusive member of the band must be over nineteen years of age.'"

James blinked. "Wesley's over nineteen."

"Yes. He is twenty-one years old."

James got up. I had stopped trying to read his expressions, but I sensed he was still cross with me.

"You're going to get me into a lot of trouble, aren't you, kid?"

"I'm not a kid —"

"Yeah, yeah, right. You're *seventeen*." James drew in a long breath, stared down at his fingers that were drumming on the table. After a moment he said, "Just don't fucking lie to me anymore, okay?"

"Okay."

Some social workers and psychologists put forward the notion that the autistic mind is similar to a child's mind. I'm not sure I understand this reference. In what respect do they mean this?

In one of Turing's papers published in 1950, he recommends computers design programs that imitate a child's mind rather than an adult one.

What is the difference between a child's mind and an adult's mind? Well, for one, the adult mind is jam-packed with preconceived ideas. With its memory full of all that learned experience, I would think it would be like swimming through a cumulus cloud that is impenetrable and fixed into place.

Turing perceived the child's mind to be much more efficient because he believed it would be more open to learning. I think maybe a child's mind is always looking to cut through all that clutter and chaos, to keep only what is needed and to throw out what isn't. So if you were going to design a computer program, in my opinion, simulating a child's mind would be the rational thing to do.

When I mentioned this theory to Doctor Bankoy he took off his wire-rimmed spectacles and let out this big sigh. "You have a lot of thoughts, don't you, Del?" He reached out and squeezed my shoulder. I let his hand stay there for just a few seconds, and then I pulled away.

"The Turing Machine Song" was obsessing my thoughts, occupying too much time and space in my brain. If I could just finish it, I could focus more on my school work.

I considered that there might be some kind of formula I might follow to write song lyrics, like haiku poetry; then I could check if what I had written was correct. But besides the syllabic counts and number of lines in haiku, I could discover no formula for the *content*. How do poets know what words to use? There were, after all, infinite possibilities. How do they know the words they have selected are the right ones? James told me to write how I feel. But how I feel about *what*, exactly? After a while I gave up. I turned off the desk light and went to bed.

But my body was humming, and my scalp was beginning to tingle to the point of itching. I wasn't feeling afraid or anxious, but just unsettled — like I was waiting for something.

When it became evident that I was not going to sleep, I got up, switched on my light, and pulled out my polynomial workbook.

But instead of working on my algebra, I started to write. After about a half-hour this is what I came up with:

> *Mathematics, certainty*
> *Algorithmic circuitry*
> *Traffic jams, construction block*
> *People puzzles, faces lock.*
> *How to act? We don't know*
> *Directions lost, where to go?*
> *Shadows, colors, voices, screams*
> *Come fly with us and see the world*
> *Inside the Turing Machine.*

It wasn't a haiku, but I now had the lyrics for the Turing Machinists' first song.

Music class was a requisite for us because the ASD Research Society revealed that when children play music together, it engages that part of the brain which is linked to empathy. I am the only one in the class who is unable to play an instrument. Does this mean I am unable to tap into the empathetic part of my brain? Ms. Biegler tried to help me, but eventually she gave up and asked me if I would like to learn music theory.

I learned much more quickly than Ms. Biegler expected. In a matter of months I could read all the different instrument parts. When I began to write music Ms. Biegler became very excited and started downloading articles and books and music for me to read and listen to. She was looking at my composition for the Turing Machinists.

"What's this, Del?"

I snatched it away. "Nothing."

She gave me a funny kind of look, then said, "You have a gift, Del." She asked me if I wanted to study music after I graduated. "You know, there are some very good music programs in Toronto."

I told her I was more interested in math. But she gave me some more books on music theory anyway. When she handed me some CDs of classical artists to listen to at home, I didn't tell her that I didn't like listening to music on compact discs, or on the radio. Neither did I tell her that my father was once in a rock band but that he could not read or write music.

"So you finally finished it, huh? Cool." James blew into his hands, then wrapped his arms around himself. "Goddammit, it's *cold*." He looked at me. "I take it this weather doesn't bother you?"

I shrugged. "I dress appropriately. And I like snow." I handed him the sheet with the lyrics.

James pushed it back at me. "You know the music. Sing it for me."

"Sing it? Here?" I cast a glance about me. At the far end of the park, an elderly couple strolled, arm in arm. To my left, a woman wrapped like a pink balloon was walking her white lapdog. Her hair was very blond and her skin was the color of an apricot. Just as I was about to say that her presence bothered me, she looked over. I quickly averted my gaze.

"You're going to have to sing in front of people eventually," said James.

I looked at the paper in my hand. I knew the lyrics by heart, but I couldn't take my eyes off the paper. "I know ... but I can't."

"Just sing, will you?" James sighed. "Look, would it help if I turned around so I can't see you?" He turned his back to me. "There. I won't watch you."

"I can't."

"Yes, you can."

I gripped the paper, cleared my throat. "Mathema-atics, cer —" My throat rasped. "I can't."

"Here. Take a sip." James gave me his cup.

I sputtered as I tasted the liquid. "Yech! What is that?"

"Some kind of Chinese herbal tea," said James. "I get it from a guy in L.A. It's ... an acquired taste."

"Is this supposed to help you not do drugs anymore?"

James rubbed his face and sniffed. "You going to sing this song to me, or what? We're running out of time."

"It's just the chorus," I said.

"Fine."

"Can you turn around?"

James sighed and turned his back to me. The pink balloon woman was drawing nearer with her dog.

"Can we do this somewhere else?" I said nervously.

"Come on, Del. It's now or never."

I had practiced singing it earlier that morning, but all of a sudden I couldn't remember the tune. "I can't remember ..."

"How about I hum the music for you?" He started humming. And when he got to the chorus, I sang. I sang the whole chorus without stuttering, without cracking my voice. When I finished, James turned around. I couldn't read his expression, so I couldn't tell if he liked it.

James got up. "You said you couldn't sing."

"I can't."

"But you just did, didn't you?" James rubbed his hands together, picked up his cup, then stood up and stretched his back. "You'd better skedaddle or you'll be late for school again."

As I hurried across the park, I glanced behind me to see James sitting on the bench talking to the pink balloon woman. I was confused; James hadn't said whether he liked my lyrics or my singing. So, was the song okay? Was my singing bad?

For the remainder of the day I obsessed about this, reciting the lyrics over and over in my head until they were etched into my brain cells. I envisioned the notes of my composition until I could hear the melody floating in my mind. In Mr. Ephron's class, while we watched slides of paintings of Monet and Van Gogh, I wrote the rest of the song.

"What's this?" Jeddy snatched up my notebook.

"Give it back!"

"*Mathematics, certainty; Algorithmic circuitry; Traffic jams —*"

I hit him on the nose.

In movies, punches are supposed to make a neat *kapow* sound. But what I heard was a kind of squishy, quiet *slacrunch* noise that didn't sound neat at all. And in movies you never see the hero holding his hand and howling in pain afterwards — which I was doing when Mr. Ephron stepped in. We were both sent to the nurse, and then, after the nurse pronounced Jeddy's nose to be broken and my hand to be only slightly bruised, Jeddy went to the hospital and I was sent to the principal's office.

What worried me most at the time was that Mrs. Seidewand, the principal, would ask to see my notebook, then figure out that I was writing a song for a rock band and that I was entering the Cubground Pub Battle of the Bands competition in Toronto. And then she would tell my parents and everyone else's parents, and we would all be in trouble and not be able to enter the competition.

As it turned out, that wasn't what I needed to worry about. What I really needed to worry about was Jeddy's father. He threatened to sue my parents and the school for damages done to Jeddy and his broken nose.

"I don't understand, Del. What made you hit another student?" My mother had that worried expression on her face that made all the lines groove across her forehead. "Maybe we should take you to see Doctor Bankoy. It might be the medication."

"You broke that boy's nose, Del," said my father. The look on his face was a new one that I couldn't read. But I couldn't detect any anger or worry in his voice. "You must have punched him pretty hard. How's your hand?"

My mother shot my father a look that made him sit back on the couch. "Del, do you know why you hit Jeddy?" she asked.

I thought about telling them the truth, but instead I said, "I don't like Jeddy. He … annoys me."

"Tell us the truth, Del. What did Jeddy do to make you so angry?"

"I didn't mean to hit him so hard," I said truthfully.

My mother sighed, and she and my father exchanged looks. "The first thing you're going to do is apologize to Jeddy," said my mother.

"Do you think that will be enough to settle this thing?" said my father.

"I'll talk to Helen." My mother had that look on her face that meant something was going to happen. I started to get those fruit flies in my stomach.

Helen is Jeddy's mother. She has short, dark brown hair and wears very dark red lipstick and dark brown eyeshadow. When she looks at me, it's like she isn't looking *at* me but *behind* me. I'm not sure I like her, but she doesn't scare me half as much as Sogi's mother. I actually think Jeddy's mother is pretty. That is, until she speaks. Her voice is sharp, like a whistle, and I have to press my hands to my ears or move away. She used to be a government lawyer. Now she's the head of the Merryton City Council. I heard my mother say she was running for mayor next year.

"You think talking to that woman will help?" my father said.

My mother got up. Her mouth was a thin straight line, and there was a glint in her eyes that always gave me a strange, foreboding sensation. "You don't think autism is a political issue?"

When I was in grade seven, my mother, Jeddy's mother, and some other people organized a charity for autism. Their platform was: *Help Piece Together the Puzzle of Autism.* At the time, the controversy over autism being caused by vaccines was an issue that was being debated hotly among local politicians. Groups of environmentalists arrived at Merryton's first autism charity fundraiser to protest the charity's stratagem, stating that there can be no "puzzle" of autism if it is caused by mercury poisoning and environmental factors. Others who advocated neurodiversity called my mother and Jeddy's mother "curebies." Autism is incurable, they protested; do yourselves a favor and accept autism and your child for who they are.

Eventually, the charity fell apart because of its backers, and my mother resigned. Jeddy's mother was the only one left trying to hold it together.

"Well, I'm not giving up hope so easily," she told my mother.

"It's not about giving up hope," I heard my mother telling Hannah's mother on the phone. "It's about accepting Del for who he is. Good God! As a mother I will never give up the hope that he will one day be able to clip his toenails by himself and eat a balanced diet. But at the same time, we do have to be *realistic*."

Food issues are something all of us in the ASD class share. Some of us, like Hannah and Wesley, have more problems than others. Wesley throws up a lot if he has too many carbohydrates and saturated fats. And I think there's a whole list of foods he's supposed to stay away from, like dairy, eggs, wheat, corn, MSG, pork, and a bunch of other stuff. I'm not sure what he actually *can* eat. His mother makes him this kind of hash-like stuff that smells like licorice. The smell is not something I like, so I'm glad he eats alone.

Hannah freaks out when she eats fruit. Interestingly enough, she can eat candy without getting hyperactive. Also, she's not allowed to drink carbonated drinks. I don't know the reason for this, but Hannah says they "fizz up" her neurons. I can't figure out the science behind this, so I can't say for certain this is true. But what it comes down to is this: Wesley throws up at certain times regardless of what he eats, and Hannah has her freak-outs even if she *hasn't* eaten any sugar, fruit, or carbonated drinks.

"Whether it affects them or not, you have to do the diet thing; otherwise you look like a bad mother," Hannah's mother once said in our kitchen.

There are other food issues we all have. Djebar will not eat foods that have been dried or have the appearance of having been dried, like apricots and dates and raisins. Darrin and his parents are vegetarians and they eat only local food. Sogi eats whatever his mother tells him to eat; but when she's not around he eats food he enjoys, which seems to be almost everything that isn't on his current diet.

I have always been a picky eater. Mealtimes make me anxious, especially holiday meals or when company comes over. My mother hovers over me, always trying to get me to eat things I don't want to eat. But I have issues with yellow and orange foods. I don't eat things like pumpkin or carrots or Cheetos, or yellow beans or corn. I do eat oranges once in a while if they're peeled and segmented and the pulp is shaved off of them.

"He'll eat them if he gets hungry enough," my father used to say.

"So what would you like me to do? Starve him so he'll eat his yellow beans?"

It wasn't until my sixth birthday that my mother noticed my eating pattern. "Look, Tom! He's picked off all the yellow and orange sprinkles. I think it's all about *color*; he doesn't like yellow or orange foods."

"That's ridiculous," said my father.

"But it's true! Look at what he does to the mixed vegetables on his plate."

When I eat I separate all of the vegetables: the corn and the diced carrots are pushed off to the farthest end of the plate, while the others are grouped by greens, whites, and reds. I eat the reds first, then the greens, then any other vegetable that isn't yellow or orange. I have always eaten in this systematic way, except of late I have begun to eat the meat product on the plate last instead of first. I don't know why. It's just sort of happened.

Most of us in the class like our food moated — meaning that we don't like any of our foods to touch or mingle. This isn't necessarily an autistic trait; lots of people prefer eating this way. The only difference might be in our reaction when one food meanders past its protective moat. Often the tantrum can end up with demands for a brand new plate or refusing to eat at all. And then there are conundrums to work out, like casseroles. For me, a casserole is just too stressful a job to eat. So I stick to the simple: meat, potato (no rice or noodles), and vegetable.

"I brought dinner!" James announced as he walked into the Minotaur. He set down two large pizza boxes on one of the tables.

"I can't eat that pizza," said Petula, looking into one of the boxes. "It has pepperoni on it."

"I'm a vegetarian; I can't have meat or cheese," said Darrin.

"What's the difference between a vegetarian and a vegan?" Petula asked.

"What kind of crust is it? I'm not supposed to have gluten," said Djebar.

"Actually, my family is ovo-vegetarian," said Darrin. "We can eat eggs, but not dairy products."

"I can't have wheat or dairy," said Wesley. "I'm not supposed to eat nitrates because they make me angry."

"What — like the Hulk?" snorted James. "Come on, guys —"

"Pepperoni has nitrates, doesn't it?" said Wesley. "I know bacon does. Is that bacon?"

"I don't like cheese," I said.

"You don't like *cheese*?" James blinked.

"Maybe you should become an ovo-vegetarian, like me," said Darrin. I shook my head. "I don't think I could give up meat."

"I'm actually not allowed to eat any part of that pizza," said Sogi with a sigh.

James stared at everyone, his mouth half open. "Come on!" He threw open the lid of one of the boxes. "This is *pizza*."

Djebar came over glanced down at the pizza. After a moment he said, "Okay. I'll try a slice."

"You're not going to have some kind of weird seizure, are you?" James said, his nose and brow wrinkling.

"Nah. Gluten just gives me the runs," said Djebar.

Sogi smacked his lips. "Well, if nobody tells my mother I think I'm going to try a couple of pieces."

The pizza did smell good. "I guess I can always scrape off the cheese," I said.

James grinned, shook his head. "Your bravery astounds me." He laughed. "Darrin? I could scrape off the meat and the cheese, if you like. Of course, that leaves just mushrooms and, uh, green and red pepper."

"Thank you, James," said Darrin.

Was there something different about Darrin? Or was I just noticing things about him now that he was in the band? He wasn't hunching over or tugging at his ears so much. He'd stopped staring, too. He was still quiet, but his voice sounded different to me. Deeper, maybe.

"If you take off the pepperoni and mushrooms I'll try a slice," said Petula. "It's from Hermione's, so it can't be that bad."

"Wesley? How about you?"

Wesley was already scooping out a piece and jamming it into his mouth. I was betting the pizza tasted a lot better than that licorice hash his mother makes him eat.

James handed out drinks, and we sat down to eat. Not together, of course. Drinking hot chocolate with other people is one thing; eating a meal is another. James sat with me and Djebar and Darrin. Neither of us are bothered so much by other people eating with us. But Wesley needs to be alone, and Petula hates anyone sitting to her right. Sogi, who suffers from a bit of food aggression, sat on the floor near the stage.

"A toast," James said, holding up his beer bottle, "to the Turing Machinists, and a successful video recording."

Djebar burped, and jumped up to go to the washroom.

"So. Is everyone ready for their close-up on Sunday?"

"What do you mean 'close-up'?" asked Petula.

"He's talking about the video recording, do-do bird," said Sogi. His mouth was full of pizza, and some of it fell out of his mouth when he spoke.

"You're disgusting!"

Wesley suddenly coughed, and then vomited onto the table. Djebar and Sogi started letting off really loud farts, and I began to scratch the back of my neck and my chest.

James rose to his feet with an expression that made me wonder if he wasn't in pain. "Okay. You guys weren't kidding me, were you?"

Turing could not decide whether computer programs, when given input, would eventually stop or run forever. This was known as the halting problem.

Even when you input all the information available, answers to some questions don't always come. Questions like, where do we come from? Why are we here? Or why are we the way we are? These are questions everyone asks *knowing* that they won't get answers. For the longest time I didn't understand this. I still don't. These are halting problems, halting questions. We try to answer them despite the fact that they are unanswerable. Why do we do this?

Theorizing about autism — what it is, what causes it — is a halting problem. The input is vast, and the information stays basically the same. And yet the solution is always just out of reach.

I watched a mother on television pronounce that she was never going to give up trying to find a cure for her child's autism. Her son, who was five, was running around the panel flapping his arms and spinning, occasionally taking a break to Velcro and un-Velcro his shoes and touch the shoes of the others on the panel. Occasionally one of the psychologists on the panel would look over and tighten up all his features and comment on the child's behavior. How the boy was acting was socially inappropriate, of course.

But of all the people on the show, the child appeared to be the most content and relaxed.

Djebar's mother came home early while we were practicing in the garage. Fortunately she parks the car outside, and because it was a cold, snowy evening, she leaped out of the car and ran around to the other side of the house. She didn't hear us playing until she was putting away the groceries in the refrigerator.

She tried the door from the kitchen to the garage, but it was locked.

"Djebar! Djebar!" she shouted.

Darrin stopped playing. He frowned, listening. Then Petula paused. Wesley stopped in mid-stroke, dug out his earplugs. We could all now hear Djebar's mom shouting from inside the house. Djebar turned white.

"What should I do?" he whispered.

"Tell her we're practicing, dimwit," said Petula.

Djebar glanced at me. "I thought we weren't supposed to tell our parents."

"Well, I told *mine*," said Petula.

We all stared at her.

"Well, they asked me where I was going last Sunday and I told them." She snorted. "The thing is, my parents never listen to me. And if they do, they never believe me, anyway."

I was suddenly glad James wasn't there. I had assured him at our first rehearsal that our parents were okay with us entering the competition and with him managing the Turing Machinists. In reality, none of our parents knew what we were doing (I suspected Petula's parents hadn't believed her), and they knew nothing about James's involvement.

"Just say you were listening to the radio," said Sogi.

"Radio? What radio?"

"Djebar! Who's in there with you? Unlock this door this minute!"

Djebar scrambled to the door. His mother poked her head in, looked at us. I could tell she was surprised because her eyebrows went way up and her mouth made a little O. "Oh, hello."

Wesley cringed behind his drum set, and Darrin turned red and looked down at his feet. Sogi busied himself with opening a caramel in his pocket, and I tried to hide behind Darrin. Only Petula stared up at Djebar's mother.

"We're rehearsing for the school band," she said.

Djebar's mother blinked at her. "You're from Djebar's class, aren't you? Are you … Hannah?"

"No," said Petula, still staring.

"Oh."

There was a beat of silence. Wesley made a gurgling sound.

"All right then," said Djebar's mother when no one spoke. "I'll let you get back to your rehearsal." She leaned against the doorframe, watching us. We didn't move.

"You need to leave," said Petula in her flat voice.

Djebar's mother's brows lowered over her eyes and for a moment her mouth got small. She looked over at Djebar, who was standing stiffly with his hands at his sides, his gaze far away. "Of course. Sorry," she muttered, and closed the door behind her.

"I'm going home," said Wesley, rising.

"It's only seven-thirty," said Sogi.

"I don't feel like playing anymore," said Darrin.

I didn't feel like singing either, and Petula started packing up her xylophone. Djebar suggested we call it a night. Only Sogi protested.

"I don't think we can rehearse here anymore," said Petula, glancing at the door.

We all agreed, even Sogi.

"I don't understand," said James. "Djebar's mother didn't say you couldn't rehearse there, right?"

"No."

"And you said she doesn't usually get home until nine-thirty on Wednesdays and Thursdays?"

"Yes."

"So why can't you rehearse there anymore?"

I thought a moment. The truth was, I didn't know why we had

to stop rehearsing in Djebar's mother's garage. Our routine had been compromised, but did that mean we had to stop altogether? James's logic was sound. Ours wasn't.

"We all agreed," I said, looking down at my boots.

After a moment James sighed. "So you're telling me you're going to need another place to rehearse."

"Did you get the firewire cable for the DVR —?"

"You already asked me that. *Twice*. Yes, I got it." James rolled his eyes. "Shit, kid, you worry. I got everything on your list. It's not like I haven't used a digital camera before."

"It has to be live," I reminded him. "No lip-synching or music dubbing. Otherwise it will be disqualified."

"*I know.*"

"The camera you rented was a Canon Vixia HF G19, right?"

"Didn't we already have this conversation?"

"You didn't get the Canon Vixia HF G10, right? Because they have almost the same features, except the G19 has 2.75 pixels instead of 1.7."

"I got the right one, Del."

"Are you sure? Because the G10 and the G19 look almost identical."

James looked at me with an expression I couldn't quite interpret. "Better get going. You're going to be late for school."

My watch said it was 8:32. "I still have a few minutes."

James slid himself to his feet, stretched and yawned. "Well, I'm heading home. I didn't get much sleep last night." He eyed me for a couple seconds. "But you already know that, don't you?"

"What do you mean?"

James snorted. "You know, sometimes I think you're hiding behind that Asperger syndrome thing so you can just play dumb and do what you want."

"I don't understand."

"Yeah, right. I think you understand more than you're letting on."

As I watched James leave, I thought about all the information I'd gathered about him from the Internet. His mother was a hairdresser and recovering crack addict living in Pittsburgh, and his father had been a jazz musician who died three years ago from alcohol poisoning. Some of the tabloids alleged that James was a cocaine addict. Others said heroin. Even if none of it was true, the mere hint of having any kind of association with illegal drugs made him suspect. One thing I knew for certain: none of our parents would allow us to associate with a suspected drug user.

Illegal recreational drugs have never been an issue with me. I don't seem to be drawn to them; I don't understand the appeal of distorting reality, especially when I am busy trying to make it clearer. Plus, I have enough of my own sensory issues and obsessions and compulsions to deal with. But then, Sherlock Holmes was a cocaine addict, wasn't he? And he was as intelligent and respectable as they come. Of course, he was a fictional character.

After Alan Turing's death there were stories about his having experimented with cocaine and heroin. But these stories, along with his alleged suicide, were eventually refuted. The coroner investigating Turing's death ruled that he had committed suicide by ingesting what they first identified as heroin. Later they discovered it was cyanide. It was well known that Turing had been electrolyzing solutions of cyanide and electroplating spoons with gold, which requires the use of potassium cyanide. Investigations into his death found that it was much more likely that Turing's death was an accident. But the coroner refused to change Turing's cause of death to "accidental," stating that the man's mind at the time was unbalanced and disturbed, as was evidenced in his eccentric behavior and the fact that he did not fit in with society.

In one of the tabloid stories about James, a spokesperson for a record label who cancelled a Magic Horse Marines music contract said James just didn't fit with their company. Another story said that the company's president's wife was having an affair with James. Some months later it was reported that he was hospitalized for overdosing on heroin. Apparently, he checked himself into a rehabilitation center, and the following day the Magic Horse Marines broke up.

I have never wondered if any of these stories about James were true. In the end they mean nothing to me. If James was or wasn't a drug addict doesn't matter to me. I don't think he is using drugs now. But what if he is? Is there really anything I can do? That I *should* do? I mean, what he does to his own brain and body isn't my business, is it?

James arrived late, sat down on the bench beside me, and closed his eyes. His face looked a little gray, and his eyes were a faded sky color, but I didn't say anything.

"Tell me about yourself, Del."

"What do you want to know?"

"I don't know. Just … distract me."

I was silent for a minute. "'Everyone goes through life dropping crumbs. If you can recognize the crumbs, you can trace a path all the way back from your death certificate to the dinner and a movie that resulted in you in the first place.'"

James turned and looked at me, his eyebrows pushing up his forehead so that two lines appeared. "Shit, Del. That's quite good. Witty, even."

"It's a passage from *Zero Effect*."

"Oh." He slid down and rested his head against the bench. After a few beats he said, "You're not going to ask me, are you?"

"Ask you what?"

"How I am."

"Why?"

"Because I'm feeling really shitty, that's why."

"But how would I know that?"

James sighed. "You're right. You're not psychic, are you?"

I was confused. "No."

"You want to know why I feel shitty?"

"No." And then, remembering a lesson in communication class, I quickly said, "I mean, yes."

He gave me a long sideways glance, then suddenly laughed. "Okay, you made me laugh. That's something." He sat up. "It's the goddamn holidays. Christmas in particular. I guess that's why I'm feeling ... blue."

"Picasso had a blue period — although he actually suffered regularly from depression."

"Yeah. Well, I seem to always get this way around this time of year."

"Is it because your father drank himself to death and your mother is a drug addict?"

James laughed. "My mother's not an addict, she's a hairdresser. And my father died of stomach cancer, not alcohol poisoning." He glanced at his watch. "There. I told you something of myself. Now you tell me something of yourself."

I thought a moment. "When I was six years old, on Christmas Eve, I saw Santa Claus on the rooftop of old Mr. Jensen's house. I told my parents, but they didn't believe me. And then the afternoon following Boxing Day, Mr. Jensen was found dead in his house."

"You saw who killed him, then!"

"It was Santa Claus."

"Or someone dressed up like Santa Claus."

"No."

"So, did your parents call the police?"

"Yes."

"What happened? Did they come to question you?"

"No. It turned out Mr. Jensen died of a heart attack."

"Oh." James shook his head. "Wait a second. What was the point of that story?"

"What do you mean?"

James smiled. "Nothing. You'd better skedaddle. It's almost a quarter to nine."

I shrugged on my knapsack and started to leave.

"Hey, Del."

I stopped, turned around.

"Thanks. You actually cheered me up."

As I ran across the park to the street, I felt lighter. My thinking felt sharper, too. It was like I'd had a brain focus adjustment. I was thinking about Fermat's theorem when it just popped into my head: the haiku for Levinson's class.

> *If you can see me*
> *Then you know I'm not like you*
> *You are like nobody too.*

I wrote it down as soon as I got to school, then showed it to Mr. Levinson during third period. He told me he liked it. "But remember that a haiku is not just about formula. Remember what we talked about? There should be elements of compassion, silence, and a sense of temporality."

"I'm not sure I understand that part."

"Read more haiku, and see if you can recognize those elements. Take time to think about it. Understanding will come after you've taken time to *think* about it."

I didn't want to read more haiku. I didn't want to think about poetry. "So you aren't accepting this haiku assignment from me?"

"It's not due until after the holidays, Del. Why don't you work on it some more?"

I didn't want to work on it anymore. Truthfully, I didn't think I *could* work on it even if I'd wanted to. "I think this poem is the best I can do, Mr. Levinson."

Mr. Levinson's expression suddenly changed. His voice lowered, his tone becoming gentler like he was afraid someone might hear him. "It's not that I don't like your poem. It's a fine haiku, Del. Really. But ... it's possible that over the holidays you might come up with something new ... something that you like better." He smiled. But it was one of those painful smiles, like Grandmother Capp's.

I looked down at the paper in my hand and didn't say anything.

"Are you going to be all right, Del?"

I frowned, looked up at him. "Yes. Why?"

"Well, you just tend to be ... you're always so ..." For a moment his brows drew together, and they formed a straight line over his eyes. "Never mind." He smiled. "Thank you, Del."

As soon as I sat down, I asked James if he had found us another place to rehearse.

"Look, I have a life too, you know. What do you think I do all day? Sit around on my ass and think about you and your fucking Turing Machinists?!"

I felt my face grow hot. I tucked in my chin, staring at the snow between my feet. My throat tightened, and my eyes began to sting. *Why couldn't I say anything right?* Under my mittens I was digging my fingernails into my palms. It was a habit I adopted after I was told to stop hitting my head.

"Aw, dammit," James muttered. "Look, Del. I'm just in a bad mood. Just … ignore me, okay?"

I didn't say anything. I was afraid I would make him angrier.

"Hey, I'm sorry. Really. It's just that …" He exhaled loudly. "I'm, like, in this in-between stage, you know? It's like I'm in … limbo. Fuck. I just can't seem to get started, you know?"

"What are you trying to start?" I asked.

He shook his head. "My life, I guess." James looked at me. He gave a small laugh. "I don't expect you to understand."

But I realized then that I did understand what he was talking about. "It's like you keep doing all these things to get your life going, but nothing happens, and you just keep waiting for your life to begin."

James smiled at me. His eyes matched the sky today. "You know, you're becoming a pretty good conversationalist."

"So did you find a place for us to rehearse?"

James threw back his head and laughed. "You are consistent, I'll give you that."

"We need a place to rehearse."

James sighed. "I'll talk to Archie, okay? He might know some places in town."

Alan Turing was a long-distance runner. Although his running style was considered awkward and some of the other runners made fun of him, especially about the grunting noises he made when he ran, his running team considered him the best runner in their group.

I hum when I run. Sometimes, if I am upset, I make gargling sounds that bring my mother outside to make sure I'm okay. One day, my father came home from work and watched me run. I was fourteen. That night he came up to my bedroom and told me that he had entered me in the Merryton Marathon.

"I don't want to run in the marathon."

"Well, you're fourteen now. You're allowed to enter."

"I don't want to go."

"Are you kidding me? I've seen you run, Del. You're going to *win* that marathon."

"I don't want to go."

"Well, you're registered." He ruffled my hair, which made my skin prickle at the back of my neck. "Look, it's not for another three weeks. You can decide then if you want to go, okay?"

The day of the marathon arrived. It was a Saturday. On Saturdays, I take the number 3 bus and go to the Merryton Public Library, and then take the number 8 bus to the Emporium where I sit down and have French fries and ketchup. As I was getting ready to leave, my father burst into my bedroom. His face was all pink.

"Okay! Are you ready? The race starts in twenty-five minutes."

"I'm not going."

"What? I thought we discussed this. You're already registered." He looked at me and frowned. "Get your gear on and let's go."

"I don't want to go. I'm going to the library."

"You go to the library every Saturday." My father opened my dresser drawers and rummaged inside. "This is special. You'll thank me for this later, I promise."

"No. I'm going to the library."

"Get your gear on and I'll drive you."

"No."

"Don't be difficult."

"No! I don't want to go!"

"Hey, don't raise your voice at me. Just put on your shorts —"

"NO!!! Leave me ALONE!"

And I ran as fast as I could down the stairs and out of the house. Instead of taking the bus I ran all the way to the library.

I like to go to the south end Merryton Public Library branch because they have cubicles with chairs that have special leather seats. But it is on the other end of Merryton. From my calculations the total distance from my house to the library is 17.3 kilometers. I made it there in sixty-two minutes and twenty-one seconds. I would have gotten there faster if I hadn't had to wait for the traffic lights along Grand Avenue.

In the 1948 Olympic Games, Delfo Cabrera, a world-class athlete from Argentina, ran the marathon in two hours, thirty-four minutes, and fifty-one seconds. Alan Turing's best time was only eleven minutes slower. Recognizing his talent for long-distance running, some of the people in the athletics department at the University of Manchester tried to convince Turing to enter competitive marathons. But he said he ran only for himself.

I can totally relate.

Archie and his wife sat at one of the tables in front of the Minotaur's music stage. Wesley was in the bathroom getting sick, and Darrin was outside because he said he felt feverish. I was drinking my third glass of ginger ale, and Petula was braiding her hair and biting her lip.

"Tell her she looks nice," James whispered in my ear.

I felt a surge of heat flood my face. I looked down at my feet.

"Djebar's out front with Darrin. Where's Sogi?" James asked.

"I don't know."

"Can you call him? I'd like to start soon."

As a general consensus, we don't call each other on the telephone. None of us like telephones or cellphones. It's very difficult for us to carry on conversations while speaking to someone on a cellphone. So I texted him, and waited.

Wesley came out of the bathroom and sat next to Archie at the table. He looked a lot less pale, and his hair was combed. I put my hand on my own hair, wondering how I looked. It suddenly occurred to me that my appearance might be important, as this was a video recording of our song.

"Don't worry. You look beautiful," said Djebar, grinning. He smelled like cigarette smoke. He smoked when he was nervous or excited. Smoking relaxed him, he told me. I tried to smoke a few times; it smelled and tasted too terrible for me to enjoy it.

"How's Darrin?"

Djebar shrugged. "He'll be okay once he starts playing." He looked around. "Where's Sogi?"

"I texted him."

"Maybe he's not going to show up?"

Petula approached. "That shit-for-brains is chickening out, isn't he?" She'd twisted small braids down the sides of her hair. I felt a surge of something strange when I looked at her.

"You look like Xena," I blurted.

"Xena?" Petula snorted. "I'm no Warrior Princess."

I blushed. I couldn't help it. Petula just made me so self-conscious.

"What is it between you and Sogi, anyway?" Djebar asked her. "You two are always picking at each other. Reminds me of my parents. Are you two having sex or what?"

Petula's mouth pressed into a thin line and her dark eyes glared at Djebar. "If you want to live you won't ask me that again." And she stalked off.

"Well, that confirms it."

"Confirms what?" I asked.

"They're having sex."

"Really?" I was confused.

"She didn't deny it, did she?"

"She didn't confirm it either," I pointed out.

"I'm good at reading people," said Djebar. "They're having sex."

Just then Sogi came in, all out of breath.

"Who's having sex?" he asked, catching his breath.

I looked at him. "Djebar says you and Petula are having sex."

Sogi laughed. "Wow. That is news to me. Although ... I wouldn't say no if she asked me. Hey, do you think she likes me?"

Djebar admitted he didn't know. "Anything with Petula is possible."

"Do you like her?" I asked Sogi.

Sogi shrugged. "She's kind of pretty, I guess."

James finished setting up the digital video camera on the tripod, then shooed Petula as she tried to adjust it. "Okay! Looks like everyone's here. Let's get started!"

My heart and stomach lurched. We all stayed where we were, as if James's words had paralyzed us.

"Well, *come on*!" said James loudly. A beat passed, and no one spoke or moved. He softened his voice. "You guys have been rehearsing this for weeks now. Pretend it's just another rehearsal."

"But it's not," said Petula.

"I said *pretend*." James sighed. "Hey, it's normal to be nervous. I would be worried if you *weren't*."

We looked at Archie and his wife and then at one another uncertainly. James didn't realize how difficult it was for us to pretend.

"All right!" James clapped his hands. "If you want to be a Turing Machinist, get on stage, now!"

Wesley started forward, leaped up on stage, and sat himself down at the drum set. We all followed him nervously. My throat was dry, and I could barely hear for the blood roaring in my ears.

Be brave, Del.

"Be brave, Del." My mother squeezed my hand gently.

The dentist approached me with the dental pick in his hand, and I screamed and screamed and screamed.

"I can't work on him like this," growled the dentist.

"Please, just let him calm down —"

The dentist peered down at me. "Del, you want to be a big boy, don't you?"

"No!" I kicked out at him.

"Now, that's enough! Sit still and open your mouth!"

"He's very sensitive. If you yell at him —"

I thrashed my body and knocked over the assistant's tray. The dentist let out a gruff curse, and the dental assistant just stared at me with big frog-like eyes and a frown. My mother started apologizing, and I leaped out of the chair and ran out of the room.

In the car, my mother was quiet for a long time. And then she spoke: "You are going to have to go to the dentist sometime, Del. I won't take you back to that dentist, but I'll find a good one — one that works on children ... like you. I'm not going to say it won't sting a little or be uncomfortable. But this is something that has to be done. So the only thing you can do right now is stick it out, and be brave."

"I don't know how to be brave," I sobbed.

"Yes, you do. Just tell yourself, 'Be brave, Del.'"

"Popcorn?" Djebar nudged the bag at me. "It's double butter."

I shook my head. I was too nervous to eat.

Archie tuned off the lights, and we all sat at the table watching the screen flick on in front of us. As soon as the DVD started Djebar began to giggle. Petula told him he was an immature ass, then leaped to her feet, twisting her hair around her fingers. Darrin was scratching madly behind his ears. As I sank down low in my seat, hooding my eyes with my hands, I wondered if Darrin had a rash and if it was catching, because my whole body was humming and I was beginning to feel itchy myself. Sogi started to say something, but James quickly quieted him. I said something, but he cut me off in the middle.

"Just listen for once, okay?" said James sternly. "This is *you*! Petula, sit down. Everyone, look and *listen* to yourselves!"

And we did.

I don't know how to describe how I felt sitting there listening to us play my music. *My* music. I watched me singing, and at first I was confused. Is that what I look like? Watching yourself on video is different from looking at yourself in the mirror. I didn't know if I liked the guy on stage singing. It felt like I was looking at my ... what was the word?

"*Doppelganger*," hissed Petula.

I stared at her. She looked back at me, her head cocked to one side. I felt a weird shudder go up and down my body. For one split second something happened between us that even later I could not figure out.

And then Djebar gave a yell. And because he was sitting to my left, my more sensitive side, the noise jarred my eardrums.

"We're fucking *GREAT*!"

Ms. Pokolopinison announced that she was ready to review the progress of our group projects. My stomach lurched, and I felt so overcome with anxiety I thought I was going to be sick. Wesley actually did vomit and was sent to the nurse's office.

"What do we do?" Petula whispered.

"I don't know," said Sogi.

"We're in big shit," hissed Djebar.

They were all looking at me. Why were they looking at me? *I* had no idea what to do.

It was Darrin who came up with an idea. "We'll tell her the game plans are on a thumb drive and Del has it at his house."

"Why is it at my house?" I asked.

"Well, you're the project leader, aren't you?" he said.

"I am?" I was stunned.

"Hey, you're the one who got us into this mess," hissed Sogi. "So you're going to have to take the blame."

"I've always thought the board game idea was a good one," said Petula. She was lining up pencil grips along the rim of the table. Djebar realigned one that was slightly askew. Petula hesitated, then went on, pulling out the pencil grips from her orange pencil case. I looked inside, tentatively put my fingers in, and pulled one out. Petula didn't do anything as I set it along the rim. Sogi reached into the pencil case. Petula slapped his hand.

"Get your fucking fingers out of my bag!"

Ms. Pokolopinison approached at that moment. "Petula! We do not use that kind of language in class."

"Okay. I'll go outside and call him a fucking bastard, then."

"Petula! That's not how young ladies speak in this class." Ms. Pokolopinison's fixed smile had turned into a grim line. "Please go to the main office."

"Can I go to the Plum Room instead?"

Ms. Pokolopinison drew in a breath, chewed on her lip for a moment. "Are you feeling out of sorts, Petula?"

"Yes," said Petula. "I am feeling out of sorts, Ms. Pokolopinison."

"Fine." Ms. Pokolopinison waved her hand at Petula. "Go."

As Petula gathered up her pencil grips and packed her knapsack, she glanced up at me, and I saw her smile. My heart skipped a beat, and I felt something stir in my groin. *Oh, Petula,* I thought.

"Del? Del? Did you hear me?"

I jerked as I felt a hand press down on my shoulder. It was Ms. Pokolopinison. "Darrin says you are the project leader." She was smiling. "I am pleased you took my business management model paradigm seriously. Is it possible to see some of what you've been working on?"

"Now?"

"If I can just see some of what you've done —"

"You can't."

"No? Why not?"

I think of myself as a bad liar, but many people interpret my blushing and stuttering as shyness and nervousness. So while I don't like lying, people tend to want to believe me. I think I could easily get away with not telling the truth — if I wanted to. Or if it was necessary.

"It's all on a thumb drive," I stammered. "And I forgot it at home."

"Oh. Well, maybe you can tell me a bit about what you're doing."

"It's a, uh, board game."

"Yes, I believe you already told me that. But do you think it would be possible for you to give me a few more details?"

I looked over at Darrin and Djebar, who had slunk away and were looking down at the floor, pretending not to listen. Sogi had snuck off to the bathroom.

"Darrin? Djebar? Maybe you can tell me a bit about your group project?"

"It's a board game," said Djebar.

"Yes, I know. But what *kind* of board game?"

Djebar looked at me, didn't say anything. Darrin kept looking down at his shoes.

"It's a music game," I said, suddenly inspired. "It's called *Dynamoelectric*."

"Oh?" Ms. Pokolopinison's face brightened. "Tell me more."

"We can show you the outline ... next week."

"Next week? We are in Christmas holidays starting next Tuesday."

"After the holidays, then," I said quickly. "It still needs ... some work." I felt the fruit flies beginning to flutter in my belly.

"But you've written a basic outline, right?"

"Yes," I lied. Djebar and Darrin nodded vehemently. Ms. Pokolopinison smiled. I wasn't sure she believed me. Her expressions were confusing sometimes. She had so many different smiles, it was difficult to figure out what each one meant.

"I'm going to need to see your outline. Remember, the review is 20 percent of the overall mark. Basically, I just want to be reassured that you've all been working on this project."

"We have been working on it, but —"

"Good. Bring your basic outline in tomorrow, then." She smiled and strolled away.

"Shit! What are we going to do?" Djebar hissed.

We brooded on it for a bit until Sogi and Wesley returned.

"I guess we're going to have to write an outline," I said.

"You're the project leader, so you can do it," said Djebar.

"Del is the project leader?" said Wesley, confused.

"We're *all* supposed to be working on this project," said Darrin.

"Did James find a new place for us to rehearse?" Djebar asked.

I shook my head.

"Why don't we all meet tonight at the Minotaur?" Wesley suggested.

We all stared at Wesley. He pressed his fingers to his lip and blinked, as if he couldn't believe what he had said.

"I think that's a good idea," said Darrin. Sogi and Djebar agreed. "Ms. Pokolopinison just wants an outline."

"I'll tell Petula," I said.

"No. *I'll* tell her," said Sogi, getting up. "I'm going to ask her if she likes me."

After he was gone, Djebar elbowed me and whispered loudly, "I think Petula likes him."

"How do you know?"

Djebar grinned. "I can read the signs."

"What signs?"

"Hey, I can read people better than you."

I hoped he was wrong.

The alarm hummed on his iPad, and Djebar returned to the screen to continue the computer game he was playing. My chest felt strangely heavy, and I experienced a sudden throb of pain crawling over the top of my head. I tuned out the sounds of the others in the classroom and sank into my own thoughts. But Petula was in my mind, so I grabbed my earphones and plugged in to my iPad. I wondered if this was how it felt to have one's heart broken. And then I started playing Ultimate Crown Mahjong, and after a while the pain in my head went away and I didn't think about Petula and Sogi until the bell rang.

Introducing computers to Aspies is something psychologists now encourage as early as preschool. The experts say computers enhance self-confidence and promote social contact. I guess computers are appealing to us because we don't have to socialize with them; they don't talk back or have any expectations you can't meet. Computers are logical and consistent and predictable — unlike people. The entire ASD class belongs to the CanCom-Aspie Club, where Aspies chat online together. But mostly we play games and surf the net. However, all of us are far more proficient in computer skills than the neurotypical students, and some of us tutor other students. Last year I tutored a student named Simon. He had one ear that flapped open slightly, and he wiped his nose on the back of his hand. This didn't bother me that much, but he tended to ask me a lot of questions that weren't about computers. And he would tell me things, too.

These were personal things about his girlfriend and his parents and how his cousin had attempted suicide by swallowing 125 aspirin. I felt anxious when he told me these things because I didn't know how to respond. But as it turned out, the less I said, the more he told me. By the end of our tutoring session, Simon shook my hand and banged his chest against mine in one of those gang hugs and told me I was an "okay guy." I might've been an okay guy, but, as it turned out, I was a lousy tutor. Simon ended up failing his course.

This year I decided to not do the tutoring. Instead I signed up for Future Careers for ASD Students, which was only forty minutes once a week, and which gave me an elective credit towards my final grade and was supposed to help guide me into future employment. Mr. Steinke told me I had "terrific prospects" for the future. But the only things I remember about his class was that Mr. Steinke had hair plugs and the fact that I had overheard one of the students say he was dating a pole dancer.

"I asked Petula," said Sogi as we were walking out of class.

"What did she say?"

He rubbed his arm. "She knows judo, you know."

"Yes, I know. She has a class at 4:15 every Wednesday."

"She's really good."

"So? What did she say?"

Sogi looked at me with a cross face. "You don't have to rub it in." He stalked off in the direction of the east wing.

Rub what in? I wondered, puzzled.

In response to the question about whether Turing's machine could play chess, Turing said that it would be able to play, but it would initially play a rotten game of chess because chess requires intelligence.

Did Turing look upon his Universal Machine as a brain that could possibly develop intelligence — like a human brain?

If it is true that autism is a neurobiological disorder caused genetically, is it possible for me to develop more intelligence than I was born with? Is it possible for *any* brain to develop more intelligence than it is supposed to have?

"I bet you do really well in school, don't you?" said James.

"Yes."

"Well, I wasn't the best student in the world, I'll tell ya," he laughed.

"But how would you know?"

"Know what?"

"If you were the best student in the world? How would you gauge that?"

James opened his mouth to speak, but he just sat there and looked at me instead. From the expression on his face I deduced that he was suddenly deep in thought. Maybe he was doing what my dad does; remembering what he was like when he was my age.

I wondered if he'd had girlfriends in high school. But I didn't ask him.

After a few minutes with us sitting there in silence, he sat up and said, "I should let you know that I won't be in Merryton for Christmas."

"My aunt and uncle are coming Christmas Day," I said. "So I won't be able to meet you that day."

"Actually, Del, I'm leaving tomorrow morning for Pittsburgh."

My heart did a little jump. I could feel the pulse in my neck speeding up. I focused on the teardrop scar in the stone of the back of the bench near his shoulder. "How long will you be gone?" My voice sounded thin and strange.

"I'll be back after New Year's, I guess. I'm not sure. It's a family thing, you know? We're all meeting at my mother's this year." He sighed. "I'm not exactly looking forward to it. But it's family, right?"

I didn't say anything.

"You know, Del, these are your *holidays*. We could have met at a later time —"

"What time are you leaving tomorrow?"

"I'm not sure. Around 10:30, I think."

"Then we can meet tomorrow."

"Well, I'm not so sure I can." James reached into his pocket and extracted a small box wrapped in blue-and-white-striped paper. The bow was one of those stick-ons, and it came off when he handed it to me. He stuck it back on. "Merry Christmas, Del."

"I didn't get you anything."

"That's okay."

I pocketed the gift and stood up. "I have to go."

"But you're on holidays, aren't you?"

"Yes."

James glanced at his watch and laughed. "Twenty minutes to nine. You're a creature of habit, aren't you, Del?"

"Yes. Well ... bye." And I gave an awkward wave, wondering why my voice sounded so strange. Once I got to the street I ran all the way home, hoping to escape the Orange Day that was following me.

Decorating the Christmas tree has become a difficult task for me since my thirteenth birthday. It is hard to describe what was in my head that year. But Bea says I 'freaked everyone out' that Christmas.

I could hear my father downstairs in the living room. "What the hell —?"

In the middle of the night I had gotten up and torn down all the decorations on the tree.

"Dellllllllll! Get down here!"

I came down, my eyes on my feet.

"Did you do this?"

"Yes."

"*Why*, for fuck's sake?"

"Tom! Watch your language." My mother studied me with that worried look she always has when I've done something out of the ordinary. "Del? Why did you take down all the decorations?"

I didn't know what to say so I just shrugged.

"Well, goddammit, you're going to redecorate it," my father ordered.

"Tom —"

"Okay," I said quickly, and set about putting back the decorations.

A few hours later, I tore down the decorations again. My parents tried to stop me, but I yelled and cried and after a while they just let me do it. After I finished denuding the tree, I immediately began to redecorate it. My mother called Doctor Bankoy, but he was on holiday in Bermuda. They called a psychiatric hotline, and they told my parents to bring me in to the nearest psych ward. My mother didn't want to do that so she called Hannah's mother, who called her doctor, and her doctor told her to just leave me alone. If I became distressed or began to hurt myself, then they should check me in to the hospital. But in the meantime I wasn't hurting anyone.

I did it six more times. And then, suddenly, I stopped doing it. That was it. My parents and Bea were mystified by my behavior. Why did I feel this need to tear down the decorations, and then redecorate? I don't know. Compulsions fog your reason, and they do strange things to your memory. Doctor Bankoy would later speculate that it was merely adolescent hormones mixing in with the chemicals of my brain.

So I usually don't trim the tree at Christmastime, and nobody asks me to. This year my father didn't join in the decorating, either.

"How about we go get some hot chocolate, Del?" he asked, coming into my room. He peered over my shoulder. "What are you doing?"

"Polynomials."

"You mean you're doing *homework*?"

"No." My father had still not clued in to the fact that I didn't do homework.

My father sighed. "Come on. Let's go for a drive."

"No, thank you."

"Come on. Get your coat."

"No, thank you."

"I'll buy you a donut."

"I'm not hungry."

"Well, I am. Get your coat. We're going out to get some hot chocolate, *right now*!"

I followed him downstairs and put on my hat and coat, and we drove to Tim Hortons.

"Do you want a donut?"

"No."

"Have a donut."

"No, thank you."

"Del, why can't you just go along with things?"

"I don't know."

An expression came onto my father's face that I didn't know. It worried me. "Find a seat. I'll bring you a hot chocolate, okay?"

He brought me a hot chocolate and a donut with green sprinkles on it. "I know you don't like orange and yellow sprinkles, so I got you the one with green sprinkles."

"Thank you." I took a sip of the hot chocolate. It wasn't hot chocolate, but it had sugar in it, so I drank it anyway.

"Listen, Del. I need to talk to you about your mom and I."

I didn't want to talk to him about them, so I ate my donut, keeping my gaze fixed on the plate.

"You're seventeen years old — old enough to have a pretty good idea of what's going on between your mom and I. Am I right?"

I didn't say anything.

"Of course, us divorcing doesn't mean we're divorcing you and Bea." He took a sip of his coffee, and his face scrunched up. He smacked his lips. "Geezus. Their coffee is getting worse every week."

I avoided his eyes and kept eating my donut.

"Anyway, we want to make sure you and Bea both know that this is not your fault, that our separation has nothing to do with you. This has to do with your mom and I. We just — well, we just don't want to live together anymore."

"Why not?"

My father blinked, scratched his head. "It's kind of complicated, Del ..."

"I bet Mom wouldn't let you leave if you were a rock star."

My father stared at me, then suddenly laughed. "Del, sometimes you say the funniest things." He rubbed the top of my head. "My little genius professor."

"Dad, I'm taller than you, now."

He smiled, took a sip of his coffee, and made a face. "This is the worst coffee I've ever had. Drink up. You can help me do some shopping for Bea."

I gulped down the coffee. Caffeine jolts my nervous system, and sometimes I get jittery and giggly. When I got up from my seat my body was humming and my brain felt sharpened and alert. But as we were exiting, a woman came in talking loudly on her cellphone, and I suddenly cringed, clamping my hands over my ears. Once we were outside I was okay again, but my father was looking at me with his brows jammed together, pushing up the horizontal lines on his forehead. It looked funny, so I laughed.

"Del? You okay?"

Bea knocked and opened the door of my bedroom. "Okay if I come in?" She didn't wait for my response, just came in and sat on the edge of my bed. I kept working on my polynomials.

"Mom's real mad at Dad."

"It's not his fault," I said.

"He shouldn't have taken you to the mall."

"We were looking for a present for you."

"Yeah?" Bea suddenly smiled. "Did you get me anything?" Her smile turned into one of those sour ones. "Forget it, sorry. Are you okay now?"

"Yes."

We sat there for a few minutes not talking. I didn't know what to say. In my mind I was replaying the incident in the mall again. I kept seeing the blinking light atop the man's head. Just for one split second I'd thought it was lightning crashing down from the ceiling. Later they told me the man was wearing a novelty helmet of some sort with a strobe light attached. I remember the sharp sounds of conversation behind me and to my right, and the contrasting musical sounds that assaulted me from all sides. My head suddenly splintered and shattered inside, and I had to keep myself together so I curled up in a ball and shut down.

"You remember that Christmas when we snuck downstairs and opened all the presents?" Bea asked.

"I was ten; you were five," I said.

"I was only five?"

"Five years, ten and a half months," I corrected.

Bea smiled. "I was such a pest, wasn't I? And you took all the blame, when in fact you were trying to make me stop. You kept saying, 'No, Bea! You're going against the Christmas rules!'" She laughed. "That was the same year Grandfather Capp bought you those binoculars. You carried them around your neck for months." She gestured to my binoculars on the desk. "Are you still spying on James Comfort?"

"He asked me not to."

A strange expression crossed Bea's face. People say my sister looks like my mother, but I don't see it. Her eyes are wide like mine, but the irises are a darker blue. Sometimes, if you see her from a distance, you might mistake her eyes for brown. Her hair is also darker than mine, and she always has rosy cheeks like she's feeling too hot. When she touches me, however, her hands are nice and cool. I tolerate her touch more than anyone else in the family.

"You've been meeting with him, haven't you?" Bea said suddenly. "James Comfort, I mean."

My heart lurched. I considered lying to her, but I did not want to be caught in a lie. And of all the family, Bea was the person I most liked to confide in. Should I tell her about the Turing Machinists?

"You and James Comfort are friends, eh?" said Bea.

I nodded.

Bea traced the planets and comets on my duvet cover. "Do you think ... maybe ... you could introduce me?"

"What do you mean?"

From downstairs we heard my mother calling for Bea. "Crap," she muttered. "I'd better go see what she wants." She turned to leave, hesitated. "One idea — if you're going to get me a present. Curls 'n' Girls has these really cool purses. I like the fuzzy pink one with the fake gold clasp and the little oval mirror inside. When you open it the theme from *Edward Scissorhands* plays." Bea sighed. "Mom says I'm too young for a purse. Sometimes I think she just doesn't want me to grow up."

I wiggled my pencil between my first and middle finger, not sure what to say. Suddenly Bea threw her arms around me. "I hope you have a good Christmas, Del." And then she bounced out of my bedroom, closing the door behind her.

I sat for a while staring at the door, rehashing our encounter, recalling that Christmas morning when she'd broken the rules and opened all the Christmas presents. My memory of that time came in a flash of scenes that evoked in me feelings I couldn't categorize. And then my mind went back to the earlier incident in the mall. But now the man with the novelty helmet was already beginning to fade. My head felt better, too.

"Del? Del Capp, is that you? Look, Djebar, it's Del!"

I looked up at Djebar's mother, then over at Djebar, who was looking off to the side. I gave an awkward wave while staring down at the brown criss-cross stitches in my boots.

"Djebar? Djebar, say hello to your friend."

Djebar gave me one of his loose-jointed waves and grinned. "Hello."

I grinned back. "Hello."

"Are you here to do some Christmas shopping, Del?"

"Yes. I have to go to Curls 'n' Girls and get Bea a pink purse with a gold clasp and an oval mirror inside."

"Well, how thoughtful of you, Del. I'm sure your sister is going to love that gift."

"She told me it plays the theme from *Edward Scissorhands* when you open it."

"Edward who?" Djebar's mother frowned.

"Johnny Depp, Winona Ryder, Dianne Wiest, Anthony Michael Hall, Kathy Baker, Vincent Price, Alan Arkin," said Djebar.

"The script was written by Caroline Thompson," I said.

"And Tim Burton."

"The screenplay credit only has Caroline Thompson."

Djebar narrowed his eyes. "You sure?"

I glanced at my watch. It was five minutes after two. "I have to go," I muttered, hurrying past them.

Later, when I got home, I looked up *Edward Scissorhands*. I was right about the screenplay credit. It was Caroline Thompson. I thought about the movie; I'd seen it only once, but I remembered almost every detail. Johnny Depp scared me, not because of his scissor hands, but because of his eyes. They were eyes that could *see*.

What I did like about *Edward Scissorhands* was the symmetry of the neighborhood where Winona Ryder and her family lived. It seemed to me an ideal place to live. I'm not sure I understood any of the characters, except for Anthony Michael Hall, who reminded me a bit of Jeddy.

My mother wanted me to come with her to Jeddy's house and give him a gift.

"No."

"It's the polite thing to do, Del."

"I don't want to do it."

"Listen, Del. We would've been in big trouble if they'd decided to sue us. They could even have brought charges against you."

"They wouldn't stick."

"You don't know that," said my mother.

"I have a disability. I'm autistic."

My mother's face took on an expression that made my heart beat a little faster. "Delmore William Capp, don't you *dare* use autism as an excuse for violence! You are who you *choose* to be, remember?"

"I don't want to go. I don't like Jeddy."

My mother sighed. "Please, Del? Do it for me?"

"No." I looked at the flat box. "What is it?"

"A Level 9 Scrabble computer game."

"Level 9?" I'd asked for Level 9. "I don't think Jeddy's smart enough for Level 9," I said. "Maybe you should just give it to me."

My mother smiled. "If you deliver this to Jeddy, I'll consider getting you one for Christmas as well."

I took the box. "Okay."

Jeddy lives at the north end of Merryton, at the end of a winding path of aspen trees. His house is at least five times the size of ours. In the small parking lot, three cars were lined up. They were all the same color of red. We had to walk up a flagstone path then climb twelve steps. Why did they make it so difficult to get to the front door?

I pressed the doorbell, and heard a sound like church bells. A couple minutes later, Jeddy's mother opened the door.

"Hello, Gloria."

"Connie, how are you?" She looked over at me and showed her teeth. She had small, wide teeth, almost in the shape of perfect squares. I liked them very much. "Well, hello Delmore. What brings you here?"

"Gloria, I'm sorry about this business between our boys —"

"Maybe we should keep it between our boys, then, yes?"

My mother ran her tongue over her teeth. She had that same look she'd had when my father told her he'd bought a new truck. "Del? Don't you have something for Jeddy?"

I thrust out the wrapped computer game.

"Jeddy!"

I cringed at the sound of Jeddy's mother's voice. Fruit flies gathered in my belly, and I felt an impulse to run away. But I stayed and waited for Jeddy to appear.

"What is it, Mom?" I heard Jeddy call out.

"Del, is here!"

"Who?"

"Del Capp! Your schoolmate," said Jeddy's mother. "Come and say hi, sweetie."

"No! Tell him to go away or I'll break *his* nose."

"Jeddy! Get out here right now, or —!"

"It's okay," my mother intervened quickly. "We'll just drop off this gift for Jeddy —"

Jeddy appeared behind his mother. "Get the fuck out of here!" he shouted. "I don't want your fucking gift."

Jeddy's mother's face got very white and tight. Her made-up eyes went flat when she smiled. "I apologize. He hasn't taken his medication today."

"That's all right," my mother said. "I *totally* understand." And then the two of them clasped hands and laughed.

I was confused; were my mother and Jeddy's mother friends now?

When we turned to leave I still had the gift in my hands.

"Del? Can you give Jeddy's mom the gift, please?"

"But Jeddy doesn't want it."

"Give it to her, please."

"But Jeddy doesn't want it."

"Del, give it to her!"

"But Jeddy doesn't —"

My mother snatched the gift from me and thrust it into Jeddy's mother's hands. They exchanged looks that made them both roll their eyes and smile.

"Day by day," Jeddy's mother called after us.

My mother turned around and gave her a nod and a wave.

It was like some secret exchange had passed between my mother and Jeddy's mother. I didn't understand it, but I had seen it often enough when the parents of the ASD class met each other. Even though some of them didn't know one another, they all acted like they were long-time friends.

On the way home I asked my mother if she and Jeddy's mother were friends now.

"Friends? Well, no ... not really. But I suppose, despite everything, we have established a kind of bond, she and I. We do have a lot in common, after all."

"I don't understand."

My mother looked at me and smiled. "I know."

On one wall of my bedroom I have a poster of Pascal's triangle. It is 36 inches by 26.5 inches, and covers a good chunk of the north wall. I was staring at the poster and thinking about Christmas dinner when the haiku came into my head. I hurriedly clicked into the Word program and started typing. About a half-hour later this is what I ended up with:

The frowns behind the tables
Disappear in light
Voices mute, hearts roar and fight.

I read it over, and found that I'd understood it more when I was writing it. But the formula was perfect with a 7-5-7 syllabic count. So I printed it out and decided to submit it for my haiku assignment for

Mr. Levinson.

I was just printing it out when my mother knocked on the door. "Del? You have a phone call."

I blinked. "I do?" I don't often get phone calls. I don't keep in touch with anyone in the ASD class, and if we do have to contact one another it is through email or text.

My mother opened the door. "It's someone named James." Her brows touched and her eyes drew in at the outer corners. My mother's face is very expressive. But that doesn't mean I can read her any better than anyone else.

I sat frozen to my desk chair. "Oh."

My mother chewed on her lip for a couple seconds. "Well, you can take the call in my bedroom, if you want."

As I walked down the hall towards the master bedroom, it occurred to me that my mother had said "*my* bedroom." Not "*our* bedroom." The pronouns were changing in this family.

"Hello?"

"Hey, Del. Merry Christmas."

I waited.

"Del? You still there?"

"Yes, James. I'm here."

"Uh, the reason I'm calling is that ... uh, I have some good news."

I waited.

"Del?"

"Yes?"

I heard a sound like a sigh on the other end of the phone. "You ready?"

"For what?"

"The Turing Machinists made the list. You're going to the semifinals!"

I was silent, thinking about what he'd just said.

"Did you hear me? The Turing Machinists made it to the semifinals!"

"Yes, I heard you, James."

A couple beats of silence passed. "Well, uh, could you do me a favor and tell the rest of the band for me?"

"Yes, okay."

Another beat of silence. "Did you have a good Christmas, Del?"

"Yes."

I could hear voices in the background. "Right. Well, I'll see you after New Year's, okay?"

"Okay."

"Congratulations, Del."

As I rang off I realized I hadn't thanked him. But even as I thought about that, thanking him felt like a redundant act. James had to know I was thankful. This was what I'd been hoping for. I threw my hands in the air and shouted, "Woohoo!"

"Good news?" my mother queried from the doorway.

"Um ..." I looked down at my hands, steepled them.

My mother smiled. "Sorry, I didn't mean to pry." She walked into the bedroom, rearranged a few things on the vanity table. "So who was that on the phone?"

Had she listened in on the conversation? I didn't want to lie to her. "James Comfort."

"Yes. But who is he?"

Bea appeared at the door. "You don't know who James Comfort is?"

"No. Who is he?"

"He's that rock star guy from Magic Horse Marines," said Bea. "He's American."

My mother gazed at me with a confused look. "But what is he doing calling here? How do you know this person, Del?"

I thought about it for a moment, then said, "He's my friend, Mom."

That night of the phone call I was beset with worry. Although I had taken an extra dose of melatonin, my racing mind would not let me sleep. I talked to myself, recalling dialogue from *Zero Effect*, which helped for a while. But then the thought of the Cubground Pub semifinals would barge in and I would get anxious again. I looked at Ol' Ben, touched the dent in its side. It was not yet midnight, and I had not heard my mother go to bed yet. Finally, I got up and flicked on the desk light, hoping no one would see it and investigate.

I pulled out my polynomial workbook. But I wasn't in the mood to do math. I decided to read. I read a lot. But I can't seem to read just one book at a time. I usually have a few books on the go: right now I have two fiction and two non-fiction books that I'm reading. I picked up *Winter's Tale* by Mark Helprin. I'd started this book at the beginning of summer and I was almost three-quarters of the way through it. I am not a fast reader. It isn't that I have difficulty reading, but I need time to digest what I read. And there was a lot of detail to digest in this book. It has been said that autistic people dwell on details, often details that don't seem to matter. But I don't think that's true. I don't dwell on details, especially if they pertain to a person. And sometimes I miss details altogether, as they don't seem to matter to me at the time. But in this book I somehow deemed the details important and urgent to comprehend.

As I peered outside my window at the duvet of twinkling snow, I knew it was the right book to read at this moment.

But I couldn't concentrate, and my legs started to get that pins and needles feeling, so I put down the book and got up and paced for a while. I did my breathing exercises, sat down and pulled out my "Dream Sweeter" assembly instruction booklet for the R29863 king-size bed. As I began to read the instructions, I wondered if I could possibly get a job writing manuals. Technical language seemed to me much less intricate than social language. As far as I could determine, most of the manuals merely repeated a series of key words such as *pull, slide, remove, fit, align, insert, repeat*, and *test*. It was a language everyone could relate to and could perform. I have come across, however, some instruction manuals which entirely perplexed me. In those instances I noticed the writer used a lot of descriptive and vague words like *skim, glide, eliminate, interweave, heave*, and *extricate*.

But this time my "Dream Sweeter" instruction manual was not calming me. I was just too nervous. I needed to run. I thought about going out to the backyard. Running in the dark was much better than running in the daylight, anyway. And I had yet to try out the new runners my father had gotten me for Christmas.

I glanced down at Ol' Ben on my bedside table. It was still too early; my mother had just gone to bed, and my father was probably downstairs watching television. Also, my parents would want to know where I was going, and then they would want to know why I was feeling anxious. My mother would worry, and I would worry about her worrying. And then she would ask a million questions, and I wasn't sure I wouldn't blurt out everything about the Turing Machinists and our acceptance into the Cubground Pub Battle of the Bands competition. And even if I did manage to keep quiet about it, my father would tell my mother to stop overreacting, and then they would argue, and in the morning they would be cross with each other and say things that confused and worried me even more.

So I turned on my computer and surfed for a while, and checked out the Aspie site where I chat sometimes. It was active. It always is in the evenings and early mornings. But I didn't feel like chatting, and so I switched off my computer and scooped out my binoculars from the bottom drawer. I aimed them at James's building.

I was staring into the dark window on the fifth floor when all of sudden light filled my vision. Someone had turned the light on in the kitchen. James was home! But he'd told me he wasn't coming home until the day after tomorrow. I kept the binoculars focused on the kitchen window until a figure passed into my view. It wasn't James.

It was a woman. I'm not good at recognizing people, but she was wearing something that I did recognize: a big pink balloon coat. She moved through James's apartment as if she knew the place. The bedroom light flicked on. The bamboo shades were half drawn, and as I spotted her, I saw that she was half dressed. What was she doing in James's apartment? And why was she taking off her clothes? I scanned the apartment with my binoculars, looking for James, but I didn't see him.

The woman disappeared for about twenty minutes, but then returned. I was guessing she'd been on the other side in the bathroom. She was wearing a T-shirt and brushing her long blond hair. A few minutes later the light went out in the bedroom.

After about an hour of staring into the darkness of the bedroom, I began to feel tired. And I realized as I turned off the desk lamp that my anxiety had leveled, and I hadn't thought about the Cubground Pub Band semifinals for the past two hours.

However, as soon as I lay down and closed my eyes, my worrying came back full force. My heart lurched in my chest, and my pulse was racing. I was beginning to sweat under my arms. I sat up, tried to catch my breath and calm myself; I knew I was keening into an anxiety attack.

I changed into my jogging pants and sweatshirt and my new runners. The bottoms of my feet tingled as they squished into the cushioned soles of the shoes. My panic attack was waiting for me, but it was being held back by my sudden sense of anticipation as I walked around my bedroom. I grew excited. I would run faster and longer in these shoes.

The stairs creaked no matter how delicately or strategically I stepped. Unlike Bea, I have never been able to master stealth on the staircase. But then, stealth is not something I will ever have. I am aware that I am clumsy and that I perform actions awkwardly. I can run, but I am not good at sports in general. I can throw and catch, but not far, and I can catch only within the visual range of my hands. All of us in the class are pretty much the same — except for Jeddy. But he cannot run distances like me, and his fine motor skills are worse than mine.

Two years ago our ASD class was involved in a research project that involved handwriting skills in adolescents with autism. The thought was that, like neurotypical people, by the time we reached adolescence we would begin to outgrow the handwriting problems we experienced as children. Our handwriting samples were judged on legibility, size, form, alignment, and spacing. Letters like S and G and Z produced the worst ratings for most of us, and cursive writing was not even close to acceptable. At the end of the study it was concluded that despite time and occupational therapy, our handwriting did not improve or develop to the neurotypical standard.

I have never been good at handwriting, and when I do write by hand, words and sentences sometimes come out jumbled, very much like a dyslexic person. However, when I type on a keyboard, I can express myself with more satisfaction. My thoughts are clearer when I use a computer, and what I write is more accurately what I am thinking.

In the breast pocket of my jacket was a piece of paper on which James had written his email address. I had forgotten it was there, as I had memorized his email address as soon as he had told it to me. James's writing was almost as bad as mine. The experts say that there is a link between bad handwriting and social abilities. From what I've seen James seems to be okay in social settings, but my mother is always saying that just because someone socializes well doesn't mean they are comfortable with people.

My sense of direction seems to sharpen at night. I don't know why. I'm sure I could find a study that has come up with some kind of reason for this. In any case, when I arrived at James's building I was hardly out of breath, even though I could see my breath snorting out into the night, it was that cold. I rang the fourth buzzer down on the doorbell panel inside (for some reason James chose not to label his buzzer).

I waited. No answer. I rang the buzzer again.

"Hello?" a voice answered sleepily.

"Hello." I cleared my voice, willing myself not to stammer. "Is James home?"

A beat passed. "Who is this?"

"Del Capp."

"Who?"

"Delmore William Capp," I said, a little more loudly.

A staticky noise sounded out of the speaker. "Oh. Right. You're that kid, aren't you?"

"I'm not a kid. I'm seventeen years old," I said. "Is James home?"

"Sorry. James won't be home until tomorrow night."

"What are you doing in his apartment?"

The woman paused. "You want me to have James give you a call when he gets in?"

"Who are you?" I demanded. "Does James know you're sleeping in his apartment?"

"Hey, kid. That's none of your business."

"It is my business. James is my friend." But as I blurted out these words my heart started to leap and pound. "If you don't leave I will call the police."

The woman uttered something unintelligible, then said, "Listen, kid, it's all right. James gave me the key."

"Why?"

I heard her sigh. "Because we're *dating*, okay?"

"You're his girlfriend?"

"*Yes!* Now will you let me go back to sleep?" I heard barking in the background. "Great. Now you woke Finnegan. Go home, kid. What are you doing out at this hour, anyway?" And there was a resounding click.

As I headed home, I went over my conversation with the woman in James's apartment. It suddenly occurred to me that I had just conversed with a total stranger. True, it had been over an intercom, but I had carried on a real conversation. *Without stuttering.*

I was so buoyed by the experience I forgot to think about my anxiety over performing at the semifinals at the Cubground Pub. I also didn't notice the figure hovering behind the deck's sliding doors when I arrived home.

"Del! Where the hell have you been!"

I jumped back and slammed my elbow into the wicker bookshelf, causing several books to tumble to the floor. The racket startled me, made me close my eyes and press my hands to my ears.

I heard my father curse and felt his hand grip under my arm. "Up you get, Del." He turned my face towards his. "Breathe on me."

I stared at him. "I don't understand."

My father laughed, let go of my face. "I thought maybe you'd snuck out."

"I did."

"I know. But I thought maybe you might have been drinking."

"Drinking what?"

"Liquor. Beer. Look at me, Del."

I looked at him. "I don't drink alcohol. It doesn't mix well with my medication."

My father sighed, rubbed his face. I couldn't tell what he was thinking; his expression was hard to read. "I almost wish you *were* drunk. At least then —" He suddenly stopped, drew in a breath. "Hey, help me put these books back, okay?"

We stacked them back on the wicker shelves, and then I excused myself to go to bed.

"Wait, Del."

I turned, and he drew me into his arms. The pressure of his hug felt good, but after a moment I felt a sudden urgency to break away.

"Well, good night, Del."

"Good night."

"It's going to be a good year, you'll see," he said. His smile was one of those painful ones. I nodded and went up to my room. I undressed and put on my pajamas and slipped into bed. It was 3:22 a.m. My sleep schedule was off, and this fact gave me some anxiety. I don't know how it happened, but I just fell asleep in mid-thought. And I didn't wake up until eight minutes after nine.

I waited for James to contact me the next day. But he didn't phone. He didn't email. I decided to go online and check the air flight arrivals from Pittsburgh.

"What are you doing?" Bea asked from over my shoulder.

"Go away."

Bea has this way of watching me so that I can almost *feel* her gaze. It has no logic, but sometimes I think she senses things in me that others don't.

"Is it true, Del?"

"Is what true?"

"My friend Izzie said her brother and his friends saw you and Djebar and some others from the Ass— ... your class at the Minotaur."

I didn't say anything.

"They said you were pretending to be a band."

"We weren't pretending," I said.

"You mean ... it's true?" Bea blinked. "You and Djebar and those others — you're actually a band? A real rock band?"

"Yes."

"Uh, but you're not going to actually ... *play*, are you? I mean, not in *public*. Not in front of everyone."

I tried to decipher her expression. Usually her expressions are quite easy to read. But now she was confusing me.

"I'm not sure I understand," I said truthfully.

Bea twisted her hair with her finger, bent down and peered at my globe. She was staring intently into the Pacific Ocean. Or was she trying to make out some of the islands? I had never known her to be interested in geography, so I was curious. After a moment, still looking at the globe, she said, "Well, you know ... you probably don't want to play in front of anyone. I mean, you don't want to embarrass yourselves, right?"

I suddenly understood what she was trying to say; Bea thought the Turing Machinists weren't any good.

"You haven't heard us play."

"Izzie's brother and his friends said you guys stunk." Bea winced, hid her face in her hands. "I'm sorry. I shouldn't have said that."

"But we don't stink, Bea."

"No, no. Of course you don't. But seriously ... you're not going to play for a school assembly or anything like that, right? This is just, like, one of those autistic research things, right? Some kind of school project?"

School project. It suddenly dawned on me that Ms. Pokolopinison still expected us to create a board game for Social Spectrum class. I had been meaning to put together an outline for her so she would think that we had been working on the game this whole time. It didn't occur to me to contact the others in the group. Outside of school, none of us really harbored any desire to socialize together. "But Djebar and Sogi are your *friends*, aren't they?" my mother would say. I never knew how to respond to this. On one hand, I wanted friends; but on the other hand, I wanted to be left alone, too. If there was one thing that kept the ASD class connected to one another, it was this paradoxical idea about socializing. This thought was the closest I've ever come to grasping the concept of irony.

"Why are you looking up flights from Pittsburgh?" Bea asked.

I minimized the screen, kept my eyes on the keyboard until she left my bedroom. For me, unresponsiveness has always been the most effective way to get my family to leave me alone. Unfortunately, silence doesn't work with Thea or the staff at Merryton Public.

Depending on the airline, a flight from Pittsburgh to Toronto could take from an hour and a half to four and a half hours. None of the sites were specific as to the flight schedule, and this annoyed me. I thought about calling up the woman with the pink balloon coat and asking her what flight James was taking. But I suddenly got too nervous and started feeling jumpy. During holidays it is difficult for me to relax, as my routine gets all mixed up and chaotic. And I'm not supposed to eat candy canes. But I always end up eating them, and my heart beats a little faster and I get hyper, and when my mother and father start arguing, I have to go outside to breathe.

I decided to go for a walk.

"Where are you going?" my parents wanted to know.

"I don't know," I replied.

But destinations, I've found, are never arbitrary. There is always a plan made up somewhere in your head. I went to the park where I usually meet James and sat on the bench where we usually talk. I sat there for half an hour. It wasn't until I got up and started home that I noticed that the snow was really coming down fast and that the wind had picked up. I was the only person in the park, and as I headed towards the street I saw only new snow and no footprints. All at once I felt strange. Until that moment I had never really known what it felt to be truly alone. No, not alone. *Lonely.*

When I arrived home I went into the kitchen and sat down where my mother was making potato soup. I wanted to hug her, but I didn't. I just listened to her warm chatter and tried not to think about James and the semifinals. And then as I was sitting there, I felt a cool hand on my forehead and turned to see my mother looking at me with some concern.

"Are you feeling all right, Del?"

My throat closed tight, and I felt my eyes sting and well up with tears. My mother hugged me. "What is it, Del? What is it, honey?"

I just cried and didn't say anything, and let her hug me.

I don't know if I was excited to be going back to school, but I was looking forward to getting back into my routine. Just before I headed off to school, I checked my computer email as usual and was stunned to find I had one message in my inbox. It was from James.

I'm back. Meet me this morning? Same time. Same place.

I don't know if what I was feeling was elation or relief. But it was that same feeling I get whenever I watch a twentieth-century *Simpsons* episode. No matter what happens to Homer or Bart or Marge or Lisa or Maggie, always, by the end of the episode, all the characters revert back to exactly the way they were at the beginning. Same age, same clothes, same everything.

Except not everything was the same this time. For one thing, when I arrived at the park, James was sitting on the bench with the woman in the pink balloon coat and her dog.

James introduced the pink balloon woman as Tammy-Lynn. Her dog's name was Finnegan.

"Like the little boy puppet from *Mr. Dressup*?" Tammy-Lynn said. "I met him, you know. Mr. Dressup."

"Finnegan was the dog puppet," I said. "*Casey* was the name of the boy puppet."

Tammy-Lynn smiled. Her face was triangular, and her eyes were long. I wasn't sure if she was pretty or not, as she wore very heavy makeup everywhere on her face. "Well, then. Finnegan is all the more appropriate a name for him, isn't it?"

"Ernie Coombs," I said.

She cast a glance at James, whose eyes were half closed. "What?" she asked, frowning.

"Mr. Dressup's name. It was Ernie Coombs. He died September 18, 2001."

"Oh. Uh, that was a while ago, wasn't it?" She picked at a thread on her glove. "So, James tells me you write music."

I was going to tell her that Judith Lawrence was the puppeteer for Finnegan, and that the first episode of *Mr. Dressup* aired forty-five years ago, in 1967. But I decided I didn't want to talk, so I just looked down at my boots.

Tammy-Lynn cleared her throat. "Congratulations on making the semifinals. Uh, what's your band's name again? Rick told me, but I can't remember …"

Something crawled up from the back of my neck, like these little feet creeping along my scalp. It was like my Spidey-sense had snapped on.

"Who's Rick?" I asked, looking at James.

"Are you kidding me?" Tammy-Lynn pulled on Finnegan's leash as a squirrel scurried across the dog's path. "Rick Turchuck? He used to play with James. Well, that's his real name. You would know him by —"

James suddenly sat up. "Hey! Shouldn't you be going? You don't want to be late for school."

I looked at my watch; it was 8:36 a.m. "I still have a few minutes. Who is Rick Turchuck?"

"Oh, I forgot," James interrupted. "I spoke to Archie, and he said the Turing Machinists can rehearse in his garage. You'll have to help him clean out his garage, but it's big enough to hold your stuff and it'll be safe —"

"Where does Archie live?"

"Uh, I think it's … Bounty Boulevard?"

"That's in the southwest end. It's too far away. None of us drive," I said.

"I can drive you, if you like," said Tammy-Lynn.

"No. I don't want you to drive us."

James frowned. "Del —"

I flicked a glance at my watch. I didn't want to be late my first day back from holidays. "I have to go."

Tammy-Lynn cast me a wide smile. Her lipstick was the color of pink putty. "Well, it was nice meeting you, Del."

I ran across the park and kept running when I hit the sidewalk. Those little feet were marching all over my scalp. My eyes stung as I began to relive in my mind the encounter with James and Tammy-Lynn at the park. Tightness clutched at my throat and I swallowed, pushing down the emotion that suddenly welled up in me. It had been so perfect before — with just the two of us. Why couldn't it have stayed that way? Why did everything always have to change?

I thought about my mother and father, then. If I could make them see that they still loved each other, that their lives would be better if they stayed together, then maybe they would go back to the way they were before.

One thing about having Asperger syndrome: it gave me a laser-like ability to focus on my goals.

By the time I arrived at Merryton Public, the little feet had stopped creeping along my scalp, and I was ready to start the day.

It was during Social Spectrum class that the first panic attack occurred. Hannah stood, told the teacher she was having a freak-out, then sprinted out the door to the bathroom. Ms. Pokolopinison's lips got thin and she crossed her arms. She looked out at us with an expression I hadn't seen before and asked the rest of the class if any of us wanted to have an anxiety attack before she began the lesson. Wesley raised his arm and promptly vomited on his desk. Ms. Pokolopinison made a sound in her throat and paged the janitor while an educational assistant escorted Wesley to the washroom. I was feeling some anxiety, but I didn't think I was going to have an attack. Djebar, on the other hand, was beginning to breathe funny behind me. After a moment he got up and left the room.

"Anyone else?" Ms. Pokolopinison asked.

Petula packed up her bag and started towards the door.

"Petula, sit down, please."

"I'm having a panic attack," she said.

"I see. Well, I'd like you to have it in here, please," said Ms. Pokolopinison. Her voice had risen slightly from its even C key, and I thought I detected a crossness in her tone.

"I think I'll have my attack in the sensory room, if you don't mind," said Petula.

"Sit down, Petula." And when Petula didn't budge, Ms. Pokolopinison said loudly, "I said *sit down*!"

Perhaps it was the sudden waver in Ms. Pokolopinison's voice that startled her, but much to my amazement Petula actually complied and sat down. Ms. Pokolopinison moved to the front of the class. Everyone fixed their gazes on her crooked French braid as she wrote the day's lesson on the chalkboard. No one else left the room to have panic attacks.

After Ms. Pokolopinison collected our completed holiday research surveys, she announced that she would be talking to the two groups about our projects. "I expect to see finished project outlines and a progress report on my desk by the end of today. Although they are not due until the end of the school year, I hope you all took the holidays as an opportunity to get together and work on your projects as I suggested."

I stared at the back of Petula's head and suddenly wished I had asked her over during the holidays. But probably she wouldn't have come. Even as I was thinking this, she turned around and stared at me. I immediately looked down at my hands, feeling my face growing hot.

Later, as we broke into our two groups, it was Darrin who brought up the semifinals at the Cubground Pub. "I googled the website. Only six bands made the semifinals," he said.

"Are we that good?" said Sogi. "It doesn't make sense. How did we make the semifinals?"

I told them the semifinal auditions would take place the first week-end of March.

"You mean we have to perform *live*?" said Petula. "I don't think I can do that. Not in front of a real audience."

"There has to be some kind of mistake," Sogi insisted. "I never thought we'd make it to the semifinals. Are we that good?"

"I'm not sure I can make it that weekend," said Darrin, tugging at his ear.

I looked at all of them. Suddenly I was gripped by a surge of irrita-tion and an anger that made me shake and stutter. "You all committed to this. This is a *commitment*. We *have* to see this through."

"Why?" said Petula.

"Because ..." I faltered. My throat closed, and I swallowed. I squeezed my eyes shut, willing myself to not cry. The truth was, they didn't have to see this through. I was counting on them to help me. But I realized they didn't have the same goal or laser focus as me. They didn't care about the Turing Machinists like I did. They didn't need the band to succeed like I did.

"There has to be a mistake," Sogi insisted.

"Why do you keep saying that? Do you think that Del would lie about this?" Petula snarled. "You're not lying, are you, Del?"

I shook my head. "No. No, I'm not lying."

"Maybe I will be able to make it," said Darrin suddenly. "The semifinals are in Toronto, right?"

"Toronto? I can't go to Toronto," said Petula, twisting her hair around her fingers.

"Why not?" said Sogi. "You know, Toronto is just a city. It's not like Hades or anything."

"Shut up," sneered Petula.

"If we stick together, we'll be okay." Darrin looked at me. "Right, Del?"

Djebar came in with one of the education assistants. His brown skin looked milky-green, but he was smiling.

"Forgot to take my meds this morning," he mumbled, throwing himself into the beanbag chair against the wall.

We were all quiet, thinking our own thoughts.

After a couple of minutes Sogi spoke: "Are you sure about this? I mean, could there be some kind of mistake? How could we have made the semifinals?"

In my peripheral vision I saw Jeddy approaching our group. All the members of his group were busy on their smart phones doing their own thing. I wondered what their group project was.

Djebar was staring at Sogi. "What are you talking about? You were the one who went nuts over the video recording. You even said you thought the Turing Machinists were fucking great!"

"Who are the Turing Machinists?" asked Jeddy.

"None of your fucking business," said Petula.

Djebar stood up. "You've never heard of the Turing Machinists? Oh, come on! They're, like, only the greatest band in the universe."

Jeddy's face scrunched up a little, like he was thinking. "Oh ... wait. Wait. Yeah, maybe I have heard of them."

"You have?" said Darrin, his eyes wide.

Petula laughed. Then Sogi and I and Djebar laughed. Darrin looked at us and then made his strange tittering sound. Jeddy's face went pink and he went away, his expression cross.

"Wow," said Djebar. "He's actually heard of us. He's a really hip guy, that Jeddy."

"There's something wrong about that," mumbled Sogi.

"Yes, there is something wrong," I said. "Jeddy was lying. How could he have ever heard of *us*?"

Djebar gave a guffaw. "Del, I was being *sarcastic*," he said.

Even though we all knew we didn't really understand sarcasm, we laughed. For we also knew that we had just managed to trick Jeddy into believing something that didn't actually exist. And that was good enough for us.

"Are we still rehearsing at the Minotaur on Sunday?" Darrin asked.

I recalled then my conversation this morning with James and Tammy-Lynn. "We might have another place to rehearse," I said. But I was cut off by Ms. Pokolopinison, who approached our group.

"Hello, everyone," she greeted. "Let's talk about your group project, shall we? Do you have your project outline finished? By the way, it was due *before* the holidays."

Everyone looked at me. My heart pounded, and I felt a surge of panic rip through my chest. I had forgotten to do the outline. I stared down at my feet. It wasn't fair. Why was I the project leader, anyway? Why did I have to make all the decisions and do all the work?

"Del? Do you have your group's project outline and progress report?"

I forced my gaze upwards so that I was looking into Ms. Pokolopinison's face. "I forgot them at home," I stammered. It frightened me how easy it was suddenly to lie to her.

Ms. Pokolopinison frowned, went to the front of the class, and announced loudly that if both groups' project outlines and progress reports were not handed in by the end of the day, each person in the group would receive a deduction of 25 percent off their final mark.

The class fell into a hushed silence. I think we were all stunned by Ms. Pokolopinison's unexpected announcement. Also, for the first time, Ms. Pokolopinison's normally composed mien had twisted into an expression none of us had seen before. None of us knew how to react, so we all remained still and silent for the remainder of the class.

"You were funny in Valtoody's class," said Djebar.

"Are we really going to Toronto to play in the semifinals?" whispered Sogi. He was looking around at the other tables in the cafeteria. If anyone had been paying attention, they would have heard him loud and clear. Sogi's whisper is even louder than mine.

Wesley, who was sitting at the far end of our table today, put down his spoon and, with his mouth full of licorice porridge, said, "We have to go to Toronto?"

Petula wrinkled her nose. "Quit being disgusting. Bleah."

"How will we get there?" Darrin tugged at his ear. He looked worried. "None of us drive."

They were all looking at me. I experienced a moment of exaspera-
tion and looked back at them in irritation. Why did I have to solve
everything?

"How should I know?"

Petula's brows drew together, and her eyes grew round and dark as
she stared at me. "Because you're the one who got us in this mess in
the first place, dimwit."

Sometimes it's like a fog flits over my eyes and for a moment all I
can see is orange and yellow and black. My heart leaps in my chest,
and the whole of my body goes rigid with tension. This happens right
before I lose my temper. Doctor Bankoy has been trying to get me to
slow down the process so I can put a leash on my reaction, which
comes out almost like a seizure. But the process doesn't always work.
Sometimes I just blow.

"Hey, look! I'm tired of making all the decisions here! If you don't
want to be in the band then go! GO!"

No one moved. I wanted to get up, but I was afraid I was going
to burst into tears if I moved or looked up from my hands. Someone
from a nearby table yelled, "Keep it down, retards!"

Djebar leaped to his feet. "For your information we are not *time
challenged*! Nor do we have burgers in our butts. We are *autistic*."

There was a beat of silence, and then someone guffawed. I looked
up and saw Darrin laughing into his hands. Petula snickered. Sogi was
grinning. Wesley kept eating his pasty porridge, gazing about him with
some curiosity. I noticed then the earplugs in his ears.

A lot of the kids in the cafeteria were laughing. What Djebar
had said echoed around us like small rollings of thunder. My heart
leaped as if starting a race. I started to get up, but then Djebar's
retort flashed in my head. It was funny. It was actually really funny.
I sat back down and laughed and laughed. And it felt good to laugh
instead of cry.

Petula moved in her chair so she was huddling closer to me.
"Maybe we should have called ourselves the Retarded Ass Burgers,"
she whispered.

She smelled like green apples and pink Play-Doh. It was a scent I was going to remember forever.

"So when's our next rehearsal?" she asked.

"Why don't you ever ask me about the Magic Horse Marines?" said James.

"Sogi thinks we should wear special uniforms for the semifinals."

"Uniforms?" James cleared his throat.

"He suggested mechanics uniforms. You know, those one-piece overalls?"

James pressed his palms to his eyes. "Okay, you mean *costumes*. Look, I'll just tell you, shall I? Rod Peel, *our* manager, called me up last night and asked me if I wanted —"

"I think it's a bad idea. You didn't wear a uniform, did you? And my father's band didn't either."

"Your father had a band?"

"Yes. My father's band was called Dynamoelectric. Have you ever heard of them?"

"No, I don't think so." He sighed. "Anyway, I just want to let you know that —"

"My father played in a rock band called Dynamoelectric. They called them 'hair bands' back then. But James, we're a *rock* band, right?"

"Rock? Uh, yeah, sure. Or maybe more … pop." He sat up, looked at me with his sky-blue eyes. "Listen Del, I have some news to share with you —"

"My father doesn't talk about his band much. He played lead guitar, and I think he was the lead singer, like me. There's a photograph of his band with them all sitting on this car. I'm not sure whose car it was, but it was a 1973 Mustang with a double white racing stripe down the middle. It's not as interesting as your Hudson Italia, but —"

"*Anyway*," James cut in, "I just wanted to let you know that the Magic Horse Marines have been asked to play at some big charity gig in Los Angeles." He stretched out his legs. "And Rod wants us to do another album. Apparently there's been a resurgence of interest in our music."

I waited a beat, then after determining he was finished, I asked him what he thought about us wearing uniforms. "I think it's a bad idea. So does Petula, but she disagrees with everything Sogi says anyway."

James just looked at me.

"But who would make our uniforms?" I went on. "How would we pay for them? We can't ask our parents." I shook my head. "I'm going to tell them I think it's a bad idea."

James blinked at me. I was startled to see his expression suddenly turn to one that I definitely recognized: he was angry.

"You could at least pretend to be interested," he said.

I was confused. "What do you mean? Do you agree with Sogi, then? You think we *should* wear uniforms?"

"Del, I don't give a flying fuck what you wear." James leaped to his feet and started walking back to his building. I ran after him.

"James? James, is something wrong?"

James stopped, looked at me with one of those expressions I couldn't read. "I was trying to tell you something."

"Yes?"

"You didn't hear a word I said, did you?"

"I heard every word."

James's brows drew together in a kind of comical expression. But there was nothing cheery in his tone. "You don't get it, do you? There are other people in this world besides you, you know."

I happened to glance at my watch at that moment. It was already twenty minutes to nine. "I have to go!" And I ran down the street towards Merryton Public.

As I sprinted across the intersecting road, I thought about what James had told me. With the Magic Horse Marines having this charity gig in Los Angeles, would James still be able to manage the Turing Machinists? Would he be going back to Los Angeles? Would this gig interfere with our semifinals entry at the Cubground Pub Battle of the Bands competition? Since none of us can drive legally, how would we get to Toronto?

While I pondered these potential new problems, those familiar words kept bouncing in my head over and over like a train stuck on a circular track.

You don't get it, do you?

As it turned out, the other group from Ms. Pokolopinison's Social Spectrum class didn't hand in their project outline or progress report, either. She extended the deadline to the next week, but told us that 15 percent would be docked off our final mark.

"This is going to pull down my average big time," said Sogi.

We were all worried about this because we hadn't even started the board game, and really, not one of us was interested in doing it in the first place.

"If we don't do it, will we get a failing grade? Or just an incomplete?" Darrin wondered.

"Wait a second, isn't Social Spectrum class an elective for us?" said Djebar. "They're not allowed to fail us in an elective."

"They can only give us an incomplete," said Sogi. "Which won't affect our overall grade, so long as we have enough credits."

Because of our extra math and computer courses, we all had more than enough credits to graduate. When we realized this, we decided not to finish the board game.

"We need more time to concentrate on getting ready for the semifinals," said Petula.

"Are we *not* going to do it, then?" I asked.

Everyone looked thoughtful and didn't say anything. I have to work on asking the right questions.

At the end of Creative Literature class, as I was packing up my books, Mr. Levinson called out to me and asked me to stay after class for a minute. I looked at my watch. Math 3, was next and I didn't like to be late for it.

"Don't worry," he said as he approached me, "I can write a late slip for your next class if you like. But I won't keep you long."

I glanced over at him and was suddenly filled with dread. My grade in Creative Literature was in the A-minus range. And I thought I had done well on the mid-term. My haiku project was worth 35 percent of my mark. Had I done that badly on the project? I searched my memory; I couldn't even remember the poem I'd submitted.

"I'd like to discuss the haiku you wrote, Del."

I looked down at my feet. My underarms broke out into a sweat, and the rims of my eyes suddenly felt hot.

"Del? Can you look at me, please?"

I lifted my gaze. Mr. Levinson has a very long, straight nose and his lower lip is larger than his top lip. For the first time I noticed that his eyebrows were very dark and as wide as my thumbnail.

"Did you write this haiku poem by yourself, Del?"

I was confused. "Yes."

"I liked it very much." He smiled. "I found it quite ... *moving*." He perched on the edge of the table, folded his hands together.

We were quiet for a long moment.

"Listen, Del, the reason I'm talking to you is that I was wondering how you would feel about submitting your poem to the Merryton Public Yeats Greats."

I stared at him. I didn't know what the Merryton Public Yeats Greats was, so I said nothing.

"I'm sure you've heard of it. It's the poetry contest we have every year for graduates."

I shook my head.

"Well, in any case, teachers are allowed to nominate a student's work they think is worthy. And I'd like to nominate your poem, Del."

I didn't know what to say, so I just shrugged and nodded. At the same time, I was trying to remember what I had written. It seemed so long ago.

"Okay, then." Mr. Levinson rubbed his long, straight nose. "I just wanted to let you know that I thought your poem was quite good." He reached out to pat my arm, but stopped himself. "Well, you'd better get a move on."

I glanced at the clock and exited the room quickly. Math class was on the east side of the school. I mapped out a route in my head and decided to take the path across the tetherball courts. At the same time I was turning my conversation with Mr. Levinson over and over in my head. When I arrived at math class (on time), it occurred to me that Mr. Levinson had neglected to tell me what grade he'd given my haiku.

But that was my fault; I never ask the right questions.

Archie's wife's name is Veda. She has short, dark blond hair that sprouts out of her head like a Chia Pet. The tips are purple or blue, depending on the light that surrounds her. In the van they sort of glowed a dark blue. Oddly enough, when I'd first met her at the Minotaur I hadn't remembered what she looked like. But now I could see she was much younger than I'd expected. I was fairly certain Archie was quite a few years older than my father. Veda, however, appeared much younger than my mother.

As if reading my mind, Petula blurted, "How old are you?"

Veda glanced at her and gave a short laugh. "You always start conversations this way?"

Petula continued to stare at her, waiting. After a few minutes of intense silence in the van, Veda said, "I'm twenty-six."

I knew we were all doing the same thing: estimating the age difference between her and Archie, making some calculations about their retirements and lifespans, and contemplating their sex life. I have read that an older male and younger female is an advantageous coupling for both partners. The man is satisfied sexually and can often still reproduce; the woman has an experienced partner and financial security.

I thought about my parents. My father was only four and a half months older than my mother. Was it possible that age was a determining factor in their marriage troubles?

Under our silent scrutiny, Veda drove with one arm on the wheel, the other on the door rest. Her nails were long and painted black with a tiny stone at the center. None of us spoke until we arrived at Archie's three-storey Georgian house.

It was big. And the garage was bigger than Djebar's *house*.

We didn't say anything as we got out. Veda had an odd expression on her face.

"You are an interesting group, you know that?"

Sogi grabbed his bass guitar from the van and frowned. "What do you mean?"

Veda grinned, shrugged. "Nothing. It was just an observation."

"Are my drums set up?" Wesley asked.

"Yup. Archie and James set them up last night," she said. "Along with the sound system."

Petula started to drag her xylophone case out of the van. "Let the boys carry that, honey," said Veda.

"My name is not 'Honey.' It's Petula." Petula tugged her case out of the van. "And I can carry my own case."

"James isn't here yet?" I cast a glance about to look again for James's Hudson Italia. It wasn't anywhere on the property.

"Yes, he's here."

"Are you sure?"

Veda laughed. "Yes. He came with Tammy-Lynn."

Everything in me suddenly compressed, and I felt a shadow of ill will creep over me. Veda eyed me curiously. I quickly turned away from her so she couldn't read my expression. I have been told I am easy to read. But what was it she would read on my face? Even I couldn't figure out what I was feeling sometimes.

"Who's Tammy-Lynn? No one said anything about strangers being at this rehearsal," said Petula.

"She's not a stranger," said Veda. "Tammy-Lynn is James's girlfriend. Del's already met her, haven't you?"

"She doesn't belong," said Wesley. He was drumming the side of the house with the drumsticks he'd taken to carrying with him. He had picked one of the pimples on his cheek and the spot was bright red and the size of a toonie. "She wrecks the entire permutation."

Veda's brows lowered and her nose wrinkled up. For a split second she looked younger than her twenty-six years. "Permutation. That's a ... scientific term, right?"

"Math term," Djebar corrected. "A permutation is basically an organized combination of numbers or objects." He glanced at Wesley. "But add something to that equation and suddenly the permutation unravels and loses order — which makes it no longer computable. Understand?"

"Does it matter?" Veda sneered. "You like to show off, eh? But just something to point out? People are not objects."

"Don't you want to play something different? Like, maybe another song?" said Veda. "I mean, what if they ask you to play something else?"

"I like 'The Turing Machine Song,'" said Petula.

"Don't get me wrong; the song's great," said Veda. "But don't you ever get tired of playing the same song over and over?"

We all stared at her and shrugged.

"Nope," said Djebar.

"No," said Sogi. "It's a cool song."

Darrin shook his head.

I shook my head. "No."

"I like playing 'The Turing Machine Song,'" said Petula. "All of us do."

Wesley, who had not extracted his earplugs, was drumming quietly on his timpani, his eyes closed.

"This song is all we have, anyway," said Sogi. "Del hasn't written any more songs."

"But surely you can play something else? Like a cover song?" Veda suggested. "Do you know any Velvet Revolver? Gorillaz? Radiohead?"

"I like 'The Turing Machine Song,'" said Darrin. "I don't think we should change it."

Veda made a noise and shook her spiky head. "I'm not talking about *changing* your song. I'm just suggesting that maybe you could try playing something else for a change —"

"Veda," Archie interrupted, "let it go, please."

Veda's face turned pink. "They just keep playing the same song over and over. I just thought that if they played something else —"

"Leave it, please, honey." Archie put his arm around her shoulders. I thought about my mother and father then; it had been a long time since I'd seen them hugging and touching each other.

James strolled in through the side door with his dark blue knapsack slung over his shoulder. Tammy-Lynn wasn't with him this time. But I was annoyed that he was late.

"James!" Veda greeted him. "James, can you tell them that they are allowed to play something else other than this fucking Turing song? Well, you spoke to Rick. Did he say anything about them needing more than one song in their repertoire to move them to the finals?"

"Who's Rick?" Petula asked.

We all looked at James. I'd heard the name before. Or read it in an email. "You mean Rick *Turchuck*? The organizer of the Cubground competition?"

Veda gave a small laugh that showed her teeth. "Oh, right. I forgot. Is he back to his real name, then?"

James set down his knapsack, opened the mini fridge, and stared at the lines of bottled water. "Where's the Coke?"

"Coke to *drink*, you mean?" said Veda with a small smile.

"We're not allowed to drink carbonated drinks," said Djebar.

"Yeah, but *I* am," said James. "I thought I had a Mars bar in here."

"I ate it," said Sogi. "I ate the salt and vinegar chips, too."

"The inmates are taking over," mumbled Veda.

James cast her a look that made me think she hadn't said something he'd liked. He bent down and snapped up an Evian. "Okay. Let's hear it, guys."

"I am not a guy," said Petula.

"Excuse me," James smiled, bowed his head at Petula. "Guys and *gal*."

Petula's brows lifted slightly. "That moniker is appropriate. I have no problem with that."

Veda made a sucking sound, rolled her eyes, and yanked open the side door that led into the green room. I had discerned that Petula and Veda did not like each other. Also, I was quite certain Veda was annoyed with us, and that she had been annoyed with us for the past three rehearsals. But I could not fathom why. Veda's face was very expressive, though. It was like being in Mr. Valtoody's class with his cut-out examples of facial expressions. I liked having her around because whatever she was feeling could be read quite clearly in the way her face moved.

After we played through "The Turing Machine Song" again, James opened his dark blue knapsack and handed us each an envelope. Inside were three things:

1) a laminated card printed with the words "Cubground Pub Semifinalist Pass";
2) a blue, green, and white strap imprinted with the word "Believe" on one side and "Coors Light" on the other;
3) a round-trip bus ticket to Toronto.

"They sent us bus tickets?" said Sogi.

"Uh, no. I bought those," said James. "Look, don't freak out —"

"I can't afford these." Petula looked down at the items, her brows low over her dark eyes. "I have to stick to a budget, you know?"

"Why did you buy us bus tickets?" I asked.

"Are these returnable?" asked Darrin. "I don't like public transportation."

"Hey, these are dated the same day as the semifinals," said Sogi.

"Why did you buy us bus tickets, James?" I repeated.

James sighed. "Okay, now. Nobody freak out, okay?"

"Why would we freak out?" Petula demanded.

"Look, I don't want you to worry. Everything is taken care of. I've set it up so that your band equipment will get there the day before your semifinal performance. All you guys have to do is get to Toronto —"

Wesley had popped out his earplugs and was staring at the bus ticket in his hand. "James? What is the bus ticket for?"

"You have to know that things do happen, that not every plan goes according to, uh … plan. You understand?"

We all stared at him, not understanding.

"For god's sakes, James." Veda, who had come back into the garage, snorted. "Just tell them."

"Tell us what?" Petula demanded.

James rubbed his eyes, looked for a moment as if he were in pain. "I know I said I would drive you to the audition, but something's come up. And, well, plans can … change, right?"

We were still staring at him, waiting for him to explain.

"It'll be okay. I promise. Just … don't freak out on me, okay?"

"For fuck's sake, James. They're not *children*," said Veda. "They're not going to freak out just because they have to take the bus to Toronto."

"We're taking the bus?" I said.

"I don't like public transportation," Darrin repeated.

"I'm not good on the bus," said Wesley in a scared voice.

"It's okay," I said. "James will be with us."

"Christ almighty," Veda muttered, shaking her head in disbelief.

James cleared his throat. "Now, there's no need to freak out —"

"Don't you guys get it? He's not going to Toronto with you," said Veda. "He has a chance to go to L.A. and restart his career — be a musician again. So you're going to have to suck it up and take the bus — on your own. No big deal."

And of course we all freaked out.

The next two days at school, nobody from the band talked to me. They didn't talk to one another, either. I tried to talk to Sogi, but he said he felt sick every time he even thought about the competition. Petula went around looking extra angry and said that if anyone mentioned Toronto to her she would stab them with a fork. Wesley spent most of his time in the bathroom throwing up until Mrs. Karroll sent him home, and when I passed Djebar in the hall, he looked like that time when he accidentally overmedicated himself. Darrin didn't show up at all. Mrs. Karroll said his parents called in to say he had the flu.

I'd thought about staying home, but I knew my parents would ask questions, and I didn't want to lie to them anymore. A part of me was wishing now I had told my parents about the competition.

But they wouldn't have understood.

Not like James. James understood.

"I don't understand," said James. "You can't be thinking of just chucking this thing. You guys have all worked so hard — and you made it to the *semifinals*."

"I think they're cross with me," I said.

"They're nervous," said James. "It's just pre-performance jitters. It's perfectly normal."

He uttered the word *normal* like it was nothing — like it was okay to say that word when he was talking about us.

"The semifinals are not for another three weeks —"

"Twenty-four days."

"Right. So you have some time to convince them." James was wearing dark mirrored glasses that reflected the snow. It was one of those cold, sunny, cloudless days, and the reflection of the sun on the snow hurt my eyes. I have tried wearing sunglasses, but I don't seem to be able to tolerate them. It is not the weight on the bridge of my nose or my ears, or anything tactile; it is merely the notion that I am watching the world through muddied air, and then my thoughts get muddy as well. Thea says I just need to get habituated to wearing sunglasses because one day I may need to wear prescription glasses. Right now I have 20/20 vision.

"What about you, Del? How are you feeling about all this?"

How did I feel about the upcoming semifinals? I had no idea. The truth is I was more nervous about having to sway the others into going to Toronto on the bus with me. And because I was focusing on that I hadn't had a chance to feel anxious about performing.

"You're not still angry with me, are you?" he asked.

I wasn't sure I'd ever been angry with him, and I was about to tell him so when Tammy-Lynn approached as if from nowhere.

"Hey, beautiful." She bent down to give James a kiss. "Hi, Del." Her dog, Finnegan, sniffed my foot. I tensed, feeling a sudden impulse to kick the dog away. Instead I got up.

"Del? Hey, it's still early," said James. "And I had this idea I wanted to share with you."

I looked at Tammy-Lynn, shook my head, and started to leave.

"You know, Del," said Tammy-Lynn, "that is fucking rude, you know?"

I turned to look at Tammy-Lynn, who was glaring at me, her coat puffing around her like a giant pink marshmallow.

James touched her arm. "Tammy-Lynn, let it go, will ya?"

She shrugged off his hand. "No. I'm sick of it. He manipulates you, and he has never uttered a civil word to me since we've met."

James rubbed his face. "Remember what we talked about the other day? You know, about —"

"You know what? That's total bullshit. I don't know that much about autism, but having autism is no excuse for having bad manners," she said. I could tell by her face she was really angry.

I recalled my mother saying the same thing a long time ago. "You're right," I heard myself say, staring down at the toes of my boots. "I'm sorry."

A peculiar expression crossed Tammy-Lynn's face. I couldn't read it at all. I have always had the feeling that she didn't like me. But I'm usually wrong about that kind of thing. I knew I didn't like her and I didn't like her dog. And my feelings about people rarely change.

"Tammy-Lynn, can you give us a minute?" James said with a sigh in his voice.

Tammy-Lynn shot me a look that I couldn't decipher and turned abruptly to walk towards James's building.

"Sit down, Del."

I checked my watch. "I only have six minutes."

"I'll talk fast. Sit down, for Chrissake, will you?"

I sat down.

"First off, don't be rude to Tammy-Lynn. She gets really pissed off when you're like that to her. Veda too." James grinned, made a snorting sound. "You're not doing so well in the girl department, are you, Del?"

"Girls confuse me."

"Yeah, well — join the club." James leaned forward. "Listen, do you and the others play poker?"

I blinked, thought about the game, and instantly went through the rules in my mind. "I know how to play, but I've never actually played the game. I don't know whether the others know how to play."

"Rod, my manager, used to play poker with me and the other members of the Magic Horse Marines whenever we got nervous and tried to back out of a gig. The thing about poker is that it is for keeps. You play, you lose or you win. If Rod won the pot, we had to go on stage; if we won the pot, we had the option of bowing out."

I was silent for a moment, waiting for him to continue. When I glanced at my watch he went on.

"He didn't always win, you know. But even when we won, we never took that option to not play a gig. Not once. But you see, he gave us the *choice* to back out. And that was what was important."

I was confused. "So, playing poker will make us feel as though we have a choice to play at the semifinals?"

"Well — no. My strategy is to win the pot and get everyone on that bus to Toronto," said James.

"But what if you lose?"

James shook his head. "You know, Del, I can't seem to think that far ahead with you guys. You're all so ... unpredictable."

Unpredictable is a tame word to use to describe autistic people; any person can be unpredictable, whether he is or isn't on the autism spectrum. In a sense, we are *less* unpredictable than a Neural Typical. What I think James meant was that because he didn't understand us he could not correctly predict what we would do in a given circumstance. But we're like anyone else; once a person gets to know us, it is quite easy to predict what will happen next. This is more true for autistic people, because we rarely waver from our behavior patterns. So the more a person knows us, the more easily he can predict what we will do.

The logic behind this premise is sound. And it *should* be true. But then, why do neurotypical people still not understand us? And why do Neural Typicals insist on thinking that we aren't any good at poker?

"Okay, first let me explain a little about the rules —"

"Are we playing Texas hold 'em? I don't really like seven-card stud or Omaha," said Djebar, sitting down.

Petula was twirling her hair staring at the cards in James's hand. "Why do you get to be the Button?"

James's brows lifted slightly. Those lines across his forehead deepened. "The Button?"

"The dealer," said Sogi. "Shouldn't we draw to see who deals?"

"High or low?" said Darrin.

James cleared his throat, glanced at me. I was sitting on his left. "Okay. So I'm guessing you all know how to play poker."

"I've never played poker," said Petula.

"Me neither," said Sogi.

"Me neither," I said.

"I played once with my Uncle Ari and his friends," said Djebar. "I won forty bucks."

"I've only played on the computer," said Darrin.

"I don't know how to play poker," said Wesley. "I don't understand games."

"Don't worry, Wesley. It's pretty easy. Let me explain …" Djebar started to explain to him the concept of the game and the value ranking of each hand.

"You have to calculate the odds, "said Petula. "If you pay attention to the flops —"

"How about we play just a simple five-card stud?" James interrupted.

"What's that?" asked Djebar.

"I only know how to play Texas hold 'em and seven-card," said Petula.

"Five-card stud: this is an official poker game, right?" said Darrin.

"How do you play?" asked Sogi.

"I'll explain it to you," I said quickly. "James told me the rules." And I repeated what he had told me the day before, word for word. When I finished they asked all the questions I had asked James. Unfortunately, he was not as adept as we were at explaining rules.

"Why does he get to be the dealer?" Petula wanted to know. "Shouldn't we be democratic and fair and draw for the Button?"

"There's nothing fair or democratic about poker," said James. "Since I am the dealer, I get to set the blind bet for this game."

"Is there a flop?" asked Sogi.

"Nope. Everything is kept close to the chest. One draw of two."

"What do you mean?" Petula wrinkled up her nose.

"You throw out two cards; the dealer deals you two from the top of the deck," I explained. "Like in the movies, you know?"

"*The Sting*!" Djebar grinned.

"Paul Newman, Robert Redford, Robert Shaw, Charles Durning, Eileen Brennan," Sogi recited. "Directed by George Roy Hill; written by William Goldman —"

"Wrong!" said Petula. "*The Sting* was written by David Ward."

"No, *you're* wrong," said Sogi.

"Wanna make a bet?" said Petula, making that sneering face at him.

"Whoa, whoa! I'm the one making the bets here," James intervened. "We're here to play poker, remember?"

"It wasn't Goldman," said Petula.

"It was," retorted Sogi. He turned to Djebar. "Djebar?"

"I don't know," he said, pulling out his smart phone.

Petula turned to look at me. "Del knows."

I did. I knew most of the movie writers. "Petula's right. It was David S. Ward."

"I think you're both wrong!" Sogi dug into his coat pocket for his BlackBerry, just as Darrin and Petula went for their phones.

I suppose we could have avoided the entire argument just by looking it up on our comps first. Although all of the ASD class carried comps with variable networks, we didn't use them as substitute brains. In the advanced math class we are allowed to use calculators, but none of us do. We are too proud of our own brains to rely on comps. As well, figuring things out, thinking problems through to their conclusion, calms me. And I suspect this is the way it is for the others, as well. Also, using our brains is often faster.

"Hey, are we going to argue or play?" said James.

"Del's right," said Djebar.

"Hey, I said it first," said Petula.

"You said David Ward," said Djebar.

"It *is* David Ward."

"It's David *S.* Ward," I corrected. But when she glared at me I wondered if it had been a good idea to point out her error.

"Okay, that's enough. Wesley, Sogi, sit down."

"Aren't we going to rehearse?" asked Wesley.

"No. We're going to play poker."

"Why? What's the point?" asked Sogi.

James took a long swig of his Heineken. "Just humor me, will you?"

"I don't want to play," said Wesley.

"What time is it?" asked Sogi.

"Time to get your ass in that chair!" growled James.

We all looked at him, taken aback by the harshness of his tone. James rubbed his face. I think he was tired, because I had noticed his eyes were bloodshot and he was scratching his forearms a lot.

"I don't have any money," said Petula.

"Neither do I," said Darrin.

"I'm not allowed to gamble," said Sogi. "Plus, I don't have any money."

"I'm broke," said Djebar.

Wesley was rocking in his chair, drumming with his hands. I looked at James, whose face had become an odd pinkish color.

"We're not playing for money," he said quietly.

"What are we playing for, then?" asked Petula.

"A promise."

"A promise," Wesley echoed.

"A promise to do what?" said Darrin, tugging on his ear. His brows were pulled very close together in a look of confusion. But there was something else there, too. Excitement?

"If I win the pot I want you all to promise that you will go to Toronto to play at the semifinals at the Cubground Pub."

Everyone was quiet for several moments.

"What if *we* win?" asked Djebar.

James shrugged. "You don't have to go to Toronto. If you don't *want* to," he added.

It wasn't much of an incentive to play, and everyone, except me, pointed this out to James. But they all sat down and played anyway.

"Well, that's that," said Petula. "I won. Fair and square."

James ran his fingers through his hair, his blue-sky eyes squinting so that I could barely see them. He stretched, raised himself out of the seat by pushing against the tabletop. His skin was grayish, and he began scratching his forearms. He glanced at me, twisted his face into an apology.

"So what does this mean?" Sogi asked.

"It means, I have to go." James looked around the table at us. "I'm sorry it didn't work out differently, but ..." he stood up, "well ... you're a ... an interesting bunch of kids."

"You're going?" asked Djebar.

"Yeah. I'm heading out to Los Angeles the day after tomorrow, and I've, uh, got things to get ready."

"But your gig isn't for another twenty-three days," I said.

James laughed. "The Magic Horse Marines are nowhere in your league," he said. "We need a helluva lot more rehearsal time than you guys." He swung on his brown leather jacket with the fleece collar. In that brief instant he reminded me of my dad in this old photograph I found stuck in the back of the junk drawer in the hallway. It had been taken before he'd had me — before he'd even met my mom.

He winked at me. "Besides, you don't need me anymore."

"Reverse psychology doesn't work on me," said Sogi. "My mother tries it all the time."

"Wait a minute," said Petula. "I won the pot, so I get to choose what we do, isn't that the way it works?"

James frowned. "Well, no. That wasn't exactly what our deal was —"

"The deal was that if you win, we go to Toronto for the semi-finals," said Sogi.

"But I won, so I get to choose what we do," said Petula.

"That doesn't sound right," said Sogi.

"Hey, no way am I letting Petula decide what *I'm* going to do," said Djebar.

James leaned in towards me. "You were right; it was a crappy idea," he muttered in my ear.

His proximity surprised me, and I instinctively shot out my hands to push him away. My left hand caught him on the chin, and he stumbled backward. No one in the room seemed to take notice of James, who cursed quietly as he heaved himself up off the garage floor.

"But," I pointed out, "if one of us decides *not* to go to Toronto, then *none* of us can go."

"So our decision has to be unanimous," said Sogi.

Darrin spoke up then. "Maybe we should just vote on it?"

We thought about this for a few moments. The truth was, we weren't used to acting as a group, and we tended to see only our own points of view. We were each habituated to making our own choices, without taking others into consideration.

Wesley stopped rocking and started flapping his hands. I realized I was flapping a little, too. And when I glanced at the others, I saw that they were stimming, as well. James was watching us with an expression I could only interpret as alarm. But I might have been wrong, because suddenly he threw his hat down on the table and suggested we do a secret ballot.

We were to write "yes" if we wanted to go to Toronto, "no" if we didn't.

"Can I think about this?" said Sogi.

"No," said James. "It's now or never."

"I don't think well under pressure," Wesley whined.

"Well, *I* don't have to think about it," said Darrin. He looked over at me, and the skin at the back of my neck tingled slightly as I watched him bend over his yellow sticky note with the pen.

"Del?" James prodded me.

I hesitated. For a brief moment my thoughts wavered. I don't like making decisions of which I don't know the outcome. Voting confuses me because there is really no way to win. You have to depend on others to think like you. To want the same thing. But I wasn't sure the other members of the Turing Machinists wanted the same things as I did.

James nudged my shoulder. There was a question on his face, and I realized I was gritting my teeth and squeezing my eyes tightly. I wrote quickly, folded the sticky note, and threw it into James's hat before I could change my mind.

My mother and father were waiting for me in the kitchen when I returned home. Their expressions made me nervous in that I knew by the way they were looking at me that I was in for a lecture. Dread washed over me as I sat down at the kitchen table.

"Del? Is there anything you'd like to tell us?"

I stared at them, my dread turning to confusion.

"Your mother got a call about you this afternoon," said my father. I couldn't read his expression. I didn't think he was cross, but I couldn't be sure.

My mother's face suddenly crumpled, and she folded her arms around me, hugging me hard. "Del, you need to talk to us about these things. We want to know what's going on in your life."

My stomach suddenly lurched. *Uh-oh. They know.* "I meant to tell you, but I wasn't sure you would let me do it. And it was supposed to be a surprise ..." My stammer trailed off as I looked down at my mother's feet. Her feet seemed smaller than I remembered. She was also wearing fuzzy pale blue slippers with tiny pom-poms in the front. Concentrating on the pom-poms helped me swallow back the lump that was forming in my throat.

"Well, it was a surprise. I'll give you that," my mother said. "My goodness, Del. You are getting so big. We're going to need to go shopping for new clothes, you and I."

My father beamed at me. "Son, we're very proud of you."

I looked over at my father. "I'm just following your dream, Dad," I said.

My father's brows sank and pulled together. "*My* dream?" He scratched his head and laughed. "Poetry definitely ain't my thing, son."

"The lady on the phone said they'd send us a copy of the *Merryton Review*," my mother said. "My son, a published poet at seventeen!"

"Fifty bucks prize money ain't nothin' to sneeze at, either." My father grinned and gave me a friendly punch on the shoulder. I stared at them as it dawned on me what they weren't talking about. But what *were* they talking about? The thoughts in my head all intersected at once, and it all became mud. My heart was racing, and a buzz of flies started up in my belly. Splashes of orange appeared in my peripheral vision. A panic attack was coming.

"Mr. Levinson said you have a real gift." My mother shook her head. "I didn't know ... Del? Would you like some raisin toast —?"

I fled up the stairs to my room.

"Listen, class, this is *serious*." The tops of Ms. Pokolopinison's cheeks had turned pink. "I need you to pay attention!" The sudden rise in volume in her voice made us zone in on her. That is not to say that we were paying attention. My thoughts were still divided. But she had *part* of my attention now.

"You are all wanting to graduate this year, isn't that right?"

We regarded her in silence, watched as she steepled and unsteepled her hands. The rosiness in her cheeks had grown to a deep fuchsia color.

"Now, I think I have been *more* than lenient about this group project," she said in her perfect C-chord tone. "I have given you *more* than enough freedom and time choosing your themes and how you conduct your cooperative efforts," she said. "But now, I would like some consideration from *you* in return. I would like you to please — *please* — work on your group projects ... so I don't have to give you all incompletes for this course."

Jeddy's hand shot up. "But this class is an elective ASD course, isn't it?"

Ms. Pokolopinison's expression changed. "Yes, but —"

"So this class won't affect our academic standing in our final grade," said Petula.

We all looked up at Ms. Pokolopinison expectantly. Her face drooped. It seemed to me that she was struggling with her features, trying to prop them up with exhausted muscles. I found, oddly, that I did not enjoy watching this. I looked away and saw Mr. Yaggi out in the yard with the snow blower. In the winter, however, all the school windows are shut tight and you can't hear anything that's going on outside. It makes you sleepy but not relaxed because you can see things happening but you can't hear them. When noises used to give me strip headaches I always wished I would go deaf. Now the thought of not hearing the world frightens me.

I looked over at the rest of the class. They had zoned out, as well. Better to just sleep the class away ...

It was when I'd gone to search my bottom drawer for an ink refill for my Paper Mate that I came across the present. Why had I tossed the gift James had given me into my supply drawer? I turned it over in my hands. The paper was blue with white stripes, the kind they use at the wrapping tables in malls. The stick-on bow had fallen to the side. I threw the bow back into the drawer and tore open the paper.

I stared at it for several minutes. But I couldn't figure out what it was. The words "Jaws Harp" meant nothing to me. On the front of the little box, underneath the words, was a picture of Snoopy playing an instrument that looked like a harmonica. I don't like the harmonica. I opened the box, pulled out the jaws harp. It wasn't a harmonica. I inspected it, tried to figure out how it worked, but gave up and opened the instruction booklet. I read it four times before I understood what it meant. I clamped my teeth down on the middle part as instructed and nudged the bar in front. Nothing. I breathed, and twanged the metal bar. It made a sound. I did it again. The sound tickled me as my mouth vibrated. I tried it again, breathing in this time. A different sound. It was like a gargle inside a tunnel. I gazed at the jaws harp with interest. *My first musical instrument.*

I got up, opened my closet door, and pushed back the clothes. I set the jaws harp down on the top shelf, next to the glass steam engine Uncle Saul had given me on my fourth birthday. On the other end was a plastic cup decorated with stills of *Scott Pilgrim vs. The World*, the movie I had almost gone to see. To the far end was a jar full of foreign coins Mr. Yaggi gave me in grade nine when he was emptying the vending machines outside the staff lounge.

My mother asked me once why I liked to hide things. "You know how many library books I've had to pay for — only to find them later all stuffed behind your bedside table? And all those beautiful carved chess pieces. Why did you hide them in your shoes?"

"I don't know." And in truth, I didn't know. I just knew that some things were too fantastic, that I needed them to be hidden away from my view, buried like a secret treasure.

I was waiting for someone to say something, to break the silence that gripped our table like a heavy raincloud. We were all edgy and excited and fearful, and desperate to talk to one another. Around us, students were chattering and laughing with such ease it made me nervous. I could not shrug off that yearning feeling that sank inside me, that was always there, like an ugly stone that never changed shape. I wanted to be a part of what was going on around me, to understand their jokes, to laugh and feel what those other students felt. As I was thinking, my gaze moved to a nearby table where I observed a tall, skinny boy wearing a baseball cap that said, "Eat This." *Eat what?* I wondered curiously. The boy noticed my gaze and stared back. His lips drew back to reveal long white teeth. It took me a moment to realize he was smiling at me. I quickly looked away, my heart racing.

"So, we're still going to do this, right?"

Djebar's gruff voice made me jump.

"Are we still going, then?" asked Sogi, looking up from his laptop.

"Are we still going, then?" echoed Wesley.

"Are we?" asked Petula.

They were all looking at me. Why were they looking at me? I didn't want to decide for them. I didn't know myself if I was going to go. I was going to say that, but instead I said, "The bus leaves for Toronto at 10:47 a.m. If we take a later bus we will miss our slot."

They all nodded. Wesley left to go to the washroom. He uses the staff washroom near the office because he throws up a lot. Sogi asked Djebar if he was going to eat his Rice Krispie square. Djebar threw it at him, muttering that he wasn't hungry. He had spent a part of the morning in the Plum Room because he had thrown his history text-book at Mrs. Karroll. Darrin announced that he had to leave for his herbalist appointment. I was supposed to be meeting with Mrs. Biegler, but I waited until Darrin had disappeared through the doors. When I got up to leave, Djebar had his earphones plugged in and Sogi was playing *Minesweeper* on his computer. I still had that ugly stone in my belly. As I walked past a group of giggling girls, I wondered if I was heading into an Orange Day.

"You still mad at me?" James asked. It was a gray day, and the snow had melted around the bench so that tufts of brownish grass were starting to push through.

I didn't say anything. The truth is I wasn't sure if I was mad at James. Or if I ever had been. I just knew that my original plans had gone awry, and it made me anxious when I realized how little control I had over what I was doing.

After a while, James sighed. "Okay, then. Since you're going to give me the silent treatment, I'm just going to say what I need to say. Okay?"

I kept staring ahead. My hands were sweating inside my mittens, and I felt waves of compressed heat under my jacket. The Weather Network had been wrong about this morning; it wasn't minus-eight degrees Celsius.

James talked for a bit, but his words floated around me and disappeared before I could make any sense of them. I started to get agitated. And then James touched my arm, and I jumped back in startlement.

"Oh, hey. Sorry," he said, looking at me, his forehead all wrinkled. "Del, you're going to be okay. The Turing Machinists are going to be great. You guys are ..." He squinted, rubbed his face. "Bloody hell, Del. If you're going to do it, do it. I can't hold your hand. And I can only say sorry so many times." His voice grew louder, more abrupt. "For fuck's sake! At least you don't have to play in front of twenty thousand people."

"Forty thousand," I said.

"What?"

"On the Internet they said they sold forty thousand tickets for your charity gig."

James groaned. "Great. More pressure." He started to scratch his arm. "Okay, listen. I've arranged it so your instruments will be there at the Cubground waiting for you. When you go in you ask for Rick Hughes, okay? I spoke to him yesterday. He'll take care of you." He glanced at his watch. "I've got to go. My plane leaves at eleven. Do you have any questions?"

Who is Rick Hughes? "Don't you mean Rick Turchuck?"

"Turchuck, right. He'll be expecting you."

I stood up and grabbed my knapsack.

"Hey, wait."

And suddenly, James wrapped his arms around me. I didn't know what to do, so I just stood there.

"Good luck, okay?"

I met his eyes, and immediately felt my throat close tight. I looked down at my boots. My feet were sweating so bad I thought maybe my boots had filled with water. When I walked away my eyes stung and my heart was pounding against my ribs. But as I broke into a run, I didn't cry, and the tingles at the back of my head vanished into the gray air. For the first time ever I didn't care that I was going to be late.

We were all standing on the east platform at the Merryton Transportation Center. All of us were nervous and cross.

"If we stick together we'll make it," I said.

"I feel sick," said Sogi.

"I think I'm going to be sick," said Wesley.

"I don't want to go to Toronto," said Petula. "You can't make me."

"I've never been on a bus like this," said Darrin. "What if I get bus sick?"

"The ride is only forty-three minutes to Union Station," I said. I was feeling nauseous, and my head was hurting. That pitter-patter sensation was taking over my body; I was having an anxiety attack. Now, more than anything, I wanted to go home.

"Let's just go home," said Djebar.

I nodded, partly with emphasis, partly with relief. "Yes. Djebar's right. Let's go."

After a minute of silence, with nobody making a move to leave the platform, Petula spoke up. "How far is it to the Cubground Pub from Union Station?" she asked me.

I focused on the map in my head. "The pub is on McCaul Street. It's near the CHUM City building," I said, kneading my hands, which had begun to ache from clenching. "I didn't figure out how long it would take us from Union Station. But I thought if we took a subway —"

"I will not travel underground," said Sogi.

"I'm with him on that one," said Djebar.

"I'm with him on that one," echoed Wesley.

"I'm not taking a subway," said Petula. "It's not safe."

"Well, there's a bus going —"

"We could walk," said Darrin, spreading the map across the magazine kiosk. "Look, McCaul Street is off of Queen Street West. Union Station is on Front Street West. We could walk it."

I nodded uncertainly. "Yes, we could walk."

"But do we have enough time?" Petula asked.

We all looked down at our watches, silently calculating the timing of our route.

"We can figure out precisely how long it will take us if I could see a map," said Petula, snatching up the map from Darrin.

We went inside the snack bar and spread the map across the table. All at once we were eager: we were engaged in a new challenge, a new project that had for the moment distracted us from the fact that in three hours we were going to have to play our music live before a live audience.

"Union Station is —"

"— on Front Street West —"

"— in quadrant T19."

"And McCaul Street is —"

" — in quadrant S18."

"They're so close!"

"If we make an algebraic equation —"

"Djebar, we don't have time. Let's just map out the streets."

"We'll have to keep the map in our heads until we get there," said Sogi. "Then we can work on the equation." We were all excited with our new thoughts now.

Somehow we managed to board the bus heading to Union Station, downtown Toronto. The ride was predicted to be forty-three minutes long. Not much can happen in three-quarters of an hour, we all told ourselves.

The Cartesian coordinate system: traditionally, the horizontal line is labeled the "x-axis" (the map letter), the vertical line the "y-axis" (the map number), and the point of intersection is known as the "origin" (the Cubground Pub).

Descartes discovered a way to represent a geometrical curve numerically by creating an algebraic equation, and vice versa. This ingenious idea forged a pathway to the concept of the simple graph. Look at a weather graph, a graph representing the weekly stock market, a graph that depicts the global rate of autism spectrum disorder diagnoses in children. Every graph you have ever seen is based on Descartes's inspiration to join together geometry and algebra to represent one truth.

This was a concept we all understood.

There is a theory that we are all born with an innate sense of personal space. Some of us require a very wide berth around us; some of us need only a small distance between us and other people. Neurotypical people have a computable vector of space that basically stays the same all around the body, like a planet orbiting a star. But people with autism tend to have uneven orbits. Personal space for us can be at once wide and small, and sometimes there is no sense of space at all. When I was younger sometimes I liked to sit so close to some people I was sitting on their laps. When Bea was a baby, my parents would often have to yank me away because I would wrap my body around her. As I got older, my need for a wider personal space grew. At the same time, whenever I was with my peers I would often stand too close, so that I was continuously being pushed away.

Our lack of understanding of personal space, the autism experts say, comes from our inability to read other people's silent signals that regularly communicate individual needs for things such as personal space. For instance, when lining up at a bank machine, people will instinctively back away to ensure that there is a certain safe distance between you and the person operating the machine. But how to calculate that distance? How do we know if we are too close? Or too far away? This is a concept that does not come naturally to us, and our inability to grasp it can be frustrating to the people around us. For people with autism, not knowing where to put ourselves in relation to Neural Typicals can cause great anxiety.

When we boarded the bus, there were enough empty seats for us to each sit alone. But then more people came. An older man wearing a thick Burberry coat decided to sit next to Petula. She glanced back at us, her brows drawn down, her mouth bunching together in a tight bow. After a moment, she got up and glared at the man, who immediately stood up and let her through. But there were no full empty seats left, so she moved down the aisle to where I was sitting.

"I like the window seat," she said crossly.

I got up and let her in. When I sat down my thigh was immediately drawn to her thigh like a magnetic positive to a negative. The entirety of my body suddenly began to hum. I imagined tiny race cars zooming through my blood, only to collide in my head. I felt light-headed. I needed some air. I wanted to touch her arm, hold her hand. Her proximity was making me anxious. I wanted to lean over and smell her hair. Play-Doh and green apples.

"I hope my xylophone is all right," she said, turning to look out the window.

I didn't say anything, as I was afraid I would stutter. I peered over the top of the seats to see Sogi, two seats ahead, setting up his laptop. Across the way, Darrin had his iPod earphones on. Behind him, Djebar was already playing a game on his iPad. Across the aisle, one seat behind us, Wesley sat, his hands tucked under his thighs, rocking. *Uh-oh*, I thought.

Petula took out her iPod, plugged in her earphones. She glanced at me, narrowed her eyes, her lips tugging up slightly at the corners. My heart skipped a beat. I wanted very much to talk to her, but instead I pulled out my Kindle and started reading the e-book Mrs. Biegler had downloaded for me. It was called *Music and Imagination* by Aaron Copland. It was actually very good. Mrs. Biegler had told me she thought I would understand it. And I think I did. Most of it, anyway. Now, I was thinking that I should have told her about what we were doing. I was pretty sure she would have liked the idea.

We were only twenty minutes down the road when Wesley had a meltdown.

Wesley couldn't tolerate anything buzzing in his ears, and he got motion sickness if he read a book or a computer screen while he was travelling. So he had brought along his drumsticks to help entertain himself. Unfortunately, he chose to drum on the seat in front of him. The couple sitting in front of him turned around and shot him a hard glare. Wesley ignored them and kept drumming.

"Excuse me! Do you *mind*?" the woman said in a loud voice.

Wesley frowned slightly, but kept drumming.

"Hey! Are you deaf!" the young man said, waving his hand at Wesley.

Wesley stopped in mid-drum. His face turned ashen, the pimples on his chin suddenly popping out like raspberries. He stared at them, his mouth slightly gaped.

"What are you? Retarded?"

The young woman punched the man in the arm and gave him a stern look. She turned around, looked over the top of the seat, and smiled at Wesley. She had bobbed reddish-brown hair and wore earrings that looked like the carapaces of tiger beetles.

"Hey, sorry for yelling at you like that." She looked down at the drumsticks in his hands. "So, are you a drummer?"

Wesley blinked. Suddenly he was out of his seat and pushing his way down the aisle towards the bathroom.

"You dumb shit princess!" Petula had risen from her seat and was leaning over me so that her lush dark hair brushed the top of my jacket. Her green apple scent very nearly made me swoon. "Who do you think you are, speaking to him like that!"

The young woman's face darkened and her eyes narrowed. "What did you call me?"

"You heard me, shit princess."

"Nancy, just ignore her," her seatmate said. "There's something wrong with them."

Petula started to clamber over me. Her hand inadvertently pressed down on my crotch, and I yelled out in surprise. She shot me a quick look and grinned, I think because she had felt my erection and because I was pretty sure my face had turned redder than a tomato.

"I'll go see if Wesley's all right," I stammered, slipping out of the seat. Thankfully, my jacket was just long enough to hide the bulge in my pants.

The older man seated in front of the washroom grabbed the sleeve of my jacket. His hands shook. "Yer friend all right, son?"

I nodded.

"He get sick a lot?"

"Yes."

"He don't look well. Better take him to the doctor."

"He's ... autistic," I said, staring at the man's bony fingers on my jacket sleeve.

"He's artistic, you say? Well," the old man relaxed his grip on my sleeve, "it's hard being disenfranchised, isn't it? Being on the outside of things." He looked up at me then and grinned. His eyes were the color of a bleached swimming pool, and his front teeth were like rotting stumps of wood.

Disenfranchised was a good word. "Yes, it is," I said. I turned to knock on the washroom door. "Wesley?"

"I'm going to stay here, Del."

"Okay," I said. "I'll let you know when we arrive."

The old man patted my arm as I started back to my seat. "You look after 'im, now."

"Yes, I will. Thank you."

"Good boy."

As I returned to my seat, I felt different. I knew it was irrational that I should feel taller and stronger. But I did. The sensation was odd, and I couldn't quite figure it out. But when I sat down next to Petula it occurred to me that while I was talking to the old man I hadn't stuttered once.

"I have to be home by four. I have karate," said Sogi.

"Twenty-three," said Petula.

"Twenty-three what?" Sogi asked.

"That was the twenty-third time you said that."

"Well, I do have to be home by four. My dad's taking me to karate," said Sogi.

"Twenty-four."

"I told my parents I would be home by three-thirty," said Darrin. "Do you think we'll be home before then?"

I'd been trying to navigate them through Union Station. The noise, the people, the smells, the flickering lights: so many sensations were bombarding me at once. Wesley looked sickly. Sogi's eyes kept darting back and forth in a way that bothered me. Darrin was alternately tugging on his ears and scratching the back of his neck like he had fleas. Djebar was shaking his wrists. Like Sogi, his gaze darted about the station. They were, like me, trying not to look scared. I wondered if I looked as scared as they did.

"I hope they didn't fuck up my xylophone." Petula was winding her hair around her fingers and tugging. I thought she looked more worried than scared. "How the hell do we get out of here?"

None of us were blessed with a sense of direction, it seemed, and when we did finally find an exit, we had to reorient ourselves as we were on the wrong side of the station.

"Why don't you ask someone, Del?" Petula suggested.

Why do I have to ask? I thought. "We mapped this out already, remember?" I was not good at talking to strangers, even to ask for directions.

"What if we get lost?" said Djebar.

"What if we get lost?" echoed Wesley.

"Let's look at the map again," said Darrin.

"Great. We're already lost, aren't we?" said Petula.

"We're not lost," I stammered. "Let's just follow the route we mapped out. Come on, guys. We'll be fine." I hoped I sounded more confident than I was. *What am I doing here? I want to go home.*

After a few moments Sogi exclaimed, "Look! I think I see the CHUM building!"

My anxiety rose twofold, but I was elated, too. And relieved. I wasn't certain how the others were feeling, but I think they were as proud of themselves as I was of myself. A part of me wanted to get this whole thing over with so I could return as quickly as possible to my normal routine. But another part of me was thrilled by the idea of this adventure. And my brain felt sharper than usual. My thoughts were crisp, clear, focused. I was feeling more confident than I had ever felt before.

And the feeling lasted up until the moment we entered the Cubground Pub.

Alan Turing once spoke to a class of freshman science students about a mathematical clan: a group of people who devoted their lives to discovering the truth of mathematics. Finding one's true family, he said, is something everyone innately strives to do at any given time in life.

But isn't my biological family my true family?

I once mentioned this to Thea, and she cited the story about the ugly duckling who was, in fact, a swan mistakenly born in a nest full of ducklings. Thinking he was a duck, he tried hard to be one, to fit in with his siblings. But he was ugly and awkward, and he couldn't keep up with the other ducklings. Sensing that he was different, the ducks criticized him and eventually ostracized him from the family. When he began to grow and change he became more and more lonely and confused, as he was looking and behaving less and less like a duck. It wasn't until that fateful day when he bumped into a creature that looked and acted just like him that he realized he was not, in fact, a duck, but a beautiful swan.

"But that story proves that I'm right. The ugly duckling's true family *was* his biological family," I said.

Thea smiled at me and shook her head. "Yes, that's true. But you're taking it too literally; you're not seeing the deeper meaning of the story. It's about finding where you belong. Or, as you put it, finding your clan."

So, were people with Asperger, Aspies, my clan, then? No, I'd decided; I didn't feel particularly close to other Aspies. And although we did have a lot of similar problems and similar interests, I don't think we were all like-minded. Maybe people with autism can't have a clan.

But as we approached the front entrance of the Cubground Pub I suddenly knew that my conclusion had been wrong, for it struck me at that moment, when I looked over at Petula, Djebar, Darrin, and Wesley, that these people were part of my clan. And for the first time ever, I was actually feeling like I *belonged*.

"I have to be home by four," said Sogi.

"We are going to leave right after, right?" Petula squeezed my arm. "We're not going to have to stay or anything, right?"

"I don't know," I replied truthfully as we approached the entrance-way. Oddly, the doors swung outward rather than inward.

The main foyer was deserted. A lonely lectern stood off to the side. Beyond it hung a dark red curtain, not shabby, but it had evidence of wear. About us there was a faint lingering odor of cigarettes and beer.

"Listen!" Darrin hissed.

We all went still. I couldn't hear anything above the rush of blood that pounded in my ears. But in some of the sensory research tests we'd undergone, it was determined that while all of us had heightened, or acute, senses, a few in our class were classified as hypersensitive, meaning that our sensory intakes and outputs were over the above-average scale. Darrin was one of those determined to be hypersensitive. My sensitivity classification was determined to be merely slightly above average.

My mother likes Darrin's parents, but my father calls them left-wing hippies because of their PETA activism and the fact that Darrin's mother and father call people with autism "super humans."

"Can you hear it?" said Darrin.

"Hear what?" said Sogi.

"Music. There's another band playing," said Darrin.

"Yes, I think I can hear it too. I think … they're using a drum machine," said Wesley. He was hugging himself, humming and rocking on the balls of his feet.

"They're called the Fuller's Teasel," said a grumpy voice from behind the curtain. "Whatever that means."

We stared at the man who strode through the split in the red curtain. It wasn't his great height or width that caught our attention (his shoulders were the widest shoulders I'd ever seen), or his hair, which sprang out of his head like a mop made out of black yarn. It was, in fact, his shirt. Or rather, what was *on* it.

"Hey! Where did you get that shirt?" said Petula with her cross face.

The man's right eyebrow shot up, and he regarded her with an expression that baffled me. "Where did I get *what*?"

"That's the 1958 map of the Island of Sodor," said Sogi.

"It's got the legend and *everything*," said Djebar.

"Wow," said Darrin.

"Wow," echoed Wesley.

"Where did you get that T-shirt?" said Petula.

The man was watching us with his squinty eyes. "My nephew got it for me. Listen, are you the Turing Machinists?" He laughed. "What am I thinking? Hell, of course you are."

"So, where did your nephew get the T-shirt?" asked Djebar.

"Huh? I don't know. He brought it back from his trip to Asia. I think he got this shirt in northern India somewhere." He glanced down at his watch. "Which one of you is Del Capp?"

My heart skipped a beat, and I missed a breath. This is what happens just before I begin to stutter. I didn't want to stammer. Not now. So I just raised my hand and nodded at him.

The man returned the nod. "Name's Burke. James told us all about you guys. You want to come in to the office and wait? Rick'll be here in about ten."

"Ten what?" asked Sogi.

Burke looked at him, blinked.

"Who's Rick?" Petula asked.

"Rick? He's the owner of the Cubground. But I thought you knew him. Didn't James tell you ...?" The change in expression on Burke's face made me believe he was truly surprised by our reaction.

But I wasn't surprised.

I didn't recognize the name at first. But when I looked it up in the *NetWet Music Star Log*, I got a hit.

Rick Turchuck was Rick Hughes; he, along with James, had founded the Magic Horse Marines in 2005. But in 2009 he'd left the band, although there was a rumor that he was actually kicked out because he was addicted to heroin. Rick and James were supposed to have been best friends in high school. There was a picture of both of them in jeans and T-shirts standing next to a black Mustang that was wearing one of those leather bras to protect the car's front grille. James, who was the taller of the two, had his arm around Rick's shoulders. The caption underneath dated it as the day before high school graduation. From the expressions on both their faces I determined that they were happy. Maybe even excited about the future.

I was getting better at reading emotions behind expressions, I think.

Rick Hughes had gotten a lot smaller since I'd seen him in the photograph online. He had shorter hair, too, and it was gray along the sides. His eyes were half moons and a color I could not be certain of. When he walked he bounced on the balls of his feet like he was dancing, and his smile was closed-mouthed and crooked. He wasn't much older than James, but he looked older than my father's friend Kent, who was fifty-six.

"Oh ho! Here they are! The Turing Machinists!"

We all backed away, staring at the man. He had a voice deep and grand like Mr. Valtoody's. But the difference was that Mr. Valtoody's voice was expected.

"Oh ho! Now, which one of you is Del?"

I could feel the blood drain from my face, and for one split second I considered fleeing. But instead I lifted my hand.

"I-I'm Del. Delmore William Capp."

Rick's smile widened. "Del! Great! Great! How about you all come into my office and we'll get things settled, then?"

"I have to be home by four o'clock," said Sogi.

Petula kicked him. Sogi glared at her.

"Hey, hey! No problem. You're going on right after the, uh, Fuller's Teasers," said Rick, glancing down at the clipboard in front of him.

"*Teasels*," corrected Darrin. "Fuller's Teasels are herbs used in cleaning textiles and curing warts."

"Curing warts, eh?" Rick laughed. "Well, now. I guess those fellas picked a perfect name for their band, eh?"

"I'm afraid I have to disagree with you," said Petula.

"I'm afraid I have to disagree with you," said Wesley agitatedly. He grabbed at his belly, a sign I understood.

"Where's the washroom?" I asked.

Rick gestured offhandedly to his right, and Wesley turned and walked in that direction. He glanced at me. "Uh, your music gear was brought around the day before yesterday. I'll get Burke and Stanley to help you get set up."

Our nervousness pervaded the room like heat waves. We were all sensing each other, and we all started stimming to relax. Rick didn't seem to notice, but Burke's face got all funny, and he leaned over and whispered something to Rick, who shrugged his shoulders.

"All right, then!" He rubbed his hands together. "Let's get this show on the road!"

"You know, Elvis and Barbra Streisand suffered from stage fright," said Burke, as Wesley circled the drum set again.

Wesley stopped mid-step. "Who's Barbra Streisand?"

Burke laughed. "You know what Elvis used to do? Before every show he used to imagine taking apart his guitar, he would label all the parts, and then put them all back together again."

"I didn't know Elvis had Asperger syndrome," said Sogi.

Burke threw back his head and laughed. "You guys are hilarious."

"I don't *feel* hilarious," said Djebar. He was gritting his teeth, and that vein was beginning to pop out in the middle of his forehead.

Darrin was tuning his guitar. He seemed all right, until he glanced up at me and I saw his eyes. They didn't look right. Probably because he was scared out of his mind.

I was staring at Burke's T-shirt when an idea came to my mind. "Sogi?"

Sogi looked over at me.

"Who created Thomas the Tank Engine?"

"Reverend Wilbert Vere Awdry."

"And Thomas was based on what class type of tank engine?"

Sogi frowned. "Class E2 type 0-6-0 tank engine. Why?"

"And it was designed by —?"

"Lawson Billington," replied Sogi.

"Lawson *B.* Billington," Petula corrected him.

"And Lawson Billington was —?"

"Locomotive Superintendent of London, Brighton & the South Coast Railway, between 1910 and 1922," said Djebar.

"1911," Petula corrected. "The E2s were introduced in 1915 to replace Class E1 engines that had been scrapped."

"All the engines had two inside cylinders and driving wheels four feet, six inches in diameter," said Wesley.

"I heard the original E1s had cowcatchers and side plates like the tram engines," said Darrin.

"I like tram engines. I think Toby has always been my favorite engine," I said. "He's based on the J70 Class engine."

"I thought Toby was based on the Y6 Class engines," said Djebar.

"Nope, Del's right," said Petula. "Toby's water tank is built between the boiler and the axles, like the J70 Class engine. It only holds about 625 gallons, which is why Toby always needs to stop for a refill at Elsbridge Station."

"I've always been a fan of Edward," said Darrin. "You know, Edward was, in fact, the first engine in the Railway Series ..."

And we spent a good half-hour discussing Thomas, Toby, Edward,

Gordon, James, and Henry, and all the other beloved engine characters we had grown up with. We all knew a great deal about the engines
and Reverend Wilbert Vere Awdry, their creator. The secret to finding
the relaxation we needed to overcome our stage fright, we realized,
was in the details. It was always the details with us. We were skilled at
reducing the sum into parts, dissecting the forest into individual trees.
This is what we understood; this is what comforted us. It was when
we had to deal with the big picture that we got scared.

When we finished "The Turing Machine Song" we knew we were done.
Without a word we packed up and headed back to Union Station.
The fact that we had played perfectly and that we had impressed
Rick and the other contest judges sitting in the audience didn't matter
to us. We had overcome our fear and had done something actually
new. For an autistic person, performing something new or stepping
into an unknown reality is a momentous occasion. We were relieved
it was over, but we were proud, too.

On the bus ride home, even Wesley was somewhat tranquil. Petula
sat next to me, even though there were empty bus seats available.
At one point, she slipped her hand in mine. Her fingers were long
and soft and warm. After a few minutes our palms were sweating
so badly they prickled. But she made no move to pull her hand away.
And so we sat there and held sweating hands all the way back to
Merryton.

I'm not sure what I felt, but when I got home all thoughts of the
band and the competition vanished from my mind. I even forgot to
think about my parents' impending divorce for a while. And when I
did think, everything got all silvery and hazy like I was in a dream.
I didn't think to check my text messages until 3:07 a.m., when I woke
up and the silvery haze had dissipated.

Rick Hughes had texted me to congratulate the band on a "show-
stopping performance!" He also wanted to tell me that the judges
had unanimously voted to allow the Turing Machinists to return to
play for the finals round. This time, however, it would be at the

Continental Gardens Center in front of a live concert audience.

I didn't text him back.

Wesley didn't make it to school the following week. All of us, including Darrin, spent a lot of time in the Plum Room because of sudden outbursts and meltdowns that had the teachers and medical staff puzzled and alarmed. On Wednesday, Petula was sent home because she had punched a Neural Typical in the cafeteria and had given the boy a black eye. By the time Friday arrived we were tense and exhausted, and the teachers and researchers were scribbling in their little books, trying to figure out why we were behaving so strangely.

"What's going on with you? Did something happen?" Thea asked me. "Why are you acting so testy?"

I didn't want to talk. I wanted to be alone. If I had been playing a Sims game, my social bar would have been filled to the maximum. Psychologists and autistic experts are always encouraging us to be more social. But what Neural Typicals don't understand is that our capacity for socializing is much smaller than theirs, which means that if we overload on our socializing capabilities, our minds get muddled and we begin to behave inappropriately.

In Social Education class, I was looking out the window, watching Mr. Yaggi digging around some cedar bushes, when I suddenly saw my parents walk by. As I watched them take the stone path to the front entrance of the school, I was gripped by a terrible sense of dread.

I waited all day for the summons to the principal's office. But it never came. I was puzzled and filled with even more dread. I didn't want to go home because I knew my parents would be waiting for me there.

So I went to the library instead.

When I returned home, all the lights were on in the house and there was a police car parked along the street. My mouth immediately went dry, and behind my ribs my heart started knocking. As soon as I stepped through the side door I looked up to see my mother's pale face contort into an expression I'd never seen before.

It took me a moment to figure out that everyone was there because of me.

"Where have you been?!"

"We thought something had happened to you!"

"Why didn't you call?"

"We didn't know where you were!"

"Where were you?"

"You should have called!"

I pressed the palms of my hands to my ears. "Leave me alone!" And I ran upstairs and slammed my bedroom door.

I had always been startled when my parents used to come to my bedroom to talk to me. That was because I was always unprepared. This time, however, was different; this time I knew what they were going to say.

My mother went first. "Del, honey? I don't mind you going off on your own, but you have to let us know where you'll be so we don't worry."

"I went to the library," I said.

My father was standing with his legs apart, his arms folded across his chest. His brows were low over his eyes and nearly touching. My guess was that he was angry. "Don't lie to us. It's eleven *fucking* thirty!"

"Tom!" My mother looked at him with that look that said she didn't like what he'd said. "Del? Please tell us the truth."

I was puzzled. "That *is* the truth."

"The library is still open at eleven-thirty at night? Gimme a break!" my father growled.

"No. The main library closes at ten-thirty. But I had to take two buses home," I said.

My mother and father exchanged glances. All of a sudden I felt that terrible sense of dread again. This time it came from deep in the pit of my stomach.

"Del, we need to talk to you about something," my mother began. She looked down at her fingers, watched them lace together then open again. For a moment she seemed mesmerized by them. "It's about your father and I." She glanced at my father. He cleared his throat.

"Uh, remember what we discussed at Christmastime, Del? At ... Tim Hortons?" My father shot a quick look at my mother. He suddenly looked like he had to go to the bathroom. My mother, on the other hand, had a very still expression, but her nostrils were flared, and her mouth was getting very small.

"Del, we think you're old enough now to understand why your father and I have decided to live apart."

I looked at my father, who was mumbling something, staring at my desk. His expression made me think he was tired. I returned my gaze to my mother. Her nostrils were still flared and her eyes had gotten bigger and harder. She looked like she had when she found out that Raymond Arbuckler had pushed my head in the toilet.

"Your father and I have agreed that I should stay here at the house," she began in a terse voice, "and I would like both you and Bea to live with me. But in a few weeks you're going to be eighteen, and that means you will be old enough to make some decisions on your own."

My father frowned, scratched his head. "I'm not sure Del is capable of making his own decisions ..."

My mother's eyes locked onto mine. It's something she's done since I was a child. It was her way of forcing me to keep eye contact with her. But it only worked with her, no one else. "Del, I want you to know that whatever you decide will be fine by me."

"What do you mean?"

"I'm moving away, Del. Into an apartment," my father said. "It's got two bedrooms, so you and Bea can come visit me anytime, okay?"

I looked down at the carpet between my feet and found that I had nothing to say. I thought when this moment arrived I would tell them about the Turing Machinists, about the Cubground Pub Band competition and the fact that we had made it all the way up to the finals. But all of a sudden I realized I didn't *want* to tell them about the band or our trip to Toronto or the contest. I didn't want them to know about it.

"Del, honey? Will you look at us, please?"

I raised my head, gazed at them. "Djebar says his mom lets him eat sugar cereals now that his parents are divorced."

My mother grinned. "That is *not* going to happen."

My father sat down on the edge of the bed. "You're taking this better than I thought you would, son."

I nodded. I was puzzled as well by my reaction. "I know."

My mother gave me a tight hug, kissed my cheek. "I love you, Del," she whispered.

My father's hug was one of those clutching hugs that make me feel uncomfortable. But I counted my Mississippis and didn't pull away. When my father finally did let me go I saw wetness collecting at the corners of his eyes.

My mother asked me if I was hungry, and I shook my head and told her I'd eaten already at Bluto's Pizza. She appeared happy — at least she seemed happier than my father, but I've been wrong often enough to know that when it comes to judging someone else's emotions I almost always have a 50 percent chance of being wrong.

I got an email from James congratulating me and the other Turing Machinists on making it to the finals. He said nothing about us bowing out of the competition, but I was guessing, since he and Rick Hughes were such good friends, that he knew we had. He told me he had decided to stay in Los Angeles, where he and the other Magic Horse Marines were going to make a new album. He wrote that he would miss talking to me and asked me to keep in touch. I don't know how I felt about his email, but I knew that it was unlikely that I would ever email him back.

Near the end of the school year, something happened that took me aback: I noticed Seth Daguerre. He was the ninth person in our ASD class, and I had never taken any notice of him before now. It was as if he had been encircled in fog, and one day the fog just lifted. Seth is short and thin and wears square wire-rimmed glasses. His hair is curly and dark brown. He sits on the opposite side of the room from me, and does not say a word. The entire time I was observing him, he was bent over his desk, moving his pencil over a sheet of paper. I asked Djebar if he knew Seth Daguerre, and Djebar's brows drew together. "Who?" he asked.

Petula knew him because he was a Non-Denominational Christian like her and her family.

"He does art. He's very good, in fact. My mother says he's mute, but I've heard him speak. He says he pretends to not be able to talk so they won't ask him any questions. He says he would rather be on his own." She shrugged. "He's no different from the rest of us."

At the end of the year each of us in the ASD class received an incomplete for Ms. Pokolopinison's Social Spectrum class. It did not affect our grade average, but the course was deemed a failure, and Ms. Pokolopinison's teaching position was terminated.

But the truth was, her class had not been a failure. Djebar, Sogi, Petula, Wesley, Darrin, and I had, in fact, worked together as a group. What would have happened, I wondered, had Ms. Pokolopinison discovered we'd formed a rock band and that we had gone together, on our own, to Toronto to compete in a Battle of the Bands competition?

Well, as it turned out, Jeddy had been right all along. Ms. Pokolopinison was, in fact, working for the Canadian Research Association for Autism Spectrum Disorder. It seems our ASD class was a test model for a Social Cooperative Education Module designed specifically for students with autism and teenagers exhibiting anti-social behaviors. Upon discovering this, Jeddy's father immediately lodged a complaint and requested that the Ministry of Education do a formal inquiry into the Canadian Research Association for Autism Spectrum Disorder concerning covert research studies at Merryton Public.

"That man is going to end up shutting down the entire research facility," my mother complained.

"And that's a *bad* thing?" said my father.

"Take a look at our son. Do you think Del would still be going to the University of Waterloo in the fall if he'd stayed in the regular public school curriculum?"

"I don't know, Connie. What did all those tests and special therapy classes do, really? How do we know he wouldn't have turned out better had we just left him in regular classes?"

"Four years we've been having this same conversation." My mother sighed. "Maybe it's time we moved on and let it go."

A beat passed.

"You're right," said my father. A minute later, I heard the kitchen door open and close, and my mother began making dinner, humming under her breath.

My father lay sleeping on the couch, mouth open, tongue lolling, head thrown back in an awkward position. On the television a woman wearing a blue apron was using a machine to cook something. Her hair and forehead didn't move as she talked. Her big white teeth mesmerized me. I noticed my father kept the television on at night. But how could he watch it without the sound?

"Del?" My father let out a small groan and coughed.

"Hi, Dad."

"What time is it?"

I cast a glance down at my watch. "2:46 a.m."

My father rubbed the back of his neck. "Can't sleep?"

"I haven't been to sleep yet."

"Hey, you want me to warm you up some milk? You used to love that when you were a kid."

"No, thanks," I said. "Dad? Can I ask you for a favor?"

My father sat up, blinked, looked more alert. "Sure."

"I need someone to take me along the route of the Merryton Marathon. I've mapped it out, but I haven't run it yet," I said.

"Huh? Marathon?"

"Yes, I'm going to enter the Merryton Marathon this summer."

My father donned an expression which I deduced was surprise. "Really? You're going to enter the Merryton Marathon?" He frowned. "Are you sure you want to do this?"

"It's only eighteen kilometers."

"Only —" My father laughed. "No, no, I don't doubt you can run the marathon. It's just that before ... well, you weren't all that keen on marathons, remember? What's changed your mind?"

"I don't know. I just want to run the marathon."

"This is great! Yes, of course I'll help you out." He grinned, ruffled my hair. "You're a great kid, you know that?"

"There's something else, Dad."

"Yeah?" His expression got a bit funny, then.

"I've decided I want to study music."

"Music?"

"Well, I'm going to go for a double major, actually. Music and math."

"Wow," was all my father said before he hugged me really tight. I counted my Mississippis and waited for him to release me.

"I love you, Del."

I was turning to go to bed when the words suddenly wizzled out of me. "I love you too, Dad." It was like when you step on a balloon to get the air out and it makes this odd kind of sound. But the air that came out was good air, and the sound was strange, but good, too.